THERE WOULD
SCANDAL

She had done a terrible thing. Deserted Freddie – dear Freddie – at the altar; disgraced her ageing father, Sir Martin Penderrick, and must have outraged his elegant second wife, Henrietta, beyond redemption. It would be said she had insulted and humiliated not only Frederick de Marchmont, her fiancé of three months, but the whole of his aristocratic line.

She rushed on half-blindly through the thickening light, a wraithlike shape, with her long train billowing and dragging behind. Her fair hair broke free of its orange blossom. Petals, like tired butterflies, drifted to the ground.

She turned a corner and in doing so caught the toe of a satin slipper on the cobbles. She fell, pulled herself up, and heard a male voice saying, 'My dear young lady, are you hurt?'

A strong arm helped her to her feet, she looked up and saw a handsome, slightly sardonic, yet amused face staring into hers.

'Come. My carriage is here. You obviously need transport.'

Also by Mary Williams in Sphere Books:

TRENHAWK
THE TREGALLIS INHERITANCE
THE GRANITE KING

Castle Carnack

MARY WILLIAMS

SPHERE BOOKS LIMITED
London and Sydney

First published in Great Britain by
William Kimber & Co. Limited 1983
Copyright © Mary Williams, 1983
Published by Sphere Books Ltd 1985
30–32 Gray's Inn Road, London WC1X 8JL

TRADE
MARK

This book is sold subject to the condition that
it shall not, by way of trade or otherwise, be lent,
re-sold, hired out or otherwise circulated without
the publisher's prior consent in any form of
binding or cover other than that in which it is
published and without a similar condition
including this condition being imposed on the
subsequent purchaser.

Printed and bound in Great Britain by
Cox & Wyman Ltd, Reading

For my friends
at Kimbers

1

1903

The girlish voice rang clear from the nave through the congregation. 'No, I will not.'

There was a hushed silence; a tense interim of horror and outrage as the vicar, who had paled visibly, reiterated, 'Wilt thou, Sabrina Ann, take this man Frederick Charles to be thy—?'

'I will not. I can't—'

Mouths gasped; elegant, beflowered and feathered heads turned. There was a furtive, astonished whispering — a cough, followed by others; the clatter of a prayer book falling. Silk rustled as the young bride turned and fled down the aisle of the Church and out of the porch to the road.

A rising mist veiled the scene, taking the Church and ancient ruined castle into grey uniformity with trees and huddled rooftops of the town. Speeding down the steep hill towards Launceston Market Place, Sabrina Penderrick felt herself in a nightmare, a yawning pit waiting to engulf her, from which there was no escape, no chance ever again of facing the world she knew or of returning to normal life.

She had done a terrible thing. Deserted Freddie — dear Freddie — at the altar; disgraced her ageing father, Sir Martin Penderrick, and must have outraged his elegant second wife, Henrietta, beyond redemption. Both had been anxious for the marriage which would have allied her to a rich powerful family and brought financial ballast to the failing Penderrick estate. The high-society guests gathered for the ceremony and reception would snigger and whisper for months once the first disappointment and shock were over.

There would be a dreadful scandal. It would be said she had

insulted and humiliated not only Frederick de Marchmont, her fiancé of three months, but the whole of his aristocratic line.

And this was the last thing she had wanted.

Until those last few reverential words demanding commitment at the altar she had believed herself to be truly in love with Frederick, who was nice looking, conventionally handsome, and who had adored her ever since she was a sixteen-year-old. He was brave too, and had emerged as a hero in the Boer War.

But — but — but — in a ceaseless refrain the one word beat its awful tattoo through her brain.

She rushed on half-blindly through the thickening light, a wraith-like shape, with her long train billowing and dragging behind. Her fair hair broke free of its orange blossom. Petals, like tired butterflies, drifted to the ground.

She turned a corner and in doing so caught the toe of a satin slipper on the cobbles. She fell, pulled herself up, and heard a male voice saying, 'My dear young lady, are you hurt?'

A strong arm helped her to her feet, she looked up and saw a handsome, slightly sardonic yet amused face staring into hers. She screwed her eyes up, and drew a hand across her forehead trying to regain composure. But of course it was useless, and she knew it. She felt, and looked, a sorry sight.

'No, I'm not hurt,' she heard herself answering mechanically, 'and if you don't mind—'

'Come. My carriage is here. You obviously need transport.'

Without argument she allowed him to assist her into the vehicle, and a minute later they were off.

So it was that on that October day of 1903 Sabrina Penderrick found herself not as the newly-wed young wife of Frederick de Marchmont on the way to a luxurious honeymoon on the Continent, but as the guest of Oliver Cavannagh, and his mother, the vague but still beautiful ex-actress Lisette Stern, at their comparatively recently acquired country residence, Castle Carnack, in the vicinity of Merlyngate, Cornwall.

'I don't see how you can possibly return to your home tonight, my dear,' Lisette said in husky calm tones, as she sat in her luxurious private drawing room facing Sabrina before dinner. They had apéritifs beside them; Lisette was wearing pastel green draperies trimmed with sequins and flowers, and her silver-pale fair hair was loosely yet elaborately dressed with a shred of chiffon and feathers. Beads and jewels glittered on her hands and at her neck. Falling from the back of her shoulders was a short fur-trimmed silk cape. Sabrina, who had been loaned a blue gown patterned with small daisies, envied her hostess the cape's warmth. Following her ordeal she felt chilled. The vast high-ceilinged room was draughty, despite the cheerful flames blazing from the immense marble framed fire-place.

Sabrina was bemused. It was as though she had escaped from one strange world into another. The whole of the ornate interior held a glittering, almost Oriental quality exemplifying wealth, and the exotic style of the new century. Flowers seemed everywhere. Shining lamp shades and screens were exotically beaded. Crystal chandeliers swung and tinkled. Ornate clocks chimed musically at different intervals. On one small carved table the figurine of a Chinese Mandarin bowed his head several times, at each drifting waft of air. The cream thick-piled Chinese carpet patterned in pale colours had been inspired by Arthur Lazenby Liberty, the English advocate of Oriental styles and objets d'art, who had already established a new vogue in current furnishing, including fabrics and materials.

No mansion in Cornwall or even London could have been more luxuriously up-to-date. The very atmosphere was permeated by wealth. Yet Oliver Cavannagh and his mother had so far failed to penetrate the barriers dividing 'trade' and the social élite. The family was self-made, Oliver's immense wealth having stemmed from the enterprising hard work of his great-grandfather Thomas, who though humbly born, had started tea cultivation in Ceylon. Through the years a fortune had been amassed, and the Merchant company now had headquarters in London and was accepted as a leading authority on perfect blending of the product.

However, merchants were after all merely merchants, without a vestige of that blue-blood quality necessary to enable their legitimate entry into the sacred circles of nobility. Money, of course, was never to be sneered at; outward respect could almost always be bought. But to 'be one' with the privileged aristocracy was a different matter altogether; especially in view of the fact that Lisette's career had been an open scandal during her younger years. Even the King, it was whispered, had been more than just an admirer. And not because of her acting quality, matron whispered to matron jealously. Lisette Stern on the stage had been merely elegantly flamboyant, oversensational and outrée, without a single genuine claim to greatness or understanding of Art.

Whatever the truth of it, she had certainly made her mark on audiences, and was now perfectly content to play her quieter role of faded lady and chatelaine of Castle Carnack. So was Oliver. He cared not a damn for the fuss-pot snobs of society. He had no need to. Women liked him for what he was; he had looks, determination, style, and millions to squander where he willed. Also ambition. Tea was not going to be his one concern as it had been his ancestors'. Already he was planning a Hotel Empire, to be founded in the south-west of Britain which was beginning to be popular with holidaymakers. A challenge! that's how he saw it — a challenge to the future.

Castle Carnack was just a beginning. Already, while retaining a large private section of the building for his own and his mother's use, he had designated the western wing for rich select guests. One or two had already stayed there and been more than satisfied. The next year there would be more, when further improvements and conversions had been made. After that, he had his eye on more southerly regions, including Falmouth.

His life, having been spent partly abroad, aroused speculation, titillated by an air of mystery amid the match-making minds of certain ambitious Edwardian matrons — Mamas, who, despite social disapproval, would not have hesitated in approving a daughter's marriage to the rich 'adventurer' should the opportunity arise.

After all, that he had a mistress in France was only rumour, which could be conveniently glossed over, once legal commitment to matrimony was avowed. In the meantime, however, Oliver Cavannagh was regarded with suspicion as an unscrupulous character likely to bring any virginal young creature to disrepute, should she succumb to his advances.

The 'advances' so far had not materialised. Simply, it was suggested, because he had his pleasures elsewhere.

'Like mother, like son,' was the adage, or, 'My dear, his place in London is nothing more than a—' the words 'whore-house' or 'brothel' were whispered on so low a key as to be unintelligible. But the inference was clear.

Yet all had to agree on Oliver's aggressive, ironic charm.

At thirty-six years of age he was broad, tall, six foot two at the least, with a flashing smile showing very white teeth, a strong jaw and cleft chin beneath a well formed nose, and a pair of clear grey eyes which could be wide and brilliant one moment, the next speculatively sensuous under narrowed heavy lids. His dark hair, curled back from a wide forehead, and side burns, accentuated his high cheek-bones. Sabrina had seen him from time to time in the past, either riding, driving, or on foot walking down a Launceston street fashionably clad in an Ulster cape over a tail-coat, striped trousers, or wearing white linen in summer. He invariably favoured a soft hat or the wide-brimmed black felt type affected by intellectuals.

Intellectual or not, he was certainly a striking figure, and Sabrina had been secretly impressed by such rare glimpses. When he came into the drawing room on that fateful afternoon however, following her disgraceful flight from the Church, she was conscious only of a confused sense of defiant shame.

'My dear child—' Lisette began again, lifting smelling-salts vaguely to her nose, 'you cannot possibly return to your own home tonight.' Her brow wrinkled distastefully, 'I suppose we must contact your parents, and then—'

'There's no need.' Oliver's interruption was firm and crisp. 'I've already done it.'

Sabrina's heart lurched. She glanced up, staring like a startled fawn into her rescuer's face.

'I've sent my man with a note informing your family you're in safe keeping and can stay here for as long as you like,' he said, with an amused twist to his lips. 'Castle Carnack, after all, is quite well equipped to receive guests. You'll not be without protection or a chaperone. There's my mother, and a well-trained staff, also keys to all doors. So relax, Miss Penderrick, I can assure you you're in no danger of assault.'

His words brought a flush to her pale cheeks.

She lifted her small head, and at that moment, had she known it, looked quite beautiful. Her face was heart-shaped, her mouth full yet perfectly modelled, above a provocatively dimpled chin. The eyes were violet, surprisingly fringed with thick dark lashes in contrast to her wealth of honey-coloured hair. The flower-like, pastel-shaded gown added to her ethereal quality.

'A Sabrina indeed', Oliver thought, 'lovely as the legendary nymph.'

At that moment, had Sabrina known it, a pattern in her life started that was to remould her whole future; and during the days following gossiping tongues not only whispered, but spat.

Sabrina Penderrick became an outcast to her own family and local society.

2

Sabrina was spared the ordeal of eating in the company of her host and hostess on her first evening at Castle Carnack. She had taken one glimpse of the vast dining room with its immense mahogany table glittering with sparkling glass and cutlery, and had been overcome by a shivering attack of nerves. The furnishing, in style, it was true, was similar to that of her own home, but more ornate, with high-backed carved chairs at either end of the polished surface, evidently arranged for Oliver, master of the house, and his mother. Without realising it she'd raised a hand to her forehead which was already aching, and Oliver had remarked politely, 'Perhaps you'd rather have a tray in your room. You must be tired, Miss Penderrick.'

'Oh yes — thank you. I really would, if it's no trouble.'

Lisette looked vaguely surprised. 'Just as you please,' she said. 'Oliver—' her voice trailed off questioningly.

Her son touched a bell which was almost instantly answered by the appearance of a butler. A minute or two later the truant bride was being escorted back to the bedroom accompanied by a superior-looking female servant, possibly an under-housekeeper.

'You needn't really trouble to come with me,' she told the woman. 'I can remember the way.'

'But you'll need attention, madam — miss — and I have to

see the bed is properly turned down, and the curtains pulled. Also you may need the fire making up.'

Sabrina argued no further. Her usual energy and vitality seemed suddenly to have deserted her like air from a pricked balloon. With the flimsy draperies of her skirt held up in each hand, she climbed the wide staircase wearily, only half aware of her surroundings. Thin fog seemed to have penetrated every small crack between panes of the stained glass windows. Ancient portraits of bygone characters stared down at her from gilt frames, misted by the cool air to an uncanny sense of movement. As she turned the first bend she was confronted by an entire wall covered by mural paintings of nymphs, satyrs, and elegantly dressed youths, half swooning over the recumbent near-naked figures of delicate pale-haired ladies. Fruit and flowers enriched the background, overshadowed by the drooping branches of exotic trees and vines. There was the semblance of a stream rippling down to a shining lake. The effect, in the blueish light, was that of a stage-set, yet in a strange way compelling; reminiscent of a past era threatening to overwhelm the present.

She was grateful to find herself at last within the bedroom — the Yellow Room — as she'd heard it referred to, and able to flop on to the bed. She lay for some minutes, limp and exhausted, staring at the high ceiling which was gold and white and encrusted with baby angels, clouds and flowers. Then she got up and moved dejectedly to the dressing table. The image confronting her through the mirror appeared, to her tired eyes, that of a stranger. Elegant, yet wan and lifeless, bearing little resemblance to the vivacious young girl who only that morning had been dressed in her wedding gown as the bride-to-be of Frederick de Marchmont.

Poor Freddie! Once more compunction flooded her, with a renewed shock of terrified bewilderment. Why had she done it? Whatever had induced her at that most sacred and emotional of moments, to humiliate him so disgracefully? They had had such fun together, been so much in love — at least she'd thought she had. She'd looked forward with such excitement to the reception, the honeymoon abroad, then returning to their gracious newly acquired mansion Rosstrellick near St Mawes. They were to have a town house, and in the winter had planned to visit Switzerland for the sports.

Now all that was over. She would never be able to face Freddie again — never. Nor her parents. Her stepmother would probably induce her father to disown her. She was a determined woman despite her composed delicate exterior, whose strong will had proved invariably more than a match for any difference of opinion between the two. And she had never liked Sabrina — perhaps because of his daughter's resemblance to her late mother, and the deep love that had existed between himself and his dead wife.

When Sir Martin had married his second wife, Henrietta had hoped to bear him a son — an heir to inherit and enhance her own position in the family. But no child had been born of the union, and although the good-natured portly Martin Penderrick expressed no disappointment, Henrietta had sensed it was there. The presence of Sabrina in the household had only added fuel to the fire of failure. Without Sabrina, Martin would naturally turn more to his wife. Henrietta was not by nature a romantic, but it was important to her to be wanted — even by an ageing man whose physical demands and desires were no longer a necessity of daily life.

Therefore, it was highly unlikely that she would willingly accept her stepdaughter's return to Fern Hill, their home. Sabrina was aware of this; she knew, also, that her father would observe his wife's wishes by managing to contrive, somehow, a place of refuge for her with some boring reclusive relative.

And that would be unbearable.

Then what would she do?

The question was tormenting her when a maid-servant arrived with a supper tray.

The meal was tastefully prepared, including fresh salmon, and a glass of white wine. The sweet, one of Mrs Beeton's specials, was liberally topped by whipped cream.

'Thank you,' Sabrina said perfunctorily, 'but I don't really want it. I'm not hungry.'

The maid retired giving a faint smile, and a few minutes later Sabrina found, surprisingly, that she had been wrong. After her first taste, her appetite revived quite astonishingly; and when she'd finished eating, nothing but a small spoonful of sweet — the hall-mark of good breeding — remained on her plate. After that she felt better.

she asked herself for the hundredth time that night, had she been frightened at the very last and run away?

Would he ever forgive her? Would he come searching for her and carry her away like a fictitious character to some quiet place where they could be married without fuss, or the smothering sensation of so many voices — so many eyes and ridiculous befeathered heads turned upon her?

Was that what she wanted? Was it?

No answer came.

No whisper, no sound, or sign. Only a muted murmur of the rising wind rustling the trees outside, and the momentary clearing of mist from the moon-streaked moors hugging the sky.

She slept intermittently that night, but in the morning woke refreshed, and after washing dressed herself in the gown put ready for her the evening before.

It was belted, high-necked, trimmed by velvet bows, and with a skirt fitting the hips then flaring to the ankles where it had a slightly longer hem line at the back, suggestive of a short train. The material was of a heavy-linen type, patterned with tiny white flowers on olive green. It fitted surprisingly well.

Sabrina giggled to herself as she puffed her fair hair out on either side, then pinned it into a knot on top. There had been tortoise-shell combs put ready, and when her toilette was completed she looked, and felt, quite a young madam. She was about to go downstairs for breakfast when a maid appeared at the door with a tray. Sabrina smiled brilliantly. 'How nice of you. But don't guests get up here for breakfast?'

'We've no other guests just now, ma'am — miss,' the girl answered, 'and madam always stays in her room till mid-day. The master's in the breakfast room though, if you want to join him.'

Sabrina sighed, recalling with a touch of confusion the circumstances of their meeting the day before, the hot searching glance of his grey eyes in the hall of Carnack later, belied so effectively by the cool polite tones of his resonant voice.

'No,' she answered, realising she was not yet ready to face him. 'As you've taken the trouble to bring the tray up I'll eat here. Thank you.'

The girl gave a little bob and departed.

The breakfast, as was to be expected, was daintily prepared

and tasteful; but the edge of Sabrina's appetite had worn off, and she ate only a little fish, followed by wafer-thin buttered toast and marmalade. The coffee was delicious — black and strong in a silver pot with a jug of thick cream beside the Georgian sugar basin. When she'd finished the meal she got up and went to the window. She pushed it open. The mist had lifted, leaving a silvered radiance everywhere. Autumn was such a lovely time, she thought absently, so rich with colour and heady earth scents of damp soil, tumbled fallen blackberries and rotting leaves. A wonderful day for riding the moors. Then her face fell. But of course her mare was not there. Not even Jody, her spaniel. Familiar memories of her home resurrected yesterday's drama.

What was to happen now?

She forced herself to leave the window and made her way downstairs. Her heart quickened as she saw the tall figure of Oliver Cavannagh examining the post on a small table in the hall. He looked up at her, and his face, for a moment, was vividly clear in a beam of early sunlight from the window. A strong, handsome, worldly face; not old, but holding a hint of — what was it — mischief? No, wickedness perhaps; although he didn't really look wicked — just devil-may-care, with a touch of laughter about his lips.

'Well, Miss Penderrick,' he said, 'do come down. What a pity you didn't join me for breakfast.'

She hesitated a second then went forward to meet him.

He took her hand briefly.

'I hope you slept well?'

'Very well, thank you. It was kind of you—'

'Nonsense.' The interruption was sharp. 'A pleasure — under the circumstances. However I suspect you may still have problems.'

He took up a white envelope and handed it to her. 'This was delivered last night, when my man returned from Fern Hill. I thought it best you shouldn't be worried until you'd had a rest.'

Sabrina held the square piece of paper in her hand momentarily, then tore it open while Cavannagh discreetly moved away. The note was penned in her stepmother's angular hand-writing:

Sabrina, your behaviour was despicable. Both your own family and Frederick's feel humiliated by such a disgraceful show of hysterics. That the de Marchmonts will ever forgive you is almost inconceivable. Frederick, I understand, is leaving for an extended holiday abroad almost immediately. I hope you fully realise, you wicked girl, the damage you have done regarding your father's good name in the county — even in London. The news is sure to be written up most scandalously. If you wish to prevent further suffering please return immediately to your own home. Your father still cares about you, though I really see no reason why he should. Still, I am writing to your Aunt Agatha in the Isle of Wight this evening, and asking her to take you under her wing for an indefinite period of time. With luck she may be able to find a worthy suitor willing to overlook your insulting behaviour to the de Marchmonts. Arthur Foster, if you remember, appeared to like you when you met last year in town. He is now fully qualified in Holy Orders, and has an incumbency promised for a parish in the island.

When you return we will discuss the matter. Your father, incidentally, is in complete agreement with my plan, and if you do not return forthwith neither of us wish to have anything further to do with you. I would remind you also, that the longer you stay at Castle Carnack, the more scandalous your reputation will become. It is not a respectable place for any young girl with her future to consider, as you must well know.

Awaiting to hear from you—

Sabrina waited a second, then tore the letter across.

'*Mother!*' she said contemptuously. 'She never was. And the Isle of Wight! Arthur Foster, that *idiot!*'

Her voice rang with scorn. Her eyes blazed.

Oliver Cavannagh ambled casually through a door on the left. His eye-brows shot up puckishly. 'I rather thought so,' he said.

She swung round on him.

'What do you mean, Mr Cavannagh?'

'Parents seldom understand,' he said ambiguously. 'Still — one must make allowances.'

'I shall never go back,' she told him defiantly. 'I shall—'

'Yes?'

'I shall go to friends somewhere, I suppose,' she said more quietly. 'In London perhaps.'

'You might find London a little wearying at the moment,' he remarked. 'Why not stay here?'

'Here?' She searched his face for any sign that he was teasing or playing with her. There was none. He looked perfectly serious, even faintly sympathetic.

'As a guest you mean? One of your — visitors?'

'A personal guest,' he emphasised. 'I'm sure my mother would enjoy a little company at times — especially when I'm away.'

'I don't know,' she answered doubtfully.

'Think about it,' he said.

She did; and the consequence was that she stayed.

3

For a few days Sabrina waited at Castle Carnack hoping half-heartedly for a word from her father, or even that Freddie would attempt to contact her. When none came she sent a reply to her stepmother, including a word for her father stating that she was remaining at Carnack for the time being. Mr Cavannagh's mother was in need of company.

—and as my presence at home would obviously only be an embarrassment [she concluded] I think it's much better to stay where I'm wanted. I'm sorry about Freddie. I'm still fond of him. But I knew during those dreadful few moments that our marriage wouldn't have worked out. I don't expect you to understand. You never have, anyway, and it's much too late to start now.

Father dear, I'll always love you. I'm sorry I couldn't have been a boy. If I'd been a boy I could have married some dull rich girl like Prissy Dukes, couldn't I? — someone with a fat dowry as fat as herself who'd please step-mamma, and get

Fern Hill properly on its feet again. Oh dear! I don't mean to poke fun. But it's better than crying, isn't it? And whatever people say, the Cavannaghs are really quite pleasant. Lisette — Mrs Cavannagh — has such amusing memories of the stage, although she's rather vague — a sort of languid lily, who trails about in draperies like Isadora Duncan.

Don't ask me what my plans for the future are. I don't know. If you're going to disinherit me, which Henrietta suggests, I shall have to find some kind of a post, shan't I, or manage to exist on the income left to me by mama. Anyway I'm not a pauper.

Take care of yourself, papa.

    With love,

        Your undutiful daughter

           Sabrina.

P.S. You can tell Freddie where I am, if he asks. Any letter addressed here will be forwarded. But if he's licking his wounds in foreign climes I expect he'll soon find some sweet shoulder to sigh on.

Oh dear! this does sound flippant.

And I don't feel flippant at all. Deep down I'm so very distressed to have created such a furore.

    S.

The letter was sent off. No reply came.

So the days passed aimlessly. During those first weeks most of her time was spent either wandering about the extensive grounds, reading when it was wet, or listening to Lisette's reminiscences. Occasionally they were driven in the landau to Bodmin for shopping, and took longer jaunts to Truro.

Cavannagh was frequently away in Paris; with his mistress Sabrina guessed. She could picture them together, and was mildly piqued by his absence. Why? the suggestion was quite ridiculous, she told herself frequently. She didn't even like him very much. Oh, he was dashing and spectacular; witty, and attentive when he noticed her at all. But certainly conceited and too sure of himself. And on the rare occasions when he was in residence he seemed to delight in discomforting her by shrewd sidelong glances, and devious double-edged remarks, though there was nothing she could take exception to in his manners or behaviour.

As the autumn days grew shorter, turning to early yellow-grey evenings burdened with lowering skies and the rotting heavy smell of fallen dead leaves, she began to feel bored and restricted by her surroundings. Lisette retreated into a mood of melancholy which left Sabrina more and more on her own. She spent whole mornings wandering about the moors and coast exploring the lonely vicinity around Merlyn Close, sometimes loosening her pale hair about her shoulders. It was easy, briefly, to imagine herself as some ghostly Guinevere or other legendary character doomed to haunt that wild forgotten region. But the passing illusion held no lasting comfort. She was flesh and blood – no ghost or long dead wraith of bygone days. The dream-lovers conjured from the tumbled bastions and ruined towers were quick to fade when memory of her true position registered. She was Sabrina Penderrick – too vividly and sensually alive to be forever dreaming. She had her future to consider.

Her thoughts invariably wandered to Freddie. She'd had an impulse, often, to write to him, but there seemed no point, because she'd no idea where he was. Anyway, there was nothing at all exciting in the idea, and that, probably, had been the root of the trouble between them. He was too predictable. She'd known him too long. If Frederick de Marchmont had possessed a shred of Oliver Cavannagh's unknowableness, maybe everything would have been different. But then things could have so easily been worse. She suspected Mr Cavannagh would be a difficult man to cross. Ruthless, a hard and demanding lover, domineering – bossy. In fact, except for his looks, there was nothing about him she could find to admire at all. His castle-like mansion was the same; flashy, without real history or roots. In spite of it, a flutter of excitement filled her every time she allowed her mind to veer in his direction.

Once, as she was standing by the window of the drawing room staring over the gardens and brown moors beyond, Lisette, who was draped over an elegant chaise-longue with a pretence of reading, looked up casually and asked 'What are you dreaming about, child? Oliver?'

Sabrina turned sharply. With her back to the afternoon light the startled expression of her fawn-like eyes, the faint pink flush, were not visible.

'Of course not,' she said sharply. 'Why should I?'

A ripple of amusement shook the delicate swan-like throat. 'Because most girls do who've met him,' Lisette answered, with no trace of expression in her voice. 'He's a very attractive man. He's had more women after him than—'

'Well, I'm not one of them,' Sabrina exclaimed hotly. 'And I'm sure I've done nothing to make you think so.'

'No, dear. I did not say you had. I was merely trying to put you in the picture. For your own sake. One thing matters to him above everything else. Business. Romance is merely incidental in his life. And don't think—' she lifted a white hand, 'that is my wish at all. I'd very much like to see him settled. I'm not a possessive mama — in any case, Oliver is hardly the type—' She smiled winningly. 'You do see what I mean, don't you, dear—?'

'No,' Sabrina answered. 'I haven't the slightest interest in your son, Mrs Cavannagh. Why you should imagine such a thing I really don't know. Obviously—' a flash of anger lit her violet eyes — 'something's given you a completely wrong impression. I suppose I've stayed here too long. But don't worry. I'll leave tomorrow—'

'But, *darling*!' Lisette's voice deepened with reproach; her arms went out pleadingly as though she was once more playing to the footlights. 'That would be most upsetting. And not quite fair, do you think? I enjoy your company. I'm fond of you, Sabrina. And Oliver would never forgive me if I said or did anything to upset you. I just—' Her manner changed abruptly. 'I know my son. He has no conscience at all where women are concerned. And you're young. You've been through a very unhappy emotional experience. I should be shirking my duty shamelessly if I didn't at least make an effort to put you in the picture. So please — *please* don't do anything drastic — don't dream of forsaking us before Oliver returns. Will you do that for me, dear? After all, we've tried to be of help.'

'I'm grateful,' Sabrina answered rather shortly. 'But I can't go on forever doing nothing, living on your charity—' she bit her lip quickly.

'Charity! what an odious word. So Dickensian and old-fashioned. I never liked Dickens, you know – especially on the stage. But then—' with an air of brightness, 'I'm not one for moralising, as I'm sure you must have heard—' Her eyes held a hint of mischief. Sabrina flushed. Before she could speak, Lisette continued, 'I well know my reputation, and I can assure you I'm not at all ashamed of it. Life is for living, and if I were ten, even five years younger—' she sighed. 'Well, never mind. One can't put the clock back, but one can endure and retire gracefully. And I don't care a fig what the dry-as-dust dowagers say of me. At heart, my dear, they're jealous. As they will be of course, of you — if you really have the courage to go your own way regardless.' There was a pause, then— 'You have the looks, you know. It would be rather fun launching you on to a career of naughty fame.'

Not knowing quite how to take the last remark, Sabrina smiled awkwardly.

'Ah! that's better,' Lisette remarked with a light laugh. 'Be happy. Don't fret, and don't believe everything I say; just a tiny portion of it. Yes? So now that's settled, now that you've agreed to stay—'

'But I never—'

'Oh yes dear; you have — of course you have. And after all we shall soon have a little diversion. Jaina will be back for half-term. Things will brighten up a little.'

'Jaina?'

'Oliver's ward,' Lisette explained, with a negligent wave of the hand. 'He more or less adopted her. He knew her mother well in Ceylon, and when she died some years ago Oliver brought the child to this country. She's thirteen now — nearly fourteen, at boarding school — a convent — near Bristol. Philanthropic of him really, but then Oliver has surprising fits of generosity when the mood takes him, and Jaina can be quite intriguing.'

'Hasn't she a father?' The question left Sabrina's lips almost unintentionally.

'My dear, he was something of a *bête-noir*, I believe. Dead; must be. I never enquire; for Jaina's sake it's best to let the past alone.'

'I see.'

The statement was a half-truth. Sabrina doubted that Lisette was telling all she knew, but realised Jaina's origins were not her own affair, and so let the question drop.

'Anyway,' she heard Lisette saying reflectively a moment later, 'you'll be able to do me a good turn by amusing her sometimes, dear. Not that I let the child intrude on my privacy when I don't want her. But she can be tiring. Not rough, or hoydenish of course. The nuns naturally teach good manners. But—' the thin shoulders shrugged under the elegant beaded georgette wrap '—she's rather compelling in a quiet way. When you meet her you'll see what I mean.'

Sabrina did.

Jaina arrived three days later. Oliver met her in the brougham at Launceston station, and together, with more luggage than was necessary for the brief week's holiday, they were driven by the coachman, Davies, cross-country through a maze of lanes to Castle Carnack.

The late-October air already held the faint tang of approaching winter. A shimmer of mist veiled the brown and green stone-walled fields, but the moors beyond were starkly clear against the yellow-grey sky, heralding rain to come. Jaina sat upright beside Oliver, her small gloved hands folded on her lap. She appeared disinclined to talk, but answered any questions with aloof politeness — a certain chilly indifference that never failed to irritate Cavannagh. She seemed so calm and in control of herself, but underneath the adult façade he knew there lurked a rebellious spirit and wilfulness that set a barrier between them.

Thank God Sabrina had stayed on, he thought, moodily. Together, the child and the girl might be able to amuse each other. Jaina could be intriguing enough when she wanted to be, and he'd sensed more than once a fiery capacity for devotion that unnerved him almost as much as her manner of pseudo-condescension. As for Sabrina! he'd have been damned annoyed — even affronted — if she'd taken off during his frequent absences from home. From Lisette he'd gathered that her mind quite often strayed to London.

'She's playing with the idea of being an actress,' his mother had informed him only recently, 'and it might be a good idea to give her the chance, don't you think? I still have a few useful connections, and even if it's only a walking-on part, the experience would ease any responsibility we seem to have assumed — or that *you* have. She won't stay here forever you know, Oliver. And to tell you the truth—'

'Mater dear, leave things alone if you don't mind,' he'd said in the hard obstinate voice that told her arguing was useless. 'How long Sabrina Penderrick stays here is my affair and mine only.'

'And hers?' The soft voice had turned ironic. 'Don't underestimate that girl. She's not just one of the many conquests to be added to your collection, Oliver. She has personality, a will of her own — and family. The Penderricks are well thought of. Any scandal in that direction might seriously jeopardise your ambitions.' She shrugged, continuing quickly, 'Oh I know you don't think much of my business sense. I'm extravagant, improvident, and if you didn't happen to be a millionaire I might have ended up in far greater disrepute than I already am. But, my dear, I do know society. Another thing—' She paused and reached for a cigarette, one of her exotic perfumed blend. He quickly gave her a light, and watched her puff a blue ring of smoke into the air.

'Yes?' His one word held the sharp impact of a pistol shot.

'I rather like the girl.'

'So do I.' The admission had even surprised himself, because until that moment he'd not seriously considered any possible involvement.

'I see.'

'No, you don't, you haven't the first clue, mama darling.'

Her eyes widened.

'What do you mean?'

He'd smiled winningly in the lazy, half cynical manner that had always proved so disarming to women of every age. Yet at that moment she had felt only irritation.

'Don't play with me, Oliver. Don't tease.'

One dark eyebrow shot up higher than the other. The flash of very white teeth had died.

'Oh, but I'm not playing. Although you'd no thought of it, you've just given me a very novel idea.'

'And what is that?'

He'd paused before replying, then he'd said as though debating some trivial business detail, 'I *might* even decide to marry the girl.'

'Marry?'

'Why not? Most men do in the end.'

He'd kissed the top of her shimmering pale head lightly.

'Cheer up, dear,' he'd said. 'As you feel her well-being to be so sacrosanct, you've really nothing to worry about.'

With which shrewd observation he'd turned on his heel and walked sharply from the room.

4

During the few days of Sabrina's first contact with Jaina, she found the child in some ways apparently naive, yet with an assessing calm look in the slightly slanted golden eyes that suggested an instinctive knowledge beyond her years. Beneath the unbecoming navy serge school dress, no figure showed. She could have been as thin as a boy. Her dark hair, parted in the middle and plaited severely on either side of her small heart-shaped face, added to the demure, prim impression. Yet when she was allowed to change for dinner on her third evening at Carnack, the difference was remarkable. Above the frilled neckline of her yellow spotted muslin dress, the delicately formed features could have been those of some portrait painted in bygone times. The shining waves had been coiled and piled simply on the top of the small head, held by a ribbon and combs. The wide silk sash tied round the waist emphasised the virginal breasts and graceful lines of the developing young figure. Mostly her expression was serious; but when she smiled the perfectly formed lips held all the allure of a trained — cocotte? Sabrina was intrigued by the idea, but she felt instinctively that Jaina was already well aware of her own sexual potential, and the knowledge was discomforting.

'Jaina likes clothes, and pretending she's grown up,' Lisette remarked with a light laugh. 'I used to myself at her age, as I suppose you did also, Sabrina?'

Sabrina agreed, remembering the several times when as a child she'd managed to purloin some of her stepmother's dresses and furs from a wardrobe, and trailed about the bedroom viewing herself admiringly in the long pier glass. Once Henrietta had returned earlier than had been expected from an outing with her father, and she'd been discovered and quite severely punished.

After that time Nanny had been strictly watchful, and life had become considerably more restricted and boring.

'Yes, I remember,' she said in answer to Lisette's query. 'But I was sixteen before I had my first real evening dress. It was of pink satin, with a wide sash.'

'How funny,' Jaina observed unsmilingly.

'Why?'

'I don't like pink; pink's babyish. I don't much like blue either. But the nuns do. It's supposed to be Heavenly. A holy colour.' She giggled softly.

'Quite out of keeping then,' Oliver observed, 'where you're concerned. But there's no need to joke about good things. It's time you learned something about values, young lady. I don't pay high school fees for nothing.'

Jaina glanced downwards. The long dark lashes cast shadows, quivering momentarily like moth wings, on her high cheekbones. A faint magnolia flush stained the ivory skin.

'Sorry, Uncle Oliver,' she murmured.

'And don't play-act either,' he said more sharply than he'd meant. 'You know very well you haven't a scrap of regret in you.'

Jaina got up from her chair and rushed from the room, slamming the door behind her. They had just finished dinner, and were assembled in the drawing room for coffee. Lisette sighed.

'I do hope we're not going to have any moods while she's here,' she said. 'If you don't mind, both of you, I'll retire. I feel tired tonight. And it would be a good idea I think to look in on the child.'

She retreated gracefully, without embracing or giving her son the usual cool goodnight kiss on the cheek.

Oliver glanced towards Sabrina. She was standing by the fireplace staring towards him with a mutinous slightly critical expression on her face. She wore a lilac high-waisted gown, frilled at the neck, with the fashionable slightly longer hem at the back which gave the impression of a train. Lisette had insisted on having it made for her, '—just a little whim of mine darling—' the elder woman had said — by her personal dresser at Truro. Sabrina had at first resisted, but had been forced to give in. Beneath her charm Lisette had a stubborn will, and as she'd pointed out, what was the use of money if you couldn't have a little fun throwing it about.

It hadn't been difficult for Sabrina to agree. The easy luxurious life at Carnack was already weaving its lazy spell about her. One day, she knew it would have to end; but for the moment there was a certain piquancy in knowing that she could have what she wanted by a simple word, or expression of a wish. Life with Freddie, of course, would have given her ample opportunity for self-expression. She would have been one of the favoured, rich élite. But compared with the Cavannagh millions the de Marchmont fortune was negligible. The thought was awesome; demoralising in a way perhaps, but subtly, and on occasions, wildly exciting. Oliver himself had something of the same dangerous reckless quality about him. From their first strange meeting, his behaviour towards her had been exemplary; his manner that of an attentive host desiring her comfort. But beneath the façade she sensed the fire – the combined concentration of will-power and magnificent physique that had produced an empire of business enterprise from Cavannagh blood. And for Oliver even this was not enough. He had to expand still, and conquer even further goals. Hotels! – a whole string of them. Further monuments to the Cavannagh name. Achievement was not sufficient, nor financial power. It was as though, Sabrina thought, that evening, he had to stamp his image on every new scrap of territory possible. And why? Even the young girl, his ward Jaina, must obey him and instantly conform. *Why?* For a second or two, as he came towards her, she resented his vitality fiercely. He should not have spoken to the child so harshly. Jaina might be precocious in a certain way, but she was also naive and impressionable. She had been hurt. And Sabrina had hated it. No one should be hurt unnecessarily – *no one*. Little sparks of indignation kindled her nerves, until she recalled with a shock, how cruelly in a different way she herself had hurt Freddie.

Poor Freddie. As always even a fleeting memory of him caused her acute discomfort. She just couldn't understand her own behaviour, or why he hadn't rushed down the aisle after her and either dragged her back by the hair of her head, or carried her away with him and somehow forced her to see reason. He could have done. He could, he *could*. For a second her head swam. She found one hand resting against the smooth marble of the fireplace, and when she lifted her briefly-drooping head, saw Cavannagh's face, licked to dramatic modelling by the leaping orange and yellow tongues of spitting logs.

'Don't get too near the flames in that gauzy creation,' he said. 'We must get the guard back. With impetuous young things like you and Jaina about there mustn't be any risks.'

'You needn't worry about me,' Sabrina answered quickly. 'I'm not a schoolgirl. And—' His eyes were suddenly so intent, so burning upon her, she paused.

'Yes?'

'I'm sure Jaina isn't quite so thoughtless either,' she told him. 'I know it isn't my affair, but I thought you were rather unkind just now.'

He smiled, slowly, yet with no amusement in his grey eyes — but something warmer, quite different; and far more personal.

'Did you now? Did you indeed!'

She lifted her chin.

'I've just said so.'

'Well, what you feel is your own business, but I'd prefer you not to show it, especially in my ward's presence.'

'And because I'm just a guest here your word is naturally law,' Sabrina heard herself saying tartly. 'I quite understand. That's why—' she broke off, biting her lip, knowing she trod dangerous ground and that she wasn't yet ready to face the issue of leaving Carnack.

There was a pause before he persisted. 'Why what, Miss Penderrick?'

'I must be free,' she answered, throwing discretion suddenly to the wind. 'It isn't right for me to stay here living under your protection, accepting your hospitality and giving nothing in return. It makes me feel quite wrong. A sort of — of parasite. I must have a life of my own—'

'Oh dear!' There was mockery in his voice. 'How dramatic!' Although she tore her eyes from his, she had the uncomfortable sensation he was laughing.

'You read too many books, Sabrina,' he said. 'Of the wrong kind. Mrs Henry Wood?'

She flushed.

'Does it matter what I read?'

'No. Providing you put real life first.'

'Life here, at Castle Carnack, you mean?' She attempted to move away, but a hand was on her shoulder — not hard or forcefully, but compellingly persuasive. Under its gentle pressure she felt electrified; hidden impulses in her stirred to life. She stiffened, against the ridiculous urge for capitulation, to feel his arms tighten about her and draw her close — so close she could no longer fight or pretend. Confusion mounted in her.

'No,' she heard him saying, 'not necessarily at Carnack. Sometimes here — sometimes — anywhere. Who can tell? The future's an adventure, Sabrina. And I think you know it. You always have. That's why you played the truant bride. That's why you tore off in the fog like any wanton gipsy hungry for gold. The silver wasn't bright enough. At the last moment you saw the truth. Maybe you knew I was around somewhere. Maybe it wasn't by chance after all—'

'You — you—' She struggled as his grip on her hardened. Her head fell back, his left hand tilted her chin up so his breath was hot on her face; her under-lip trembled; against his evening jacket her heart pumped heavily.

'Yes' — his voice lowered — 'I'm all you think, and more, much more. King — brigand — one who knows what he wants and gets it at any price — call me what you like, it doesn't matter a damn; because we're two of a kind, Sabrina — adventurers needing the right to live by our laws — with just one difference. You happen to be a woman.' He paused. Beneath the fiery grey eyes the brilliant violet of her own intensified, lit by quivering spots of gold.

She stared for a second before his mouth came down on hers, enfolding her lips sensuously, draining their sweetness and all resistance from her.

After a few heady seconds he released her.

'Here's a pretty kettle-of-fish,' he said.

Momentary shock in her turned to indignation. She opened her mouth, but no sound came from it. What was there to say? How to treat a man, who could behave so passionately one moment, the next as though she was some light pawn in an amusing game.

She turned and walked quickly to the door. He strode after her and pulled her back.

'I – I – you—'

'Sh-sh!' His lips were gentle now against her cheek. 'Don't fight. There's no need.'

'But—'

'And no buts, I'm a man of honour – in my own way.' The teasing note had returned. 'Caught in my own net, though,' he continued. 'No matter! once for everything.' He grinned.

She lifted a hand to slap his face. He caught it and held her wrist tight.

'Marry me, Sabrina.'

She was so astounded she simply stood dazed, glaring at him. When she saw he really meant it, a rich colour flooded her cheeks. Her heart had started its wild hammering against her ribs.

'Don't be ridiculous.'

'Oh I'm not. All things considered I think we might make a pretty successful couple.'

'Successful!' In spite of the scorn in her voice, its excitement did not escape him. He drew a hand across his forehead.

'Well – I'd rather hope so. I don't usually back a pig-in-a-poke – and I'm not a liar. I've never asked a woman to marry me before—'

'So that's it! a new experience.'

'That's it exactly. I think I'm in love with you—'

'You think?' She was aware of a curious disappointment clouding exhilaration into prosaic reality.

He smiled again. 'Sufficiently sure to take the risk.' A finger touched her cheek lightly. 'I'm no adept at this sort of thing – probably not half as good as your Freddie was, at making romantic speeches to lure you to the altar. But you can take it from me – once there you couldn't escape. No running away into another man's arms. Hell no. That's the difference. What I want I take and keep. And if I can't get it, I'm no longer interested. So no games, Sabrina. Just say yes or no. And—' his glance was quizzical. 'You'd better be quick about it, or someone will be in to spoil things—'

While her mind raced this way and that, her instincts – heart – senses – whichever it was – already knew the answer. And suddenly, hearing footsteps in the hall, the words came.

'Very well. Yes — if you really mean it — I'll marry you—'

A moment later there was a knock on the door, and a maid entered with a tray.

'I'm sorry, sir—' she said, sensing — as she put it later to the cook — a kind of atmosphere. 'I can come back later. It was just to collect the cups—'

'It's quite all right, Annie,' Oliver told the girl, casually. 'Carry on with your work. Miss Penderrick and I are retiring to the conservatory—'

He offered his arm. Sabrina took it, and with extreme decorum he escorted her from the dining room.

At last, in the green carefully tended wilderness of flowering blooms and hot house plants, he turned and took her into his arms. The humour of the little charade had not escaped them; both were smiling.

Then the mood changed. There was a long moment of silence between them before he said, 'I'll do my damnedest to be a good husband, Sabrina—'

'And me — a good—'

His fingers went to her mouth, 'Shush, my love, make no promises you can't keep, just be yourself. I'll see to the rest.'

She sighed in acknowledgement.

5

Lisette received Oliver's news with mixed feelings. He did not tell her until the following morning, after her usual breakfast in bed. He was waiting for her in the 'garden-room', a lounge where it was her habit to open any personal correspondence, and to supervise the display of flowers from the grounds or greenhouse. They were put ready in vases, but Lisette seldom found their arrangement completely to her satisfaction. That day she appeared very like some exotic fading blossom herself — wearing a loose lilac-coloured wrap over pale blue silk.

She wrinkled her fine high-bridged nose distastefully.

'Ella still hasn't learned the art of discrimination,' she said critically. 'There is a time and season for all things. And chrysanthemums should not be mixed with leaves, however colourful.' She dislodged some sprays of orange and yellow herbage and loosened the flowers so they drooped more gracefully in sprays. Then she divided the roses and placed some in a spare crystal bowl. There were always one or two additional containers placed on the tray by the housemaid. Madam's idiosyncrasy for having to alter any floral design — however tasteful — was well known. So Oliver simply stood with his back to the fire, watching her with a contemplative smile twitching his lips, and waited for the task to be done. When she turned to look at him, he went forward and kissed her cheek dutifully. She smelt very faintly of lily-of-the-valley.

'Well, Mater? And how are you feeling today?'

'As usual, Oliver, thank you. A little weary, but after a cup of coffee I shall feel better.'

'Good. No headache?'

Her delicate brows lifted.

'I haven't noticed one. Why? Do I look so *fatiguée*?'

He shook his head. 'Not at all. But I have news.'

'News? So early?' Her vague eyes sharpened. 'Nothing wrong, I hope?'

'No, no. No. I've made a decision.'

'What do you mean?'

And then he told her.

She stared at him before any reaction came. Her voice when she spoke was cooler than usual, even a little chilly.

'Are you sure you're wise? You hardly know the girl.'

'That will soon be remedied. I hoped you'd be pleased; it was you who put the idea into my head. Remember?'

'I recall the occasion. But don't try to make me believe anything I ever said made a jot of difference. You've always done exactly what you wanted, and this, I suppose, is just another of your reckless gambles. Well — I hope you're not let down.'

His mouth tightened slightly. 'I'll see I'm not. You should know that I seldom back a loser.'

'Sabrina Penderrick is not a horse.'

He laughed. 'It hadn't occurred to me she was. Come on now

you should be pleased. A girl of good breeding, family, and beauty! what more do you want?'

She sighed. 'I suppose you're right. But don't count on the family, Oliver. She's burned her boats very effectively in that quarter. And marriage to you isn't going to remedy it.'

He frowned.

'Don't be too sure. Money talks.'

'And so do tongues.'

'Let them! What the hell do they matter? They never have, up to date.'

She allowed herself to smile faintly.

'That's true. And of course there'll be advantages on my side. Sabrina certainly has a way with Jaina. The child's growing up too quickly. I find her quite exhausting sometimes. I think you may have problems there, Oliver, I only hope you're able to deal with them without too much fuss when they arrive. She certainly won't be content to live at Castle Carnack just twiddling her thumbs.'

'I can't see that happening,' Oliver said shortly. 'She'll be a beauty in a few years. A good marriage shouldn't be difficult to arrange.'

Lisette gave the semblance of a laugh. 'What a hypocrite you can be. A good marriage! *arrange*. Remember this—' she lifted a finger warningly '—women aren't just goods to be packed and disposed of conveniently to the most available purchasers like packets of your precious tea—'

'*Our* precious tea,' he interrupted. 'If it wasn't for Cavanagh's Select Blends we would never have acquired this stately home, and you − mother dear − would not have been in the position of playing the stately chatelaine.'

Forgetting the question of Jaina, she flung him a coquettish glance. 'Don't brag, Oliver. I may be your mother, but I was young once. And my potentials then were quite − dazzling. If it hadn't been for your father I would probably have ended up as Lady Smith-Durrant with two stately homes and one in Scotland. Wilfred adored me, poor darling.' Her expression had become vague and retrospective. At this point Oliver generally managed to extricate himself by some sudden switch of conversation. The name of Wilfred Smith-Durrant − otherwise his Lordship − had become, through the years, Lisette's most familiar weapon for combat in any social argument.

'And you might *not* have done,' he said bluntly. 'Anyway I haven't time to discuss your torrid past, or Jaina's future. You know now about Sabrina. We shall be married probably before Christmas—'

'And then you'll take her out east I suppose for a prolonged honeymoon? Leaving me and only that ineffective Miss Willis to cope with Jaina.'

'I doubt it. I've two trips to the Continent planned. Sabrina will go with me I expect — once anyway.'

'France?' That one word was sharp with irony.

'Perhaps.'

'How brave of you.'

'Now, Mater—'

'Oh, don't try to hoodwink me, Oliver. I'm quite aware of what's been going on these last few years. I'm not a fool. And I hope you won't be. I hope too, that with marriage in the offing you'll determine to give Ceylon a miss.'

'Temporarily maybe. Not for ever. Having a wife is one thing. Business interests quite another.'

'Two different compartments. I see.'

'No, my dear. You do not. But you can take it from me that I intend to make a success as a husband, and Sabrina will be content.'

'Happy also?'

'Now what makes you question it?'

'You do, Oliver. I doubt very much that you're capable of giving what she needs. What she wants? — yes, for a time. But Sabrina Penderrick has a heart. And I think you're quite capable of breaking it. You've caught her on the rebound, and she's reacted as any wayward sensitive girl would. When she wakes up though — just take care, if you can. Still, as you've obviously made up your mind I suppose I can do nothing to change it. You have my blessing, both of you, although I still think the affair is a mistake.'

Oliver waited a second before answering abruptly, 'Thank you. You've made your point. So let's forget the moral issue shall we, and get down to brass-tacks. The servants will have to know, sooner or later. Sooner preferably. I'm sure I can rely on you to start the ball rolling.'

'And Jaina?'

'Leave Jaina to me,' Cavannagh said. 'She'll revel in the news.'

'Are you sure?'

'Where she's concerned I'm sure of nothing. But she goes back to school in a few days. She'll have plenty of time before Christmas to get used to the idea.'

Lisette shrugged. 'You don't think you may be putting the cart before the horse?' she suggested after a pause.

'What do you mean?'

'I mean, my dear, suppose Sabrina changes her mind?'

'She won't. Not this time.'

'Ah well—' Lisette once more sighed resignedly. 'You never could resist a challenge. It's the—'

'Nature of the beast,' Oliver interrupted. 'Like mother, like son.' He was grinning again.

'How can you say that? After what I went through in my younger days—'

'Loving it, the whole exciting business of fighting your own subtle little battles — scheming and planning and having men swoon round your feet — you were tough, my love. And you're tough still, thank God, beneath that beautiful wilting exterior.'

She flushed faintly, inwardly gratified.

'Go on with you, Oliver. No soft soap, if you please. You have a wily way with you. You should be in politics.'

She spoke quite innocently; but his reaction startled her.

'I *may* be too. In the not-too-far-off future.'

She dropped a spray of hot-house flowers to the table.

'Whatever do you mean? You're joking.'

'No. Liberalism is strengthening. The old order's changing. The aristocracy may not realise it, but only three things are needed to bring the rival party into power again — brains, personality, and sufficient wealth to back them. Victorianism's already on its last legs. Edward's of a happier breed — more democratic in outlook, and far more adaptable to a new image. Working people can't be kept down forever. Campbell-Bannerman knows that, and I've a hunch he'll form the next government—'

'But you—'

'I was talking to a crony of his in Truro recently. He dangled a bait. But I've not bitten yet. Still — I'm thinking about it.'

Lisette threw up her hands. 'And with all your other commitments. The estate, the company – the hotels – will you ever stop, Oliver?'

'I hope not, Mater.' He lifted a hand warningly. 'And don't say "no man can have everything" – because this man's going to have a damn good try – when the right moment arrives.'

He patted her cheek, took a cigar from a gold case, lit it, and while she still watched him, slowly shaking her head – he turned deliberately and left her to the whirl of her own thoughts.

News of the impending marriage soon spread through the whole household causing surprise, a good deal of whispered gossip among servants, and a certain secret envy in female quarters.

'A kind of plot, if you ask me—' Nellie, a kitchen girl, remarked to a housemaid. 'She meant to get him, and that's how she did it – causing an upheaval with all them dramatics at Church.'

Cook, who overheard, said tartly, 'Enough of that, Nellie Oaks. You get on with your work and stop putting wicked thoughts into others' heads. Miss Penderrick's a very nice young lady; and if you ask me the master's a lucky man to get her.'

There was a muttered grumbling that finally died into silence.

Jaina, meanwhile, who had learned the news from Oliver only a short time before, had wandered out into the gardens to get her feelings under control. She had quite liked Sabrina until he'd told her. Now inward resentment niggled her. Since being a tiny child Uncle Oliver had been someone very special to her, and she'd believed she meant the same to him. But of course getting married would make everything different. She would have to take second place; he might hardly even notice her at all. And she was growing up. Her shape was changing. Her face had lost its early plumpness and was showing signs of beauty. Even her tilted eyes appeared larger and more luminously dark in contrast to the magnolia clear skin. When she lifted her head and arms, and twisted this way and that before the mirror, the developing young breasts were obvious above the flat stomach and slender waist. It was silly, she thought then, that other people didn't seem to realise it – especially Uncle Oliver. Stupid too that she had to wear her hair mostly in pigtails when she could look so enticingly grown-up with it pinned on top of her head.

There was so much about herself that she didn't understand at that time — most of all the deep secret realisation that it was nice to be admired by men — even if they were far beneath her, and not worth noticing, like Nicholas Carne, the stable-boy. He had been watching her every time she passed the stables recently. She hadn't let him know she knew, but had gone by with her chin up, feeling his eyes boring through the back of her head. Was this what the nuns had warned her against at school last term? Telling her to think good thoughts only, and never be conceited — never put earthly desires before God? Well she didn't. She didn't desire Nick at all. But she was deeply confused. It had all started about the same time — perhaps a little before — when the bleeding began, and in the middle of class too. She'd been terribly embarrassed by that, and frightened.

Sister Monica had done her best to usher her out of the schoolroom so the other girls wouldn't notice too much, walking closely behind her like a mother-hen pushing a solitary chick to safety. Then there'd been all the explaining — the reassurances that she wasn't ill, she wasn't going to die from some strange disease, but that the bleeding was just a sign from God that she, Jaina Lee, would soon be turning from a little girl into a young woman, and therefore must be more than ever careful to act modestly in the company of boys and young men.

Sister Monica had said a good deal else, but much had been so veiled in mystery and parables that Jaina had forgotten. One thing she had learned — and more from her own instinct and snippets of gossip recollected from other girls than from the good Sister — being unwell once a month was something to do with having babies.

Having babies was important of course. But Jaina was not particularly interested in tiny children. It was herself who mattered, and the strange exciting longings deepening so mysteriously inside her — making her want to race and run with excitement one moment — the next casting her into a well of gloom because she felt suddenly lonely and lost, unsure of anything that lay ahead.

It was in such a mood of vague melancholy that she wandered for a walk towards the moors, on her last afternoon before returning to school. She wasn't supposed to go further than the boundaries of Castle Carnack grounds, because a tinker woman and her son lived over the ridge just beyond the high lane, in a shack where they made brooms, baskets, and kept goats. There was a copse nearby, enclosing a green clearing which in the spring was thick with daffodils. At that season they gathered the blossoms, bunched them, and took them to the nearest villages or suburbs where inns, boarding homes, and shops were glad to pay. The son was industrious at various crafts. He was a dark-eyed curly-haired young man, handsome but rather surly-looking with no apparent interest in the outside world except to make what he could from his own skill.

He'd visited Carnack twice, and been rebuffed so sharply by a manservant and the housekeeper, that he'd afterwards kept his distance from the 'big place'. But Jaina had glimpsed him from a corridor, and thought him somehow exciting. One day, she'd decided, when no stuffy grown-ups were about, she'd go and find out for herself the kind of place they lived in.

That certain afternoon — when everyone seemed still so concerned and occupied by the affair of Uncle Oliver and Sabrina — seemed a propitious time. So she took a narrow side-path that eventually led between larch trees, willows and sloes, upwards towards the more open and wilder landscape. The air was very still under the golden autumn sky; ahead of her she presently glimpsed the white thread of lane winding ribbon-like through the wind-blown trees. She loosened the cape collar of her coat, and impulsively unbraided her hair. She'd left her ugly stiff-brimmed hat behind. Miss Willis, the stodgy governess who had been retained at Carnack as sewing-lady and assistant supervisor of domestic and certain social matters, would have had a fit — almost — Jaina thought, with a surge of triumph. She was such a boring prunes-and-prismy creature. Secretly Jaina had always despised her, and it was fun for once to be able to outwit her and be free of the wretched headgear. She couldn't understand why Lisette kept her on at all. Whatever else she might be, no one could call Aunt Lisette stodgy. It was Uncle Oliver, of course. He seemed determined these days to keep her Jaina, forever a little girl. And she was already nearly five feet tall. Her dresses were growing tight too and showing little slits at the bodices, between the buttons.

She smiled secretly to herself, and it was just then that she noticed the pool. It was under a bend of the moor, overhung by drooping branches of willow, very near to the lane above. In the pale hushed air it glittered with the brilliance of a painting, through the networked shadows of the trees. She paused, staring, remembering something; something of far-off earliest childhood, only half visioned, as though from another land — another world far away. There was music too. Tinkly music, and a painted beautiful face with flower lips; she could feel her baby hand reaching out, and the touch of something sweet and soft — flowers on silk — or was it water? Just pictured water from an artist's brush? The vision was so vivid for a second, she could not move. Then the illusion passed. She shrugged, pushed a branch aside, and took a closer look. It was a real pool after all; a lonely looking clear pool with tiny shapes darting beneath the slipping shadows. It would be nice to take her shoes and stockings off, Jaina thought, and feel the ripples between her toes. One day she would — in the spring perhaps when the sun was warm. She might even bathe. The thought was exhilarating; the impulse to plunge her naked smooth young body into the cool clear water almost overwhelming.

With an effort she tore herself away, and returned to the path. She had only walked a few yards when she heard the rumble of an engine, the grinding of brakes, and looking up saw one of the new strange motor cars drawing to a halt in the lane.

She stood still, wanting to giggle. It was such a funny looking thing, red with the driver sitting high up above the engine, under a canvas cover. He was wearing a light coat that looked like a macintosh. Uncle Oliver's chauffeur had one almost the same, a 'dust coat', he called it, though she didn't know why, and she didn't think it at all smart, much preferring the coachman's canary coloured uniform with the smart tall hat that looked so grand when she and Lisette went driving in the carriage and pair.

This young man wasn't a coachman though, or a chauffeur; she could tell that instantly. No servant would wear such a very large check cap surely? Or such immense goggles. When he clambered from the driver's seat Jaina saw he was tall, with a fair moustache curling up at the ends. She watched him take off the cap, and wipe his forehead as though he was very hot. He bent down to inspect the front of the car, then stood up. When he turned towards the path, Jaina went forward. In spite of his odd-looking clothes she saw that he was very handsome, with thickly waving hair and sideburns the same shade as his moustache. She went forward then, to meet him. There was a half open gate in the fence bordering the property. She stood there waiting as he approached. He looked rather nice, she thought, friendly.

He smiled down at her.

'Hullo.'

Her heart quickened a little. There was something exciting in meeting such a distinguished looking young man under such unexpected circumstances.

'Hullo,' she said shyly.

He paused a moment before continuing, 'I'm looking for Castle Carnack. Must've taken the wrong road though—'

'Oh you have, if you want the front way,' Jaina told him. 'This is the back. There's a path down, but you couldn't take that — that—'

'My car?' He laughed. 'By Jove no. The old girl — or rather I should say young lady — I haven't had her long — wouldn't be up to bashing through trees. She's had about enough already. How far is it to the main entrance?'

Jaina shrugged.

'Quite a long way I should think,' she answered vaguely. 'But if you want to see anyone — Uncle Oliver, or — or—'

His fresh face turned slightly more pink.

'As a matter of fact I wanted to talk to Miss Penderrick, Miss Sabrina Penderrick. My name is Frederick de Marchmont.'

He held out his hand. She gave him her own which he grasped firmly. Her mind whirled. Freddie! this was the Freddie that Sabrina had treated so cruelly. How could she? He had such blue eyes and such a kind smile. Not a dull looking young man at all. A wild thought occurred to her. Perhaps if she could find Sabrina and bring her up to the moor, Freddie would make her fall in love with him again and take her off in the funny looking car so they could get married as they planned. Then Uncle Oliver would be free and she, Jaina, would have all his love for herself. The idea just for a few seconds seemed a brainwave and quite possible.

'I could find Sabrina, I think,' she said, 'and bring her here. Would you like me to? I know she's thought about you a lot.'

'Has she now!' The nice voice was more grim. He frowned. 'No, it would be better I'm sure if I called at the house. Obviously—' his glance became curious '—you know all about our sorry affair.'

'I think most people do,' she answered. 'And everyone believes she treated you very badly.'

'Oh, I don't know. Women you know – nerves! it could have been an attack of the vapours.'

'She shouldn't have had them in Church,' Jaina stated critically. 'I know I wouldn't. I'd have known who I wanted to marry before I did anything so awful. Of course, I'll probably not marry at all.'

She lifted her head purposefully an inch higher, revealing through the transient light her own exquisite youthful profile. She could feel Frederick's eyes for the first time fully aware of her; could feel a deepening interest in his gaze and manner.

'I'm sure you're quite wrong,' she heard him saying. 'You'll have suitors galore in no time, and be able to take your pick from the whole bunch of 'em.'

'Oh, I didn't mean that. I mean – marriage isn't the only thing, is it? There are so many more exciting things to do.'

She had no idea what impelled the observation, what deep instincts and inbred secret knowledge stirred her.

'Yes I suppose so,' he agreed. 'I must say you seem to be a very – observant young lady. And I don't even know who I'm talking to.'

She smiled her wise half-child, half-woman smile, knowing she was charming him.

'I'm Jaina,' she said. 'Jaina Lee. Mr Cavannagh's niece.'

'Oh.' He looked surprised. 'Then I'm very lucky. You'll be able to show me down, won't you?'

'This way?' She frowned doubtfully.

'There's a path, I suppose?'

'Oh yes. But – someone might see you, from the kitchens. Or the stables.'

He laughed. 'I'm not about to plunder the larder or commit a jewel robbery. By Jove, you surely didn't imagine such a thing?'

Reddening with confusion she answered, 'Of course I didn't. All right—' pulling herself together, 'follow me.'

She turned swiftly, pushing restricting claws of undergrowth and trees aside.

'Let me go first,' he said, when the track suddenly narrowed, 'or you'll get your face torn.'

She allowed him to play the chivalrous gentleman with one strong arm lifted to make an arch of the branches overhead. She passed underneath feeling suddenly grown up and cared for — picturing herself as Sabrina might have been — a bride walking from the altar on Frederick de Marchmont's arm beneath an arc of regimental swords. Sabrina had been stupid, she thought with a tinge of contempt. Life with Uncle Oliver wouldn't be nearly so romantic. He could be bossy when he felt like it, even a little cruel. And yet somehow he managed to charm everyone. There was something 'different' about him — an energy and infectious zest for life that made everything either glow a little brighter, or else dark as doom. She had adored him when she was living at the mission as a tiny child in Ceylon. His visits had filled her with pride, raising her above the orphan status of the other young children. But, as she'd grown older, strictness in him had increased, and since her coming to Castle Carnack his sternness had often reduced her to secret tears.

Why? She didn't know, except that he was something special to her — or had been, until she'd heard of his engagement to Sabrina.

Silly Sabrina, she thought again, walking with Frederick de Marchmont through the trees. But perhaps her marriage to Uncle Oliver wouldn't come off after all. Perhaps she'd run away again before it happened. If she tried then Jaina determined she'd do all she could to help her; she was sure it might save a good deal of unhappiness for both of them. The decision prompted her to ask Freddie bluntly, 'Do you still want to marry Sabrina?'

He glanced down at her, taken aback by her nerve. What a question, he thought. Was she trying to goad him, or being merely precocious?

The cool golden eyes staring up at him appeared quite without guile. The flower mouth had a faint expectant smile at the corners, a certain innocent friendliness that moved him strangely.

He cleared his throat with a short cough and looked away. 'We shall have to see,' he said, adding after a moment, 'I take it you know her quite well?'

'Oh, I wouldn't say that. I'm at school you see. This is my half term. Most of the time I'm with the nuns, at Bristol.'

'By Jove! are you now,' a statement more than a query. 'A convent?'

She nodded. Her smile widened. 'Yes. You sound surprised. Why? Don't you think I'm good enough?'

He laughed outright.

'I've not had much chance of finding that out.'

She shrugged. 'No. We're terribly restricted there. And these clothes are awful, aren't they?' She glanced wrily at the serge coat. 'But it won't be for long now. When I'm fifteen I expect I'll leave. That's only another year.'

'So you're fourteen?'

'Yes — almost.'

'And what are you going to do then,' he asked, 'after you've left school?'

Again the characteristic shrug. 'I've no idea. Stay here, I suppose, while Uncle Oliver and Aunt Lisette try and find me a rich husband. Of course I shall make up my own mind. I'm not going to be palmed on to just anyone with money. And there'll be an argument, I suppose—'

'What about?'

'About leaving. Aunt Lisette wanted me to go to Paris for finishing off—' she suddenly giggled '—that sounds awful doesn't it? Like being shot, or a cake or something having icing put on? But Uncle Oliver didn't agree. And I know why.'

'Oh?'

'He wants to keep me under his eye. Because of my mother, you see.'

'Your mother? Doesn't he like her?'

'She's dead.'

The abrupt statement silenced him momentarily, then he said politely, 'I'm sorry.'

'You needn't be. It was a long time ago, when I was a baby. I can't remember her properly at all, but I think she was what's called a bad influence.'

'Great Scott! what gave you that idea?'

'Things — the way Uncle Oliver looks at Aunt Lisette sometimes. Just words, and kind of secret remarks. And nobody ever telling me anything. Oh, I think she was wicked. And beautiful

I expect. Yes, I'm sure she was beautiful. She smelt nice. And sometimes I seem to be looking at a picture — when I'm half asleep mostly. It's a funny feeling, like staring deep down into the sea with flowers and feathers — peacocks' feathers — waving in the water. And yes — very dark eyes. I used to tell them about it — Aunt Lisette and the Nanny I had when I first came here. But they said it was a dream. I expect it was.' Her voice had saddened and become very soft. A brief feeling of enchantment fell upon him. As she lifted a hand to brush a spray of leaves away, he noticed how slender the fingers were and delicately formed, like those of some frail porcelain figure. He quickly pulled himself together. What a strange young creature she was. And too grown up by half to be still at school. Just then the trees and bushes abruptly cleared, and the back of Castle Carnack emerged grey and imposing below, beneath a sloping stretch of grassland and terraces. There was a paddock at the left, where someone — a groom probably — was exercising a horse.

'That's Frank,' Jaina said. 'Trying out the new filly, I suppose. She only came on Monday.'

'Does your uncle ride much?'

'No. He hasn't time. He's always buzzing off—' she gave a soft laugh, 'that sounds like a bee doesn't it? But what I mean was he has such a lot of business. He travels all over the world. Of course he can ride.' She sighed. 'He can do most things I guess. Perhaps it will be different though — when he marries Sabrina.'

A hand went to her mouth quickly as she realised what she'd said.

He stopped walking. 'What did you say? Marry Sabrina?'

She hung her head. 'You didn't know, did you? Oh, I'm sorry I didn't mean to—'

'Hm!' When she lifted her head she saw that his face had paled. For a second or two he looked almost hard, and years older.

'I shouldn't have told you,' she continued. 'It slipped out.'

She waited for him to speak. When he didn't, she resumed 'Would you rather go back? Perhaps—?'

He gave a jerk of his shoulders and started walking again 'Certainly not. I think she at least owes me an explanation.'

'Yes.'

He forced a faint smile and touched her hand. 'Don't worry. I'm glad you've put me in the picture. We'd better hurry in case she spots me and tries to escape the Big Bad Wolf.'

'You're not a big bad wolf,' Jaina told him. 'That's more like Uncle Oliver. He just — well, he's used to having what he wants. Very rich people grow like that, I suppose.'

'Some maybe.'

He quickened his pace so that she had to run to keep up with him.

When they approached the first terrace a figure in riding kit cut from the paddock through a gate towards a side door of the house. Near the steps he turned his head and looked directly towards them.

'There he is,' Jaina said, 'there's Uncle.'

'How very convenient.'

De Marchmont's pace increased. Cavannagh took a few steps to meet him.

Oliver offered a hand. His expression was bland.

'Good afternoon. I think we do know each other — by sight. But I didn't realise you were a friend of my young niece. Jaina—' he dismissed the child with an authoritative gesture, 'run away, quickly now. Your aunt wants you.' Reluctantly Jaina obeyed.

'We met by chance,' the other man said coolly when they were alone. 'My car's parked in the lane above. I made what I thought was a convenient detour from the main road. As it happened it was quite a long way round. Still—' He took Oliver's hand. 'How d'you do! You'll guess my business without being told, I expect?'

'I'm sorry, de Marchmont, I'm not very bright at riddles. Hunches are more in my line. Yes. I've a hunch. To see Sabrina. Miss Penderrick, your erstwhile truant bride.' He smiled without humour, and continued, 'My dear fellow, you've left it rather late in the day, I'm afraid. Sabrina's a proud girl. You should have up and followed her and shown her what was what in the least gentlemanly way if necessary. She would have forgiven you a spanking, sir. But certainly not scorn and neglect. I'm sorry, but that's the truth. And now she's quite committed in another direction — to me.'

Frederick flushed.

'Be damned to you, sir. I've a right to put my case, and if I know Sabrina — which I certainly do — we've been friends since childhood — she'll be wanting to talk. So if you don't mind—'

'I do mind. And so does Sabrina. She's quite finished with you, de Marchmont. I have her word — and believe me, I'm no liar. She wants nothing more to do with you.'

'I don't believe you.'

'That's your business. Whether you do or not doesn't affect me in the least. But as this is my land I'd be obliged if you'd leave the way that you came as soon as possible, before Miss Penderrick is embarrassed by your unwelcome appearance. She's out for a drive at present. But I expect her back quite shortly.'

Freddie gave a shrug.

'Don't worry. I've no wish to force a confrontation. Duels are no longer à-la-mode. Good day to you.'

Frederick de Marchmont turned on his heel and strode smartly back the way he'd come, realising he'd made an error in trying to manipulate a meeting with Sabrina on that 'jumped up brigand's' own terrain. He didn't doubt the man's assertion — certainly not the young girl Jaina's that Sabrina had become involved with him. She had always been impetuous and the victim of her own emotions. This made the fellow more than ever an upstart in his eyes. No gentleman would take advantage of any woman in such circumstances. But then Cavannagh was not, and never would be a gentleman; and Sabrina had proved great instability of character in falling victim to his glib persuasiveness and oppressive charm. Still, there was time yet somehow to put a spoke in the fellow's plans, although during the last few weeks de Marchmont had seriously wondered whether the effort was worth it. He'd been in love with her; he was hurt. Certainly his vanity had suffered. But the world was wide, and full of attractive women. His spirits always sank a little when he reached this point of reasoning. He loved her — or he had. Sabrina in every way was beautiful and unique. The fact remained though, that she'd let him down. And come what may, he doubted he could ever feel completely the same about her.

If she wrote to him, or apologised — thought up some explanation that would suffice and allay any doubts he had of her integrity — would he capitulate once again and be able to resume where they left off? Probably. But deep down the wound would still fester. Damn it all — he was human. Perhaps the trouble had been that they'd taken each other too much for granted. It was true, that during recent months something of the mystery — the first excitement of being in love — had worn a little thin. But that was life, wasn't it? No man expected high romance to last forever. He'd looked forward to sharing the pleasurable colourful routine of other young married couples of his circle and class — riding, hunting, house-parties — holidays abroad, and in due course children to fill the stately home with their pranks and laughter. What more could anyone want?

He smiled to himself grimly.

Sabrina apparently demanded excitement of a very different kind. So perhaps in the end all had happened for the best. His own conclusion reassured and fortified his smarting ego; and as he pushed his way back through the trees to the lane his mind switched abruptly to his chance meeting with Jaina. A child only — but of a rare type. A last dying filter of sun, shining gold through the interlaced branches, revived a startling memory of the fey slanting eyes in her tilted face. She had seemed lonely and vulnerable. So young, yet in a deep instinctive way already aware of womanhood's flowering. A nymph on the verge of waking to reality. Unintentionally his senses stirred. He found himself picturing her in six months — a year; could almost feel the slim limbs pliant in his arms — the gentle golden sheen of soft thighs and virginal breasts responding to his touch.

The next moment he cursed himself silently for being a fool. What tommy-rot and impertinence. The sort of indulgence no decent man allowed. Thirteen years old! Nearly fourteen, she'd said — and he twenty-five. All the same he'd suspected a knowing look in those strange eyes once or twice — a certain unavowed coquetry that belied, in a subtle way, her appealing innocence.

When he reached the lane he jerked the car's engine suddenly to life. Presently he was forcing it to a maximum speed along the high moors. He felt curiously and irrationally perturbed. Not because of Sabrina. Sabrina lingered as a beautiful and upsetting memory — but vividly real. His emotions following the interlude with Oliver's intriguing niece were entirely different;

intangible and too remote to define. He was a practical man — by nature easy going, yet quite capable of dealing with most situations in a down-to-earth fashion. Now a whole host of fresh and hitherto unknown instincts stirred him, in which normal codes of behaviour and reasoning had no part. Although so outwardly possessed — Jaina, that child in the unbecoming serge coat — had seemed for those few minutes to be more at one with the cloud-ridden sky, great boulders of the brooding hills and distant scars of ruined mine-stacks, than with the imposing massive structure of Castle Carnack. A savage wild countryside this, he decided, forcing his thoughts to other channels. The sooner he got back to Falmouth the better. He put on an extra spurt. The engine groaned and suddenly stopped. He wasted five minutes' energy again in trying to get it started, then gave up and set off on foot to find help. His first sign of any was a remote inn, The Queen of Prussia.

By then Frederick de Marchmont's nerves and temper were on edge. Blast all women, he thought. It was the last time he'd have anything to do with the Cavannagh breed. His decision, genuine as it was at the time proved ineffectual, although it was not until the following spring that the pattern of events showed how wrong he was.

6

Sabrina and Oliver were married in November at Truro Registry Office, with the minimum of fuss, and completely without publicity, due to Cavannagh's influence and manipulation of the press. Sabrina wore a blue velvet three-quarter length coat, tightly waisted over a gown of the same material with a spreading embroidered hemline just brushing the floor above the tips of pointed buckled shoes. Her hat had a wide brim, pushed upwards over her curled fringe of pale hair. It was liberally topped with flowers and fruit, and worn slightly sideways, at a coquettish tilt towards the back of her head. Fox furs draped her shoulders, just below the high lace yolk of the gown which was stiffened by bone supports at the neck. She had slept very little the night before; nerves, combined with the structure of her fashionable ensemble made her stiff and exhausted before she dismounted from the limousine for the ceremony. Her chin was forced erectly upwards above the throat. She felt smothered.

'You look entrancing,' Lisette had told her before they set off. 'Quite queenly in fact.'

Oliver had echoed his appreciation on the return journey to Castle Carnack, but sensing her tension had added, 'Cheer up, my love; you can soon rid yourself of the trappings.' And she had blushed.

There was a reception in the dining room and great hall, attended by servants and staff. No visitors from outside had been invited, but one or two guests — including a wealthy count from France who had decided to spend Christmas in Cornwall — were included in the celebrations.

Sabrina, who had quickly changed into a cream silk picture-dress, felt dazed, exhilarated, and a little frightened at the same time. When she heard Oliver and herself toasted as Mr and Mrs Oliver Cavannagh, her pale cheeks flamed. Mrs Cavannagh! for a wild moment she had an impulse to rush from the exotic surroundings as she'd rushed from Freddie in Church only a few months before. She glanced round at the swimming assembly of smiling faces, the glasses raised, feeling the perspiration pricking her whole body. Her eyes closed briefly then opened slowly, to find Oliver's brilliant gaze firmly upon her, in so concentrated a look of desire, she flinched. She smiled mechanically, as he whispered, 'No magic allowed any more, darling — no disappearing trick.'

There was amusement in the undertone, but something else also — a warning. And for the first time she realised the full extent of the commitment she'd undertaken.

His wife! Oliver Cavannagh's wife.

It had all happened so quickly. Recalling the circumstances a tide of panic rose in her. She felt trapped — bewitched — although not entirely unpleasantly so. She was thrilled as well. But what had she let herself in for so heedlessly? Oh God! What would marriage to Oliver be like?

That night he gave an effective demonstration, and through

her bewilderment, pain, shock, and ultimate reciprocation, was a wild sense of physical awakening that took her to another dimension — another completely new state and knowledge of herself that left her weak and shaken; no longer Sabrina Penderrick the wilful and defiant girl who had so easily abandoned one lover for another — but a woman unrecognisable to herself; a sensual creature woken for the first time to her true potentials of sexual awareness.

As his lips and hands traced the soft sheen of flesh, exploring and caressing every secret intimacy of her womanhood, she withdrew at first, shuddering and frightened of abandonment. But his breath was warm on her cheeks, neck, and shoulders; the pressure of his mouth and tongue firm against her breasts, as one arm slipped round and beneath her, encasing her buttocks, drawing her ever closer — closer — until against his demands she weakened, and collapsed, abandoning herself to their mutual need. Her womb's pulse leaped and became a living fountain of desire. After the agony, exquisite waves of passionate fulfilment encompassed and drowned her. She closed her eyes, and when the dark tide receded, found her arms still round his neck, her thighs defenceless, entwined under his. As her breathing quickened she looked up, and he eased himself above her. Between the heavy lids his eyes gleamed, slits of possessive mystery — hypnotic and primaeval. The eyes of a master. Then, very slowly, the sensuous lips smiled. He released her and rolled away, with an expression of quiet indulgence on his face. The skin of his broad chest had a mahogany sheen in the muted glow of the bedside lamp, each fine hair touched with gold. He lifted his hand and forced her head round so her chin was tilted upwards towards his mouth. His lips came down upon hers again, and the kiss this time was slow, and calculated to win once more her submission. She looked very beautiful — a flower-like nymph roused from lily-white to rose-and-silver from his ravishing.

'Sabrina!' he whispered. 'Oh my Sabrina.'

She did not ask him if he loved her. The question somehow — even the word — would have seemed trite, mundane. For the time being it was sufficient to have been wooed and won by this magnificent man who was her husband.

It was only later when he said abruptly, 'Time for sleep,

darling. I've things to attend to in the morning before we leave—' Facts slipped into place with a jerk of reality. 'Things to attend to!' Commonplace, everyday things. Business matters that had nothing to do with marriage or their trip to the Continent. How much, in the future, she wondered, would his true environment — the world of high finance and his own business empire — intrude upon their mutual personal life?

A faint shadow clouded her imagination. Long after he slept, which was almost instantly, she lay awake, physically at peace, but intangibly mentally perturbed, because she had given herself so completely, and he had been able to switch his mind elsewhere at a second's notice.

Men! perhaps all men were alike — perhaps even Freddie at heart. Poor dear Freddie! a tinge of remorse niggled her. Against her will she found herself thinking, 'I could have managed Freddie. But this one — never. He will always be top. Always the leader — master. Unless—' A hint of the old wilful spirit rose in her. He did not know her yet — not properly. One day he might find she surprised him.

The imp of mischief in her deepened, refortifying her ego. Soon, with a little smile on her lips, she slept. She did not wake until the morning, when winter sunlight filtered the curtains, casting a tracery of shadows round the room from the networked branches of the trees outside.

7

The first week of the Continental honeymoon passed, for Sabrina, in a dream. They visited France, Spain, Germany and Austria, returning to Paris, where they spent Christmas. The passionate tempo of love-making retained its zest following periods of lazing or sightseeing under the most luxurious and comfortable conditions. Days and nights seemed to merge into one. Under the heady influence of wining and dining at the most expensive restaurants or artistic pensions, the world assumed a magical aura through which everyday life registered only as a mundane memory. During that period Sabrina felt she knew every inch of Oliver's lithe body, yet every time he made love to her his expertise swept her to new rapture. She held nothing from him, denied not an inch of herself to his demands. He taught her all the subtle facets of stimulus and awakening to desire. She knew instinctively what was coming, but was always surprised.

However, as the time for leaving Paris for home arrived, she sensed an instinctive change in him. He became slightly more abstracted. It was as though a trespasser had at last softly penetrated their intimacy, bringing at moments a veiled look to his eyes.

So she was not unduly surprised, just mildly depressed when he said one afternoon, 'I'm sorry, darling, I'll have to leave you for an hour or two — a damned nuisance, but there's a man I have to see for dinner tonight. I've kept putting it off, but business is business.'

'Oh.' Her spirits sank. 'Yes, it is a pity. Can't I come?'

They were in the bedroom. He touched her chin teasingly. 'No, you can't. Sometimes men have to be alone. I shan't be late back. You're not frightened at eating on your own for once, are you? I'll tell Jules to take special care of you and serve his most delectable menu.'

'You needn't,' her voice was a little sharp. 'I may decide not to stay in the hotel. Eat out, I mean — at that intriguing little café place we found yesterday.'

'I don't want you to. Ladies don't dine out or take supper on their own. Do you understand, Sabrina?'

'Very well.' She appeared to agree. But her eyes were colder than usual, reflective, and a little remote. Against her will she was recalling the unsavoury gossip concerning his French mistress, and was suspicious.

So suspicious in fact, that after he'd left about six o'clock, she did what normally was quite alien to her nature — started searching among a few odds and ends and private papers in a pocket of his smaller travelling case. There were a few scribbled notes — a memorandum from the past, pencil, pen, a business diary, and casual recordings of figures. There was also a small black book with a gold clasp, which included items that meant nothing to her — until she reached the end. And then she was certain she had found it, a strange address which ran simply:

> Lili Leblanc,
> Café des Fleurs,
> 3 Rue Violette,
> Montmartre,
> Paris.

She stared at it resentfully, with a disconcerting wave of jealousy rising in her. The paper had been carefully folded, and she fancied a faint drift of perfume still lingered there — a subtle insidious scent reminiscent of feminine allure and secret bedroom intimacies that were echoed somehow in the thin fragile writing which certainly was not Oliver's.

She debated for some minutes on how to treat the matter — to disregard it if possible, or act heedlessly on intuition. The former proved to be impossible. It was not Oliver's way normally to lie or prevaricate. But this time, tired physically, but with her senses overstimulated from the wild impact of passionate experience, she felt he was doing just that — partially, anyway.

An ungovernable irrational sense of betrayal seized her. She could be wrong of course; most women, she knew, would be content to turn a blind eye to any possible secret infidelity — the excitement and considerable advantages of being Mrs Oliver Cavannagh far outweighing any manly moral lapse. But she could not calmly accept such a situation. She had admittedly been aware from the beginning of his reputation. But a honeymoon surely demanded complete undivided attention and faithfulness. In any case, she argued, he could at least have been honest with her. She was no prude. She might have listened with restraint and somehow beguiled him into disregarding the odious Lili — yes, the other woman had already become that to her — a scheming beautiful creature like so many French women were, determined still to lure Oliver from her side, and impinge on their life together.

She, Sabrina, hated her. The sense of outrage was so intense, that on the brink of dressing for dinner at the hotel, she changed her mind, knowing she could not eat, and that she had to find out for herself if what she suspected was true, and the nature of her husband's involvement with Lili Leblanc.

It did not occur to her, at that point, that he could have been telling her the truth; the tiny slip of paper was sufficient to show he still treasured the relationship, or he would have thrown it away months ago. Possibly, she thought, as she dressed herself in a blue velvet costume, he took it out at moments just to sniff the lingering sickly smell of perfume. It had obviously been lying near some personal memento — a scrap of lace handkerchief probably, that she'd found on the floor near his case before leaving Castle Carnack. She'd thought nothing of it at the time, elated as she'd been by the excitement of events. But now the memory of the fragile thing registered as further proof of his duplicity. She stared at herself through the ornately framed mirror, and was gratified by the reflection. Proud head with lips set determinedly above the furs, eyes brilliant, kindled to sparkling pools of different shades beneath the tawny gold fringe of hair. She reached for her hat, tilting it slightly to one side, and put a pin in, securing it firmly, so the curling ospreys swept from the crown over the brim to a shoulder. Spots of brilliant colour flamed on her cheeks. She pulled on a pair of cream kid gloves, took her gold link bag, with cosmetics and money in it, then went downstairs, treading carefully with her skirts held up elegantly by one hand, revealing just a few inches of embroidered petticoat.

When she reached the desk she told the receptionist she would not be in for dinner.

'I am dining with a friend,' she announced, noticing the man's obvious discomfiture.

'But, madam—'

'My husband is fully aware of it,' she lied, 'I expect he neglected to inform you.' She smiled so sweetly Oliver's instructions were instantly forgotten, or conveniently ignored, and a minute later a cab was heralded to take her to her destination.

Although the weather was cold the lights and evening mystery of Paris gave the glow of warmth and excitement as the cab threaded its way through the maze of streets to the artists' quarters. Pin points of stars pierced the deep blue velvet night sky; a moon was rising, casting strange interlaced shadows from the trees over the cobbles. Mellow lights streamed from cafés and wine shops, blending with colourful walls — the blue and pink of doors and windows, reflecting interiors where flowers mingled with the glitter of glass and wine bottles, and patrons unconventionally attired ate their meals in an atmosphere of intimate bonhomie. This had been the world of Van Gogh, Lautrec, Renoir, Signac, and many other impressionist painters. The little tables at the side of the streets which would appear again in the spring had mostly been taken inside now, but the romantic atmosphere remained, and as the vehicle neared its destination, Sabrina's niggling worry over Lili Leblanc temporarily abated. The horses' hooves echoed and clippety-cloppetted down shadowed byways and lamp-lit corners. Then, rather abruptly the vehicle stopped. The driver heaved himself down and pointed ahead, round a sharp turn. 'That's it, madam' he said, moving his hand vigorously, 'La Rue Violette. Not far. You go. I wait here. Yes?'

'Oh!' Sabrina was momentarily taken aback. 'Very well. The restaurant, or café – do you know it?'

He nodded.

'Many cafés there. All together. *You* find. Too—' he opened his arms expressively then drew them together. 'Too – how shall we say? – Too narrow, yes, – to turn.'

Lifting her skirts Sabrina alighted from the cab, and a moment or two later had made her way round the bend. From semi-darkness she suddenly found herself again in a subdued golden flood of light, intermingled with a spilling stream of orange. As she screwed up her eyes scanning the lettering in windows and above coloured doors, the muted sound of chatter and laughter reached her. A half-tipsy portly figure in a black jacket wearing a beret over one eye bumped into her, bowed, made a profuse apology, and went on again, swaying from one side of the pavement to the other.

Not more than a dozen yards ahead Sabrina located the Café des Fleurs. It was a low building compared with many others grouped round it, with an entry running down one side. The main window though was wide, painted deep blue, lace curtains were half-drawn across the glass panes, taking figures inside into blurred silhouette. The door, which was pink, was half open.

Sabrina pushed it wider and went in. She found herself in a passage having white walls almost covered with pots of trailing plants. A yard or two ahead, doors on opposite sides led into rooms beneath hanging baskets of flowers. At the far end of the corridor was a reception desk where a woman sat under a red swinging lantern. Beaded curtains divided the back portion of the small restaurant from the front. But it was possible to glimpse shadowed figures moving, and catch the murmur of conversation, which was intermingled with the tinkle of pots and cutlery. The air was welcomingly warm, intermingled with a savoury smell of cooking and beer.

As she stood pondering which room to enter, a young woman appeared carrying a tray. She pushed past the receptionist, and approached Sabrina.

'Yes, *madame*?'

At first Sabrina could not speak. The girl was so very beautiful — dark hair drawn in two curves to the back of her slim neck, glossy and glowing as birds' wings. Her mouth was full and exquisitely curved in the suggestion of a half smile, her eyes a very clear gold, black lashed, large and limpid. She was slender, but not thin; a lace apron tied at the waist over a blue gown emphasised her alluring form — the full yet trim breasts, curving gently from neat shoulders and rounded throat, were invitingly obvious, but not distastefully so. Only a French woman, Sabrina thought with a pang of envy, could appear so innocent yet compellingly seductive. If this was Lili, no wonder Oliver had felt impelled to pay her a visit. A visit? And what else?

Her voice was cold when she said, 'I would like a glass of wine, and perhaps a sandwich, or—'

'Ah yes, *madame*. You wish refreshment? But *certainement*. This way if you please.'

Still with the tray in her hand she indicated the room on her right. Sabrina entered, and saw that it was larger than she'd thought, and divided from the back portion of the building only by the multi-coloured bead curtains.

She found the most secluded place possible at a small table in a corner nearest to the frail barrier where movement of the figures behind, though blurred, was visible. As she relaxed she realised that she had no concrete plan. When she'd started off from the hotel in such a confused state of jealous reaction, her one idea had been to confront the detestable Lili — even Oliver, should he be there — with some trumped up excuse on her lips.

Now, she discovered, a believable explanation would be difficult. She could only say she had been bored and decided to make a tour of Montmartre's night life on her own, as Oliver was not there to accompany her. He would be extremely annoyed probably; but he could hardly accuse her of lying, only of disobeying his instructions; and he would be in the weak position of having his false story about dining with a business acquaintance revealed. So! she sat back as brief anxiety stiffened again into indignation. She kept herself well shadowed in the dim light, and when wine and light refreshments were brought she toyed purposefully at eating, keeping her attention constantly on the interior beyond the curtain.

For almost half an hour nothing remotely suspicious occurred. There was a coming and going between tables and the far back of the café, where steam emerged as a door opened presumably from the kitchens. The beautiful girl appeared several times with her wine-tray, and Sabrina also glimpsed the broader form of an older woman busying herself to and fro behind. A waiter — very French looking and efficient, passed by on quick soft feet, at intervals; from the other room across the corridor violin music started up — a nostalgic melody in a minor key, accompanied presently by the husky voice of a woman singing. The sensual, nostalgic atmosphere intensified. Sabrina, lulled by the colourful yet dim lighting, music, and potency of the wine, felt a creeping sense of drowsiness overcoming her. She pulled herself together abruptly, and caught the murmur of conversation from the back.

She turned her head, and went rigid. The half silhouetted form of a man in a dark coat, entered from a recess, or door — whatever it was, leading from the left of the corridor into the private portion of the café. For a second, as the young woman went forward to meet him, his features were not visible. But when he bent his head, kissing her on both cheeks — the warm glow of a swinging lantern lit his profile for a quick instant to unmistakable clarity. Even through the narrow chink of the curtains his identity was unmistakable.

Oliver.

With a trembling hand gone suddenly cold, Sabrina pushed the beaded strings an inch wider, watching with cold, petrified attention the lift of her hands and lovely chin — then the affectionate linking of arms as they turned and receded into the violet shadows. Violet! soft and secret, a subtle colour – turning to deepening dark crimson behind Sabrina's eyes. Her lids closed briefly. She felt mildly faint. She had half expected the revelation. But the reality of the disclosure was worse – far worse – than she'd anticipated, and far too unpleasant for physical confrontation. She knew in that brief interim that she was incapable of facing them. Her body had become icy cold. Her mind was frozen. So this was what her life was to be – a humbug affair of physical ravishing at Castle Carnack, interspersed by constant periods of boredom while Oliver bestowed his sexual prowess elsewhere.

Perhaps he was even in love with the girl – woman – or whatever she was. Then why hadn't he come out into the open and married her? The answer was obvious of course. He needed a wife of breeding and family, someone with sufficient standing – however much she might have disgraced her reputation – to give him a 'leg-up' – wasn't that the vulgar expression used – in the social world? Well, he would have a shock, she told herself bitterly. In future Mr Oliver Cavannagh might not find her body so available whenever he felt inclined for a gratifying session in the marriage bed.

Marriage! it was merely an experiment to him – a gamble.

Presently she got up, paid her bill, and left.

The cab was still waiting round the corner. She gave instructions for her return to the hotel in cold clipped tones. The man glanced at her for a second with curiosity. Under the lamp light her face was hard and set. She could have aged ten years in the brief interim of her absence. He shrugged, heaved himself to the driver's seat, and the next moment they were jolting down the cobbled streets towards the main thoroughfare.

At the hotel Sabrina took her key from the receptionist automatically, and made her way under a veneer of haughty indifference to the lift.

When she reached the bedroom her defiance was weakening, leaving her utterly exhausted. Her aptitude for planning seemed completely to have deserted her. She did not undress immediately, but lay on the bed for a time until commonsense told her Oliver might soon return, and she had no intention of his finding her fully attired and at the mercy of questioning.

She got up and divested herself of the velvet gown and constricting underwear. Then she slipped on a silk nightdress and wrap, and sat before the mirror, unloosening her hair. Its sheen glowed in the lamplight like a shroud of pale satin as she brushed it automatically, sweeping its silken masses down both sides of her pale face over her shoulders.

How white she was! strained and remote looking, like a waiting, watchful ghost.

When Oliver came in she was still seated there, idly toying with cosmetics and applying salve to her lips. She had used more perfume than was necessary. Its odour filled the air. A bottle had overturned, and she had simply placed it upright again without troubling to replace the stopper.

Oliver stopped abruptly behind her chair.

'Heavens,' he muttered. 'Are you trying to seduce me?' His voice verged between irritation and amusement. 'There's really no need, my love.'

He went to the window and opened it. When she said nothing he frowned slightly, returned to her side and kissed the top of her head lightly. Then he forced her eyes to meet his.

'What's the matter?'

'Nothing,' she told him coldly, turning away.

His hand slid to a breast, enclosing it possessively, but with firm gentleness.

'Oh don't, Oliver,' she said shortly. 'I'm tired. I don't feel like—'

'What?'

'That sort of thing.'

'Oh!' he stared at her, perplexed. 'Why so chilly all of a sudden? What have you been doing with yourself?'

She got up and walked towards the bed, with her back turned deliberately to him. She'd no wish to see the ardour in his eyes, watch the sensuous lazy smile curve his lips so calculated to charm her. Beneath the thin wrap her gracefully curved figure was provocatively defined. Alluring creature, he thought. Playing with him, was she? He had an urge to slap her, but instead controlled the instinct, and simply took her by the shoulders, and forced her round, trying to draw her close.

She resisted.

'I told you, Oliver. I don't feel like—'

'Loving? Or intercourse? Is that all it means to you? While I dined with Louis Monière, have you decided after all that golden boy de Marchmont would have been the better gamble for you? Oh, I've no doubt his manners and instincts might be finer, and that as a gentleman I don't quite make the grade. But then—' against her will he drew her tight against him '—you didn't want the gentleman did you? Or you'd have married him. Surely you're not regretting it already? Sabrina—'

His lips were suddenly warm and demanding on her mouth. She could feel the heavy pumping of his heart against her breasts, and the fiery longing it stirred in her roused her to irrational anger.

'Go away. Leave me alone.'

'The devil I will! − when I choose to.' His face had turned a ferocious red. Hurt and intense humiliation filled him. Yet he still controlled any physical outburst.

'Sabrina, I don't know what the hell's got into you, but one thing's for sure, I don't intend any romantic yearnings for a former lover to come between us. No comparisons understand? No lusting in your heart for another—'

'And what about you?' she cried heedlessly, forgetting discretion and all her former determination to be cold and unobtainable. 'How *dare* you criticise me when − when—' she paused to get her breath, half choking from the lump in her throat.

'Me?' He appeared genuinely confused.

'Yes *you*!' The jealous little demon urged her on wildly. 'Your dinner with that − that Louis someone or other − it was all lies, wasn't it? Just a cover up so you could carry on your disgusting affair with the Lili creature. How could you, Oliver − and on our honeymoon—' she broke off, swallowing hard. Then automatically a hand went to her throat. What had she said? Heavens! he'd know now. Her own words had betrayed her. She glanced round desperately. The tell-tale scrap of paper had fallen from the dressing table to the floor, and lay there as condemning proof of her action. Oliver's case, too, was not properly closed. The pause, the silence, seemed to her interminable. For minutes − or it could have been only seconds − he stood perfectly still, as though carved in stone. Only the glance of his eyes moved, travelling from her face to the condemning evidence.

He stared at her again, then said between the hard line of his lips, 'You deceitful, crafty little madam.'

She winced, as he approached and backed nearer to the bed, collapsing on it as he approached meaningfully. She fell on her back. He grabbed her by the lacy neck of her nightdress and jerked her up again. 'So that's the kind of woman I've married,' he said. 'A cheat. Did your parents never teach you that nice girls don't steal or pry into anyone else's business.' She simply stared at him, wide-eyed, lips slightly parted. He smiled sardonically. 'Well well! obviously not. A pity. Because now, my darling, I'll have to do it myself.' He pushed her back against the pillows, tore the flimsy garment from her body and without tenderness or consideration ravished and took her to him.

She made no sound, but gritted her teeth until it was over. Then she said, 'I hate you, Oliver Cavannagh.'

He smiled wrily. 'At the moment I hate you too. Never mind my love, no doubt we shall manage to fool the world, and in the end even tolerate each other—'

'I won't—'

'Live with me? Oh, but you will. I told you at the beginning there'd be no escape this time, and I meant it. So get up, make yourself look respectable for the night, even if you're not. We both need sleep. Tomorrow, after this wretched experience, we'll return to Castle Carnack.'

It was only later, as she lay sleepless beside him that she realised how completely he'd won, and that he had made no attempt to explain his interlude with Lili Leblanc, except for one brief allusion to the visit as a 'purely business matter', a statement she could in no way disprove.

7

Sabrina writhed and chafed inwardly at being 'hauled back', as she considered it, to Castle Carnack a week earlier than had been planned. She resented being treated as a naughty child, when the whole business had resulted from Oliver's secret visit to see his mistress. That Lili Leblanc was the woman gossiped about by ill-meaning matrons and uncharitable society, she had no doubts whatever. Therefore — although she was inwardly a little ashamed of having rummaged through Oliver's things — the blame really was on his side. Before their departure from the hotel she managed to adopt and retain a manner of cold dignified scorn. When he attempted to touch her, or win a smile by some veiled compliment or hint of humour, she drew away.

He was chagrined, but not perturbed, telling himself he'd soon woo her back to his arms once they had crossed the Channel and were back in Cornwall. She was undoubtedly spoiled. Her wilfulness, apart from its frustrating effect, mildly amused him. He had as well other things on his mind. He'd planned when they first set off on their honeymoon to make an extended trip of it, travelling further afield so that additional business was incorporated. But if little madam Sabrina wished to poke her nose into his affairs so cunningly he was certainly not prepared to put up with her tricks and emotional scenes.

Lisette sensed that something was awry during the first evening of their return. Sabrina had a remote air about her. Although tired, there was a challenging gleam in her eyes. Her chin was set, and her smile appeared slightly false.

'You look a little — exhausted,' Lisette said later, after Oliver had left the drawing room to have a look at the stables and chat with the men. 'Still,' she forced a cheerful note into her voice, 'that's only to be expected. Did you enjoy Paris?'

Sabrina, who was wearing olive-green chiffon, answered brightly, 'Of course. It was interesting. Picturesque — and stimulating. We visited most places of interest, the Folies Bergère, and the Moulin Rouge; and of course the Eiffel Tower.'

'Oh dear! how trying for you.'

'Not really. It was such a marvellous view at the top.'

'Yes.'

'I didn't let Oliver know I'd been before. We used to go for holidays to France sometimes when I was young. Well – Brittany really, which is quite different. But still we generally had a jaunt to Paris as well.'

'Whyever didn't you tell him?'

Sabrina shrugged.

'I didn't want to spoil his pleasure. He likes to think he knows all the ropes.'

Lisette's eyes sharpened as they slid sideways to Sabrina's face. 'He generally does, you know. Oliver's very au fait with the world. I've got used to it. I know my son. No doubt in time you'll learn.'

'I've learned quite a lot already,' Sabrina said, not intending to.

'And what does that mean? You get on, I hope? Everything's all right between you?'

'You mean in bed?' Sabrina said bluntly.

'My dear!' Lisette's eyebrows arched disapprovingly. 'I never enquire about such intimacies. I wouldn't dream of it!'

Sabrina smiled again, and this time her amusement was genuine.

'Mother-in-law – or Lisette – I'm sure that's what you wanted to know, and I can assure you that between the sheets everything's fine. I don't want to sound crude, but Oliver's proved himself an adept at love-making.' The smile faded. 'You knew he would, didn't you? You knew very well what a deal of useful experience he'd had.'

Without waiting for Lisette's shocked reply, she thrust out an arm and said, 'May I have one of your cigarettes, please? I feel like a soother.'

Grudgingly, Lisette passed her mother-of-pearl and gold case. 'Does Oliver know you smoke?' she asked, relieved to avoid the first question.

'No. But he'll soon find out, won't he?' Sabrina attempted to blow a ring into the air, failed dismally and started to cough.

Lisette turned away, hiding her smile, and the next moment Oliver came in.

He sniffed. 'Good heavens! I didn't know I'd married an addict. And in the drawing room too. Mater dear—' turning to his mother, 'I'd be obliged if you'd very discreetly point out the rules of the house to Mrs Cavannagh junior. I doubt if she'd listen to me.'

'Oliver—' Lisette picked up her lorgnettes from a small nearby table and scrutinised her face closely. 'No sarcasm if you please; I'm sure Sabrina will listen to anything you say — in reason. And I don't like moods. At this hour they can be very wearying. Obviously you're both on edge and irritated from the journey. My advice is to retire and have a good night's sleep.'

Oliver did not at first reply. Then after the brief pause he said, 'Well, Sabrina?'

'Just as you like,' she answered meekly.

He went to the door, opened it, and held it while she passed through; then he returned to give Lisette a peck on her soft perfumed cheek. 'Don't worry,' he said. 'Everything's very satisfactory.'

'Are you sure?' Her voice was tart. 'Be careful, son, or you may have a problem on your hands.'

'I have one already, but I'm quite capable of resolving it.'

He left her, and followed Sabrina upstairs, leaving Lisette staring after him thoughtfully.

He found Sabrina already pulling a gauzy nightdress over her head when he entered the bedroom. She had thrown her dress carelessly over a chair, and was obviously trying hard to be safely between the silk sheets before he arrived. She moved to the other side of the immense bed, stooped quickly and unfastened corsets and underwear, letting them fall unceremoniously to her feet. Then she hastily picked them up and threw the garments after the dress.

Oliver smiled lazily, and had captured her before she was under the eiderdown.

'No.' She stiffened in his arms. 'I don't feel like it. I'm tired. Your mother knew. Please let me go, Oliver.'

Without demur he released her. 'Very well. If that's what you want.' She climbed into bed. His face hardened. 'I'm just wondering how long it's going on?'

'What?'

He stared at her wrily, noting the defiant glint in her eyes, the tightly clenched hands gripping the nightgown at her neck. 'Your evasion, darling, the capture-me-if-you-can mood. Don't tempt me too hard.'

'I don't mean to tempt you. I'm not like that — that—'

'Yes? Go on. Finish what you were going to say. That what?'

'Lili Leblanc,' she said recklessly. 'The woman you went to see that night. And don't deny it, Oliver. I have proof. I *saw*.' Her cheeks flamed.

The flesh round his mouth whitened. His eyes were cold and inscrutable as he said very clearly, 'Repeat that, will you? You said you *saw*? You mean you were *there*? You followed me?'

She didn't reply. He took her by the shoulders and shook her.

'Yes, yes,' she confessed when his reaction became too much for her. 'What did you expect? You left me on our honeymoon, for another woman. I knew about her of course—' Her voice quickened into an excited flow of words. 'I'd heard. Everyone knows. Don't you realise that? It's common knowledge. But when you said you loved me I thought you meant it. You didn't though, did you? I was just another conquest, another — another—' she turned her head away, sobs mingling with the tumultuous heavy breathing.

She waited for him to strike her or offer some explanation. But he did neither.

'You little fool,' she heard him say, with withering contempt. 'You should have had more discretion, Sabrina, at least have feigned a sense of honour. Such a sordid little game. Well, it didn't pay, did it? And it's not going to. If you expect me to cooperate with your scheming blackmail you're very much mistaken. You can brood and think what you like, and I hope it brings you most unpleasant satisfaction. This time, for the sake of peace and quiet I'll try and overlook it, but if you ever dare to pry into my private life again or fumble through my personal letters I can promise you'll need feather cushions to sit upon for some considerable time.'

He turned, went to the mirror, and jerked his tie loose. Then he went to the small adjoining door, opened it and told her, 'I shall be sleeping in the dressing room tonight. See you wake up in a more congenial frame of mind. At the moment I almost envy de Marchmont his escape.'

The door snapped with a sharp click.

He had gone.

8

Although Oliver and Sabrina came to an uneasy truce concerning the Lili affair, the hidden battle of wills between them remained. Their love-making — physically — was satisfactory. But as winter passed to early spring Oliver became increasingly aware of Sabrina's determination to assert herself as an individual in the domestic establishment. Before his marriage wheels had run smoothly enough; Lisette had been perfectly satisfied to keep to her own personal domain, attending only to the elegant details of running Carnack, such as flower arrangements and seeing that any valuable pieces of sculpture and china were placed in complimentary lighting, according to the weather and time of day. Domestic affairs had always bored her, and in the person of her housekeeper she had a prize. The servants were well used to the routine. When a maid left, due to some unwanted pregnancy or other mishap, Lisette, after Mrs Drew's thorough inspection of the replacement, always gave a brief interview to the new girl. At such times she took care to appear especially gracious and glamorous, inspiring immediate awe, and sense of admiring envy in the humble heart of the newcomer. Lisette, from the first, had proved herself to be a subtle and expert actress. Her smile radiated confidence and respect of the other's station in life, while retaining her own special aura of queenly superiority. Her rare visits to the kitchen were hushed affairs, accompanied by little bobs and 'madams' and mistaken 'ladyships' which though incorrect gratified Lisette immensely. Her draperies, silk shawls, and flashing jewellery relegated her from ordinary life to a completely different sphere of existence — a magical realm of the past when mediaeval kings and queens ruled their subjects with a wave of the hand or a single expressive word.

Because of this, servants at Castle Carnack were content to go about their duties to the best of their ability. If there was a grudge, they knew it would be listened to fairly.

But Sabrina changed everything.

After the first two months she found life boring and lacking purpose. Without meaning to she trespassed into matters that were not her concern. The curtains in the small drawing-room needed cleaning. There were plants in the conservatory that should be put out for fresh air and rain. A stair-rod was unsafe, — two of the pictures on the main landing needed re-varnishing. Windows should be opened more, and greenery in the bedrooms at night was not healthy.

However right her judgement might have been, in Mrs Drew's opinion she was interfering, and eventually Lisette had to agree. After ineffectually pointing out the problem to Sabrina but with no satisfaction whatever, she was forced to tell Oliver.

'What do you expect me to do?' he asked bluntly. 'I should have thought Mrs Drew was quite capable of handling things.'

'She is — but I don't like to see her becoming irritated. I don't entirely blame Sabrina of course; you *are* out a good deal, and topics of conversation between her and me have become exhausted. She needs something to do. You're going abroad shortly, aren't you? I hope you'll take her with you.'

'I'm afraid not, Mater.' His tones were short, almost curt. 'Sabrina, as you've pointed out, is quite a positive character, and my next trip will be entirely business. Divided interests would be distracting.'

'Divided! and so soon after your marriage.' She stared at him very directly. 'Is the novelty already wearing thin, Oliver?'

He paused before answering. 'You know me better than that. It's because I find my young wife so uncomfortably distracting that I have to put her out of the picture for the time being. Apart from that it will do her good.'

'Are you sure? And what do you expect her to do in the meantime? Quite frankly, Oliver, I don't intend to play the watchful duenna whenever you feel like abandoning the responsibility. Far too exhausting.'

He smiled placatingly, and took one ringed hand in his.

'Mater dear, I don't expect it, and Sabrina certainly wouldn't allow it. Next week remember, we have half a dozen guests arriving. Let her take a hand in entertainment — act as unofficial hostess when the opportunity rises. She'd enjoy it and probably be a great success.'

'She might, and she might not,' Lisette said cryptically. 'It would depend on the guests. Sabrina easily gets bored—'

'Then don't give her the chance. Pack her off to make peace with her family. It's high time something was done about it.'

Lisette laughed shortly.

'Can you see her doing that? I can't.'

'I'll have a word with her,' Oliver said.

That same day he put the suggestion.

The sudden flood of warm expectancy in Sabrina's violet eyes when he mentioned the European visit, died to cold ice grey as he informed her she would not be accompanying him.

'Why not?' she asked. 'Oh *please*, Oliver. I wouldn't be in your way. I'd promise not to intrude on your — your business meetings. There are so many places I've never seen. I could amuse myself—'

'Yes. You've put it in a nutshell. One dose of your self-amusement tactics has been more than enough.'

Sabrina flushed.

'That's not fair.'

'Darling, darling, don't pretend. On your own you're a menace, and a moral gamble. No, don't try and persuade me. The matter's decided. You'll remain here at Castle Carnack and help please any guests we have. That shouldn't be difficult—' the whimsical smile returned to his lips, '—in fact I'm taking a damn gamble that you won't become involved with some business magnate, or play fast and loose with the emotions of some unsuspecting heir of a wealthy house.' There was a brief silence before he added, 'You won't of course, or there'll be one hell of a reckoning when I return. Anyway there's something else.'

'Yes?'

'Your family. I'd like you to go and see them, Sabrina. You've got everything on your side, nothing to lose, and everything to win—'

'For you, do you mean? Your standing? Your *politics*?'

He smiled blandly. 'Politically, yes. Can't you do that one thing for me?'

She hesitated.

'Why should I? — so — so humiliating somehow.'

'As my wife? Nonsense. And remember; any success on my side means success for you too. Also — there's your father.'

Her mouth hardened.

'What about him?'

'I've heard he's not been too well lately. Material matters aside — you were fond of each other, and I think you've fretted.'

She glanced away, but not before he'd glimpsed the softening of her expression. When she didn't speak he enclosed her shoulders gently with an arm. 'Come along, Sabrina. Promise me — please.'

'I wouldn't know what to say.'

'My love, I'm pretty sure there'd be no need for anything. One look at you and all would be forgiven.'

His eyes were warm. He was trying to win her by flattery of course, and she knew he'd already succeeded. Despite her disappointment, faint humour rose in her. But she managed to say without showing it, 'So I'd be forgiven. How nice. Why do you always put me in the wrong, Oliver?'

He laughed, 'My sweet I don't have to, you're quite an adept at doing it yourself. Anyway, what about it?'

'Very well, if that's what you want. I shan't enjoy it, and my stepmother will start one of her interminable lectures — Papa will try to ease matters by bringing out the madeira, then he'll say, "Well, you two girls, I'll leave you to have your pow-wow," or something just as ridiculous, and go off to the billiard-room or library for a smoke. Imagine it! — girls! *pow-wow!*' She smiled reminiscently. 'My father was never a brilliant conversationalist, and Henrietta's effectively done in what initiative he ever had.' She sighed. 'Everything at Fern Hill is so boringly predictable.'

'Then stir things up again. Put on that red cape thing you brought in France, wear your furs and feathers and make your debut as the proverbial scarlet woman.'

'Oliver!'

'Go on, darling. Do it. The servants will be thrilled.'

'But you didn't like the coat when I got it.'

'No, I thought it atrocious.'

'Put it in a box room you said, for theatricals and Christmas time. Then why—'

'Quite right. And I meant it. You should know how to dress, for Pete's sake. The blue then. Forget the red. Be your own natural alluring self. Do you understand?'

She smiled at last.

'I'll try. And you're right of course about my father. I didn't know he'd been "off-colour". Poor Papa. If only he could assert himself more.'

'With you out of the way he possibly has a better chance now,' Oliver said drily. 'Anyway to carry on with a feud is ridiculous. Life's far too short.'

Yes, Sabrina thought glumly, and too short to spend weeks apart from Oliver when he could so easily have taken her along with him on the forthcoming trip.

But she gave up arguing, and tried to rid herself of the jealous idea that somewhere on his travels Lili Leblanc might cross his path again, or that he might make it his business they should meet. How far she could trust him Sabrina hadn't yet decided. The niggling idea that her own attitude was becoming that of any upper-class conventional housewife wanting to keep tabs on her husband's activities, was distasteful and boring. The thought of a jaunt to Fern Hill therefore proved a way of escape. Lisette, too, was in agreement.

'Quarrels, my dear, are odious,' she told Sabrina when the subject came up. 'You won't be welcomed with open arms, naturally. But I'm sure your charm will overcome resentment. You should try — for Oliver's sake.'

'Why for Oliver?'

Lisette lifted her still beautiful chin an inch higher, placed her long jade cigarette holder between her lips, puffed restrainedly, took it out again, and said, 'You know very well, darling. He needs you and the assistance of your well-bred connections.' She paused, adding after a sigh, 'He has it in him you know to become Prime Minister one day if he really wants to be. I don't agree with the idea at all. Politics bore me stiff, and I think if it happened, he'd soon get sick of the whole devious calculating business. Then — when, and if — he'd make some dramatic exit in true Cavannagh style and conquer some other highly original field. Well — millionaires can afford such diversions.'

'As long as the diversions don't happen to be women,' Sabrina said bluntly.

'Oh dear! you shouldn't think that way. It's not only unfair, but extremely limiting — for you. Oliver's no serious womaniser, and never has been. If a girl likes him and he responds, he shows it. He's all male, my dear. But never doubt his passion for you. I've never before seen him so obsessed by any woman. I was quite alarmed at first when he spoke of marriage. Tea and this hotel business — the Stock Market — the shares — the gallivanting out East and dabbling in new ventures and companies seemed his life. And I knew you were not the type to take a back seat like the others—' she broke off, taken aback by her slip of the tongue.

'The others? Yes. Oh, don't worry,' Sabrina said, in purposeful casual tones. 'I'm quite aware of Oliver's women.' In spite of herself her tones were brittle.

Lisette's eyes became briefly hard — the eyes of a doting possessive mother hen. 'You're speaking nonsense. There are no other women now. And you have no right — *no right at all*, Sabrina, to delve and conjecture about my son's past. He's not been a monk of course — you wouldn't want that or expect it, would you? If so you're a fool.'

Sabrina stared. The vague elegant creature Lisette had formerly appeared to be, was no longer there. Instead, an erect defensive woman of glowing cheeks and blazing hot-tempered eyes confronted her.

'You'll have to learn to put up with any idiosyncrasies my son has, and accept that you're not perfect yourself,' Lisette continued sharply. 'All things considered I think you've done quite well for yourself, and you should make an attempt to keep harmony at Carnack, instead of disrupting it.'

Sabrina was dismayed.

'I didn't know I'd done that,' she said in more conciliatory tones. 'It was just—'

'Just that you wanted everything on a plate and to your own tastes.' The interruption was sharp and cutting. 'No one can have that, you know. I had a few things to come to terms with when I married Oliver's father. So did he. But after a few violent rows we settled down quite amicably, learning to respect each other's private whims and indulgencies. Turning a blind eye when necessary is an important virtue in a successful marriage. It's like—'

'Making a cake?' Sabrina suggested with a sudden quirky hint of the underlying humour that never fundamentally deserted her.

Lisette suddenly relaxed. 'Yes, my dear. Oh yes — exactly that.' She smiled and patted Sabrina's arm. 'Thank God you've got a laugh in you.' She sighed. 'Do you know this has all been quite exhausting. I hate lectures and arguments. I'm not at all the lecturing sort, as you must know. I think we should celebrate our — past. Madeira? Or sherry? Or shall we concoct some glorious mixture, for old times' sake? Mine, I mean. I remember when I was in my heyday at the Haymarket—'

'Sherry please,' Sabrina interrupted, feeling she could not tolerate a dose of Lisette's oft-repeated stage reminiscences. 'And you needn't worry, I shall go and see my parents as soon as Oliver leaves.'

He departed on an early morning in March when the air was faintly suggestive of spring, and the ditches and lanes below the moors were already starred by pale primroses and the deeper gold of celandines. Gorse flamed on the brown hills, and the sky was a hazy blue above the distant sea. An exciting, adventurous kind of day, Sabrina thought, regretfully, as she watched Oliver driven away in the landau. They shouldn't have been separated at such a time when all nature was stirring and waking, on the brink of blossoming. However, he'd gone now, and there would, after all, be a certain stimulus in arriving quite without preliminaries at Fern Hill.

She ordered the carriage and set off shortly before eleven, wearing blue, as Oliver had suggested, and a small boat-shaped hat tilted coquettishly towards one eye. It was composed almost entirely of forget-me-nots, with a shred of veiling half shading her eyes. When they reached the drive of her old home which was picturesquely situated in a wooded valley, she pushed the veiling up and regarded the familiar scene with an unexpected sense of affection. The house had been built in Elizabethan days. One small wing remained almost intact, displaying its original character, the rest had been added to rather indiscriminately at different periods — mostly mid-Georgian. But there was nothing startlingly out of harmony about the whole. It was just an old house with gardens that needed some attention, and renovations to the older portion of the roof.

Sabrina felt almost guilty as she dismounted from the carriage in her luxurious velvet, diamonds flashing from her ears and from her left hand. The coat was trimmed with ermine, and one hand was encased in a small silk-lined ermine muff. She had wondered, before setting off, if the fur was in keeping with the forget-me-nots. But the effect was certainly impressive, and this was what Oliver wished, she told herself. So she walked very erectly up the steps to the Georgian portico and front door. The bell clanged as she pulled it. Almost immediately steps echoed down the main hall. A strange girl — probably a housemaid, let her in. Her face was unfamiliar, and Sabrina wondered what had happened to Parker, the footman. Had he been retired because of his age, or because her father could no longer afford the salary?

Certainly, after the ostentation of Carnack, the interior had a certain sad, fading gentility. If she had married Freddie everything could have been so different. Sabrina could not help a brief feeling of regret. Then the door of the small lounge opened, and Henrietta appeared. She dismissed the girl immediately, and said coldly, 'Oh. So it's you. I rather expected you'd come earlier since your father has been so unwell.'

'I knew nothing about it,' Sabrina remarked with the old sense of antagonism rising. 'If you'd let me know I would have.'

'Would you?'

'Of course.'

'Well — come into the room. We don't want the staff to overhear private discussions. There's been quite enough gossip already.' She held the door open, and Sabrina passed through, followed by Henrietta. The latch clicked behind them, sending a scurry of fresh chill air across the carpet. A fire was burning in the grate, but the sense of spring seemed suddenly to have departed. Henrietta's unspoken censure chilled Sabrina to the bone.

'Well, Sabrina?' the older woman asked when they were seated. 'What have you to say for yourself? No apology I suppose — although there should be, considering the pain you've caused us all.'

Sabrina observed that her stepmother did not actually appear at all dispirited or dejected. She had, in fact, put on a little weight. Her fine complexion was clearer, her eyes brighter, and whatever the problems of Fern Hill's financial standing, she was wearing a maroon-coloured silk dress of the very latest style, obviously new.

'I did write and apologise,' Sabrina pointed out, 'and I can't do any more. I called so we could perhaps make peace — for father's sake.'

'Hm. And how is marriage suiting you? I must say you look extremely — affluent.'

Sabrina coloured.

'Those forget-me-nots, though, hardly match the ermine. Still, your taste was always inclined to be flamboyant, and I suppose living with that — that actress and her notorious son have encouraged it.'

'I wear what I choose myself,' came the stiff reply. 'Actually, I'm quite free to lead my own life, which is a change. And if it hadn't been for having Freddie thrown at me so obviously and so much, I'd probably never have got engaged to him in the first place.'

Henrietta shrugged. 'I can hardly believe that. He was a catch for any girl. I was extremely surprised — and gratified, naturally — when he chose you. Sophia Clarke-Davies was quite infatuated, you know. And I believe — though I can't be sure — that they've become friendly recently. He calls on us sometimes.'

'Freddie?'

'Yes. He's really a very charitable young man. In his place I'm afraid I'd have avoided Fern Hill like the plague.'

Sabrina, most annoyingly for her stepmother, laughed.

'But Freddie isn't that sort of person. He never bore grudges and I'm sure you needn't feel the de Marchmonts will blackball you from any notable function simply on my account. They probably think their son and heir had a lucky escape, and feel sympathy for you and Papa. So let's forget all that social misdemeanour stuff, shall we? I'd like to see my father. Is he about? Or in bed? Or—'

'In the smoking room, I believe,' Henrietta said coldly. 'I'll break the news of your arrival, and fetch him — provided he wishes to speak to you—'

'No.' Sabrina jumped up. 'I'll go and see him myself.' And before Henrietta could delay her further, she had gone.

The reunion was natural, simple, and touching.

Sir Martin had obviously lost a little weight. He looked paler, and considerably older than when his daughter had last seen him.

There was no longer any necessity for words, explanations, or excuses. Mutual affection was sufficient to allay any lingering resentment or annoyance from the past.

'Good to see you,' he said, after the first greetings were over. He heaved himself to his feet, and poured two glasses of vintage wine. 'A moment for celebration, what?' He handed her a glass, took one himself, and when they were both seated told her, 'I started to write to you once or twice y'know, but I was never good with the pen, and your mother — your stepmother — generally spotted me and managed to put me off. Don't know why. She shouldn't have. But she's got a will of her own, Ninny,' — unintentionally his old nick-name for his daughter slipped out, 'and a very clear head. Logical.' He lifted a hand. 'Not that I'm complaining, mind you. She looks after me well, she runs the house on a minimum — she's a good wife—'

'Papa—' Sabrina interrupted, 'if things are really difficult for you, I can — I can help. There wouldn't be any problem, honestly. You know how rich Oliver is — and I have such an enormous allowance. I'd like to—' she was breathing quickly. Her enthusiasm restored extreme youth so vividly, she looked for a moment almost a child again.

Her father's face softened.

'No, no, child. I know you mean it well, but I'd have to explain, and you can guess what Henrietta would say. Personally I've no feelings whatever against Cavannagh. But his family y'know—'

'You mean the *tea*? What's wrong with tea, Father? We all drink it.'

'His mother. That's the nub of it. They say she came from—'

'Oh damn her origins.' Sabrina's voice was fierce. 'She's as much a lady as Henrietta. If we all fussed and delved into our pedigrees I wouldn't wonder a prostitute or bastard appeared every so often to liven things up.'

A hint of humour lit Sir Martin's small tired eyes.

'You've become quite worldly all of a sudden, been digging into history, have you? Kings and Queens, and bastard probing?

All that? Shouldn't have thought it was your taste at all. "Don't give me that old stuff," you told your governess more than once, when she tried to din a few facts and figures into you—'

'Oh, that was different. Old Ponty was such a bore—'

'Ponty? Ah I remember her name now. Ponting.' He gave a little grimace. 'Don't blame you really. But you had to be punished. Didn't agree with that. Still—'

'Never by you though,' Sabrina reminded him. 'You were always kind.' And weak, she added to herself, always ready to take the easy way out of a difficult situation. She smiled. 'That was a long time ago.'

'Not to me. The older you get the quicker time slips by.' When he breathed she noticed his chest made a faint rattle. Recalling the true motive of her visit she asked quickly, 'What's been the matter with you? Is it your lungs, or just a cold?'

He shrugged. 'Just the years telling me to go slow,' he told her. 'Saw old Patterson the other week, and he said there was nothing organically wrong. Age, that's all.'

'But you're not really old.'

'I'm not young either, my dear. Anyway there it is. Had to give up hunting y'know—'

'I didn't, but I'm glad. It's a horrible sport. I always said so—'

'Mustn't let Henrietta hear you say that—'

'Oh, bother Henrietta. She's just a snob.'

'Sh — sh—' Sir Martin looked warningly towards the door. There was no sign his wife was about. But indignation forced Sabrina to exclaim, 'Why are you so nervous of her, Papa? You're master here, it's what you say that matters, not dear step-mama.'

'I know, I know. But the years are on her side, Ninny, and I haven't the energy left in me to go working out problems and asserting myself. Mind you, child, if you really need me any time I'll always be here, and—' he moved his head closer to hers confidentially — 'she won't get everything when I go, y'know. She thinks she will, but—' he tapped his head significantly, '—you'll have half, I've seen to that; all signed and sealed. Not that there'll be such a lot, as things are today.'

'Stop,' Sabrina said. 'Don't talk like that. I hate it — just thinking about wills and dying is somehow so sordid and sad. And I shan't need money, Papa. Have you forgotten? I'm rich.'

'Yes of course. The tea-magnate.'

Sabrina laughed. 'So let Henrietta know she's your chief beneficiary, if you've got to dwell on such sad things, and maybe she'll like me better.'

He paused before saying, 'Perhaps you're right. Perhaps. We'll see.'

There was the sudden trilling of a bird from outside. The song, throaty, sweet and clear, pierced the drift of air from the narrow slit of open window, holding the joyous challenge of spring. A blackbird, Sabrina thought; soon there'd be the cuckoo's call, and the frail heady scent of blue-bells from the lush woodlands. Would Oliver be back by then?

She got up, walked to the window and pulled the curtains wider. Everywhere patches of palest green penetrated the darker tones of last year's decay. The grounds and distant fields showed a patchworked quilt effect; and beyond, the early flame of gorse was already interspersed with stretches of purple heather. Fresh, yellowish green feathered the lean branches of the nearby trees. The distant glint of sea shone silver against the far horizon. How beautiful, suddenly, the world seemed to be, and how wrong that Oliver was not able to share those vivid moments of acute awareness with her.

Her expression was ruminative when she turned and returned to where her father was still seated. He must have noticed something. His next remark gave her a mild shock.

'Are you happy, Sabrina?'

'Of course. Wildly happy. We really are suited, Papa, Oliver and me. The only snag is that he has to go away rather a lot. Still—' she shrugged. 'I expect I'll get used to that in time.'

'You must come here as often as you can,' Sir Martin told her. 'It'll do me a world of good, and give you and Henrietta more chance to get to know each other better than in the past. She's a fine woman, y'know — at heart.'

'Yes, I'm sure she is,' Sabrina agreed tolerantly.

They chatted for a time after that; then, following a further, slightly more amiable, interlude with Henrietta, Sabrina left.

The carriage had just turned the corner of the drive leading into the lane, when she saw a man's figure walking towards them, from a motor-car which was parked rather precariously near a ditch. He wore a check cap, long dust coat, and was swinging a pair of goggles from one hand.

Freddie!

Her heart lurched. She gave a brief command to the coachman.

'Please wait a moment — I must speak to — to Mr de Marchmont.'

She inelegantly opened the door herself, scrambled down and hurried fifty yards or so towards the familiar figure.

Freddie stood completely still, staring for a minute, then rushed ahead again, with an arm stretched out. There was no malice or condemnation on his face. He was grinning. And the grin was more obvious, because he'd shaved his moustache off.

'Sabrina!'

She felt her palm crushed, and experienced a great flood of relief.

'Oh Freddie, what a surprise. And how — nice.'

She really meant it. It was so comforting somehow to have him near to her again, his handsome face beaming on her, the last terrible embarrassing incident between them apparently forgotten.

His eyes travelled from her somewhat absurd forget-me-not hat, to the tips of her shining pointed boots beneath the velvet gown.

'How are you feeling, Sabrina? Happy?'

She nodded. 'Mostly. Although I shouldn't be, should I, after the awful thing I did?'

'Oh, rot. Forget it. I understand. I'd be an ass not to.'

'What do you mean?'

He touched a cheek lightly with a finger. She glanced back to where the coachman was sitting rigidly upright on his box apparently unaware of the small intimacy.

Sabrina tucked her arm into Freddie's, and diverted him to a less observed place behind the car. A spray of blossoming thorn from the hedge partly shadowed her face.

'If *you* understand,' she continued, taking up where they'd left, 'I certainly don't understand myself; and that's the truth.'

He shook his head. 'My dear girl, your instincts suddenly sprang to life, saving us both a pretty dim future, I'd say.'

She was momentarily taken back, even faintly chagrined.

'You mean you felt the same? You didn't want to marry me after all? Are you telling me it was a relief?'

His face sobered. 'No. I loved you, Sabrina. It was hell at first — for quite a time. Then I realised we'd got mixed up, both of us. I mean — we'd always been such good friends, and dammit, any man in his senses would want a girl like you. As a kid you were a tormenting little hoyden. But later you were so stunning I — well, I just fell hook, line and sinker, and I guess that was about it. But did we think about it properly? Did we ever ask ourselves "Is this right? Is it everything? Is there some facet of love missing?"' He broke off, studying her face intently. She looked suddenly serious.

'Perhaps not. *Do* people?'

'I don't know. Maybe they should.'

'So you're saying really that you don't think it could have worked ever?'

He smiled gently. 'Obviously you thought that.'

'But you?' she persisted. 'When did the light dawn?'

He turned his face away, pretending to notice the swaying of a branch overhead when a bird fluttered its wings for a second before flying away. Small white petals scattered the air; he was recalling, against his will, Jaina's young pale face staring up at him, so innocently, yet with such deep feminine knowledge, from the trees' shadows — experiencing the mysterious awareness that had flooded him — the brief recognition of his own subtle emotional potentials — longings that had hitherto been dormant and therefore unknown.

During the difficult days abroad following Sabrina's rejection and social humiliation, he had lived wildly for a time, trying to erase the affair. But it was not until the chance meeting with Cavannagh's niece that he'd been able to review matters with healthy objectivity. Since then he'd found his mind straying at intervals to the haunting incident on the moor that lingered like an elusive dream — discrediting forever his former faith in his own rational commonsense attitude to life.

He turned again to Sabrina. Obviously he couldn't answer her question truthfully. Truth would sound ridiculous, and if he put it in a nut shell could be extremely hurtful. He could hardly say, 'You're still very beautiful Sabrina, but you're not the woman I thought you were. Something's gone — or changed, I don't know which. Maybe it's just me. You look — obvious somehow. Sophisticated, and just a little too brilliant and assured. You've matured. You're Sabrina Cavannagh now. There's nothing in the slightest sacrosanct between us any more. We can always be very good friends. I hope we will be. But there's something else. Someone quite impossible. A mere dream really — but the dream's taught me to know myself. So don't question me.'

No. He could hardly be so brutal.

'Well?' he heard her persisting, 'you haven't answered.'

'There's no answer to give,' he replied. 'To be intense is futile, don't you think?'

She shrugged, slightly put out.

'Perhaps. Oh well,' her voice brightened. 'It's been good seeing you again, Freddie. You must call again — soon, at the house. Why don't you? I'm sure Oliver would be pleased to meet you, when he—' she was going to say 'gets back.' But Freddie interrupted her.

'We've already met,' he said. 'Didn't he tell you?'

She looked astonished and was conscious of a quick wave of anger. 'No. When was that?'

'Oh, I don't remember exactly,' Freddie replied evasively. 'It was just a social overture. I took the wrong route and arrived in the lane at the back of the hall. I met your — Cavannagh's niece — Jaina.' The name came out with difficulty. 'She was taking me down, when your — husband — appeared from the stables.'

'And he never even told me.' Her voice was shocked.

Freddie grinned. 'I'm not surprised, come to think of it. A very jealous man, Mr Cavannagh. He told me in quite clear tones to clear out, which I did.'

'I do apologise, Freddie. It was unforgivable of him. I shall certainly tell him so, and see that—'

'Tell him nothing, Sabrina. You wouldn't do any good. Anyway, d'you think I cared?'

Sabrina shook her head. 'No. Why should you? A de Marchmont and a Cavannagh! Oh, I know what's said about Carnack. I don't care generally. But you're an old friend, and I simply won't have you being slighted.'

'My dear girl, I wasn't slighted in the least. Just a little — sorry for you perhaps.'

'You needn't be,' she said tartly, lifting her chin a defiant inch or two higher.

'I can see that now. And it's a relief. So we'll let bygones be bygones, shall we? By the way, your father must have been glad to see you.'

'Yes.'

He smiled, thrust out his hand again, and said, 'Bye then, for the moment. You'd better be off or your horses may get restive. I'll tell your pater we met and all's well.' He paused, before kissing her lightly near one temple. There was no passion in the gesture at all. She couldn't help feeling slightly mortified.

'Goodbye then, Sabrina, look after yourself, and see you obey your strong man.'

She smiled mechanically.

The next moment he turned and left her, walking with head and shoulders thrust forward, towards the car.

She paused waiting for him to look round once more. When he didn't, she made her way back to the carriage and got in, glancing at the man's face suspiciously. His expression was dead pan, telling her nothing. She knew he wouldn't speak of her encounter with Freddie. If tales were spread to Lisette or Oliver there would be trouble, and this particular servant was trusted and well liked by Cavannagh. He would certainly not risk his job through tittle-tattle.

So she was safe.

However, the ride back to Castle Carnack was in a vague way discomforting.

She had expected Freddie to miss her more.

As it was she felt any serious sympathy for him had been misplaced. There was no need to continue thinking of him as 'poor Freddie'.

Men, indeed, could be faithless creatures.

Especially Oliver.

'Can't you drive a little more quickly?' she suddenly demanded of the coachman, tartly.

Not looking at her, the man cracked his whip. There was a rattle, and increased clip-clop of horses' hooves. Sabrina sat rigidly upright, wishing she had not bothered to speak to Freddie at all.

But when she reached Carnack she had relaxed, and was chiding herself for her mean thoughts. It was Oliver of course. If only Oliver was back.

A little smile curved her mouth. It wouldn't be long now, surely. And when he arrived she'd show him, somehow, how much he meant to her, and she'd find comfort once more in his arms.

9

Jaina returned to Castle Carnack a fortnight before Oliver, owing to an epidemic of chicken-pox at the convent which meant the Easter holidays were precipitated, to save unnecessary risk of the infection spreading.

Lisette, therefore, was more than relieved to have Sabrina available; and Jaina was delighted to be able to abandon the unbecoming uniform for less restricted clothing.

'Couldn't we go shopping though?' she suggested to Sabrina one day. 'To Falmouth perhaps. I've saved all my pocket money — well, most of it, and it would be exciting to have something new.' Her strange eyes glowed; there was an elfin smile on her lips that was peculiarly beguiling. Sabrina agreed. She had found Lisette's company, recently, extremely boring, and helping entertain the few 'guests' on those early spring evenings even more so. There were no more than thirty of them at the most. Two or three rich ambitious mothers with plain daughters on the look-out for eligible husbands, a peppery colonel, elderly bridge-playing dowagers with gossipy tongues, a wealthy but dull middle-aged couple with an anaemic looking son who was mournfully on Sabrina's trail whenever she appeared, and the lascivious-eyed count who gave her suggestive glances each time she caught his eye. There were luckless over-vivacious spinsters inwardly dreading being left on the shelf, and a few wary-eyed males of dashing mien, playfully yet cruelly leading on the hopeful females with hints of romance that never matured.

Following dinner, concerts were arranged in the large guest lounge, where the audience sat under potted palms listening to ballads that brought tears to the dewy-eyed younger element.

A yellow-haired soprano with quivering bosom sang woeful ditties of tragic love, and a middle-aged man with curling moustache gave an off-tone rendering of 'Mandalay' and 'Come into the garden, Maud.' There was an impresario, and duettists accompanied by a flamboyant pianist who at intervals struck the wrong note. Then the recitations! — 'Barrack Room Ballads' mostly, by Rudyard Kipling, and the Colonel's insistence that he took part in the proceedings by a dramatic rendering of 'Gunga Din'. Oh the drama, the emotion, and the wildly beating hearts!

Sabrina found it all mildly ridiculous, and was determined that when Oliver returned she'd make it quite clear to him that she had no intention whatever of being embroiled any longer in the social events of Castle Carnack.

In the meantime she made Jaina's company an excuse for getting away as much as possible during the daytime. 'Yes,' she told Jaina when the shopping expedition was broached. 'We'll have a jaunt out if you like. Not Falmouth though, too far for just one day. Truro. Why not? And we could have lunch somewhere.'

And so it was arranged.

They set off early on a fine calm day when only a few stray cotton-woolish clouds sprinkled the sky, and the whole landscape and air seemed to quiver with waking trembling excitement.

The ditches and hedgerows now were alight with the pushing pale heads of curling fern fronds; foaming wild cherry blossom and misted blues and purples of heather above the stone-walled fields. Through the splashed radiance of early sunlight the gaunt mine-stacks were lit briefly to fiery gold on the rising hills. Pools of light and shade dappled the curling lanes. Briefly, at intervals, the far distance became a transient area of shimmering white, where clay workings emerged as a mysterious moon-landscape, fading again with each turn of the carriage towards the town.

Jaina, full of excited chatter, at moments would lapse suddenly into dream-like silences that made Sabrina enquire once, 'Now what are you pondering over? The new clothes?'

Jaina shook her head.

'No. Just things.'

There was no way of expressing what she felt; her ponderings were a mystery, even to herself. Occasionally a queer sense of familiarity — of things far far away — a world she'd once known, long before her time as a child at the Mission — held her transfixed, desperately trying to remember. But it was no use. There were no concrete facts to recall; just feelings and a sense of 'knowing' — a secret realm that had no shape or form, but fleetingly sprang to life as an impression of magical awareness, of belonging. Half-formed recollections flowed through her mind, like a stream or river momentarily bright with the floating shapes of lily-buds reflected through clear water. The intermittent shadows became eyes watching — golden eyes flecked with violet and deepest green — the colours of earth and sky. Then they had gone, and with the fading of the vision it seemed that a deep longing, and a potential hungry capacity for love had also flown, with the sad beauty of a bird's wings disappearing into the summer mist. She had felt such emotion on the day of her meeting with Frederick de Marchmont, and Sabrina's question had suddenly jerked the memory to life again. He had been so gentle, and deep down so hurt. She had felt it. He had stared at her for one quick instant as though she was not a child, but someone much older — someone needing so very much more than the nuns or even Uncle Oliver could give her. She'd wanted to lay her head against his coat, take his hand and say, 'I know, I understand.' She did of course. At such rare moments she understood in her own strange way, things that other girls of her age never seemed to bother about. Why? Because they were different. They hadn't the first idea of the true Jaina lurking beneath the schoolgirl — the young woman who in reality, despite her innocence, was years and years ahead of them, and already passionately searching for individual secret fulfilment.

Sabrina was nice of course, much nicer than she had imagined when they first met. But there was no way of properly confiding in her, because Jaina had not yet learned any way of communication; there were certain things, she guessed, that never could be explained anyway.

So that day, apart from her short ambiguous answer to Sabrina's question, she remained uncommunicative except for factual allusions to clothes, and where they would have their luncheon. How warm and lovely the sun was, and how she hated the thought of going back to school after Easter.

'Perhaps I shall develop chicken-pox at the last moment,' she said once. 'Then they wouldn't want me back for ages. The nuns are very funny, you know.'

Sabrina smiled.

'What an unpleasant thought. I'm sure I'd far rather have school than all those nasty red spots and having to stay in bed.'

'But you're not me; I'm tired of lessons. And the other girls don't like me much. I wish—'

'Yes?'

Jaina suddenly diverted the subject by asking very directly, 'Why did you run away from Freddie in Church? Was it because you'd already seen Uncle Oliver and fallen in love with him?'

Luckily Sabrina was spared the embarrassment of having to concoct either a plausible answer or give a sharp rebuff. One of the horses, startled by the sudden darting of a fox across the road, jibbed, and the carriage drew up for a moment while the man got everything under control.

When they started off again Sabrina immediately started a new trend of conversation dealing with the day's programme. Jaina's youthful interest responded, and by the time they reached the town all niggling and despondent reflections of school had lifted as effectively as a passing cloud dispelled by the sun.

Sabrina was generous with her purse. They had a meal at the most select hotel — an expensive coaching house, and spent the afternoon shopping, buying not only dresses, but materials and frivolous accessories of veiling, lace, and silk underwear that brought muffled sighs and squeals of delight from Jaina's lips.

'I don't know what Uncle Oliver would say,' she told Sabrina, when they were out in the street again. 'Aunt Lisette would understand — well, she's lived so long, hasn't she? And met so many different people. But Uncle Oliver can be so prim and bossy when he feels like it — especially about me.'

Sabrina smiled, although her thoughts were mildly ironic.

'I don't think he's really prim,' she said. 'He probably pretends to be, because you're young, and I suppose he thinks you need guidance.'

'I'm sure he doesn't,' Jaina replied with such certainty Sabrina was startled. 'He's not that kind of person. Nuns give guidance. It's their religion, isn't it? But Uncle Oliver isn't religious. He always does just what he wants — well generally, anyway. Of course you can understand it. He's so—'

'Yes?' Sabrina prompted her curiously.

'Well—' Jaina paused before concluding, 'fascinating, I guess. Sort of compelling and magnetic. He came to the convent once and all the girls simply fell for him.'

'Fell?' Sabrina laughed. 'What an expression.'

'You know what I mean though. They were watching from the window, and he looked so handsome coming up the drive, Caroline Carne nearly dropped dead.'

'Did she?' Laughter bubbled from Sabrina's throat. 'And how do you know?'

'She closed her eyes, and gasped, and said she was all fluttery. Of course—' Jaina's face sobered, 'she could have been acting. Caroline's awfully good at that. She tells awful fibs to the nuns, and they believe her because she looks so innocent.'

'And how old is Caroline?'

'Older than me. Fifteen. She's not in my form, but we know what goes on in our dormitory. Sometimes she goes out at nights. She crawls through the library window, and meets Willy.'

'Who's Willy?'

'A gardener. Not the proper one — he's old and fierce. Willy just helps. And they go to the greenhouse. They do things there.'

There was a silence before Sabrina asked, 'What do you mean, do things?'

Jaina shook her head. 'I'm not sure — actually. Make love, I think — that's what Olivia Jarret said. Olivia's the only friend I have. But I don't really think she knows what happens. Making love sounds so — exciting and wonderful, doesn't it? But the older girls nudge each other and whisper and wink about her, so maybe I'm wrong. Maybe they don't make love at all. What do you think, Sabrina?'

'Oh, I've an idea most of the stories about Caroline are just gossip,' Sabrina prevaricated. 'If you haven't seen anything yourself try not to listen.'

'I haven't seen anything,' Jaina answered. 'Except Caroline creeping down the side path in her dressing gown. Our window faces that way, and there are trees. Everything's in shadow generally, but one night there was a moon. I couldn't sleep. So I got up and looked out. The light was suddenly very bright when the clouds passed, and it was then I saw her face. Just for a moment. It was Caroline.'

'Did you tell anyone?'

'Of course not. That would have been cheating, and the nuns can be strict. Caroline would probably have been expelled or have had to do some terrible penance. It was funny though, she was so conceited and kind of stuck-up the next day. If she and Willy had been making love she wouldn't have been, would she? She'd have looked beautiful and gentle and sort of — mystical, like the painting of the Madonna in the Lady Chapel.'

Sabrina grasped Jaina's hand. So strange, she thought, to be conversing about such matters in a town thoroughfare, during a shopping expedition.

'Love isn't always gentle,' she heard herself saying. 'And I wouldn't worry too much about Caroline, if I were you. She doesn't sound a particularly nice person.'

'She isn't. A lot of them aren't. That's why I want to leave. I don't like the way they tell things and I don't like being told I'm a sinner. I want to find out about love for myself. I used to think I knew. That's when Uncle Oliver was so nice. But he's not nice to me any more, not often.'

Sabrina made no comment except to say, 'Doesn't that box of bon-bons look tempting?' She indicated a pink box tied with satin ribbon in the window of a confectioners.

Jaina nodded. 'Can we carry it?'

Sabrina laughed. 'You can, I'm sure. My arms are quite full. But the carriage is only just round the corner. Come along. We'll get it.'

By the time they had started the return journey to Castle Carnack, the sun was already sinking, leaving a reddish glow in the sky. The dampness of the earth and warmth of the afternoon had brought a haze that would later become deepening mist to the countryside. The vast wild area of Bodmin moor seemed to descend and encompass the district taking the rocks, standing stones, and menhirs into a mysterious uniformity that gave even the clippety-clop of horses' hooves and carriage wheels a weird intensity.

The journey from village to village was a solitary one. Sheep occasionally wandered from a gate, followed by a farmer or shepherd. The only sounds to be heard were those of cattle or mournful crying of gulls overhead. As they neared Carnack, Sabrina and Jaina had settled into reflective mutual silence. Sabrina was thinking of Oliver; Jaina, in a kind of half-dream found her mind wandering once more to Frederick de Marchmont, then back to things much further away — impressions of sound, and scene, and touch, that had nothing to do with the present world. At a certain point everything dimmed. It was like a brief mirage almost visioned, then completely lost. Such experiences always left her mildly troubled. If only she could remember. She longed, through her bewilderment, for babyhood once more — to have the wonder in her grasp again — to feel the softness of satin against her cheek, and the glitter of rain-drops or coloured leaves drifting from the sky. But perhaps they weren't leaves at all — perhaps they were butterflies, and the tinkly far off music was a fountain splashing. Why did the beauty of those lost years have to fade so abruptly? It was like a curtain falling, or a cold knife suddenly cutting off a part of her life forever.

Involuntarily she shivered.

Sabrina noticed. 'Are you cold, Jaina? This mist does hold a chill.'

Jaina shivered. 'Not really, I'm not.' She sat up, very straight and stiff, and trying to change the trend of thought said, 'Look, it's as though those stones are moving, isn't it?'

She was pointing at a broken circle of granite columns which in the thickening light did appear to encroach a little towards the passing carriage.

Sabrina laughed. 'Just stones. Ancient menhirs. On certain evenings and early mornings they cast funny shadows. There's a legend about them in an old book I have. I'll find it for you.'

'What does the legend say?'

'How the daughters of the High King of Cornwall in ancient times disobeyed their father on the Sabbath, and were turned with their lovers into stones. Once or twice a year they come alive again to pay respect to their father and the old gods.'

Jaina was silent for a minute then she said, 'I thought there was only one God. That's what the nuns say.'

'Of course,' Sabrina agreed. 'What I've just told you is only a story. Something made up in Celtic times. Imagination, if you like.'

'Like my dream.'

'Your dream?'

Jaina nodded. 'I have very strange dreams sometimes, Sabrina, about a place I never knew. And eyes — there are always eyes looking at me.'

Sabrina shrugged the statement off lightly.

'Ah well, we can all have weird experiences in sleep.'

'Do you?'

'Sometimes. But I don't let it bother me.'

'Neither do I. But I *wonder*, all the same. It's not always easy to know what's real and what's not. Have you ever thought that?'

Sabrina's hand lightly touched Jaina's. 'Yes. When I was your age I felt the same. In a year or two you won't wonder at all. You'll know.'

Jaina's mood suddenly changed.

'I do now. About the real part.'

'Oh?' Sabrina glanced questioningly, with rising curiosity at the younger girl. 'Tell me.'

Jaina shook her head.

'Not yet. It's something deep down. A secret.' She sighed, with a kind of rapturous longing. She was thinking of Freddie. Sabrina sat back, realising there was no point in further questioning. Twilight was quickly encroaching upon the mist. The pace of the carriage slowed. At each bend of the lane the coachman tightened the reins, emitting a soothing warning to the horses as they took the corner. His voice was sufficiently clear for any wandering itinerant, farm-labourer or shepherd to hear.

When at last they reached Castle Carnack it was almost dark.

The weather next morning was unruffled by wind, and warm for the time of year. The sky, silvered at first by mist, lifted to hazy gold by ten o'clock. A letter arrived for Sabrina from Oliver, headed by the address of a Spanish Hotel elegantly embossed in gold.

He told her he would be back shortly, and that business (whatever it was) had been successful. He was making a brief call in Italy before crossing to England, and would not be bothering about France this time. She hoped the letter was true, and tried to believe it.

> I miss you, Sabrina, [the note concluded]. Never a day passes that I don't long to have you in my arms again. Be good, behave yourself, and see you look your ravishing best for our reunion. (That flimsy black chiffon thing you wore on our first night together might be a good idea!)
>
> Au revoir darling. Let me assure you, all your naughty misdemeanours are forgiven, up-to-date. I take it you feel the same.
>
> As ever, Mrs Cavannagh,
> Oliver.

So typically evocative. So brief, so subtle, so — vividly Oliver.

Sabrina's face was rosy when she'd finished perusing it. Her eyes flickered over the bold writing a second time, then she placed it in the envelope again, and put it in a dressing table drawer.

Later, over mid-morning coffee she mentioned the communication to Lisette, adding, 'He doesn't say one word about Jaina.'

'Does he know she's back?'

'No. I suppose not.'

'By the way, where is the child this morning? I haven't seen her at all.'

With a jerk of surprise Sabrina recalled that neither had she.

'She's probably in the garden or at the stables,' she said. 'Or perhaps she's merely having a lazy lie-in. I'll go and look for her. She'll be pleased to know Oliver's on the way home.'

Jaina however could not be found.

This was understandable.

Quite early the young girl had left by a side door from the house and hurried secretly up the path leading to the moor. All seemed hushed and sodden and very still. No leaf seemed to stir. There was only the brush of dewy undergrowth where she walked, and at one moment the startled movement of a deer as it sprang gracefully from thick curling bracken and raced ahead of her towards the lane. Through the silvered air to her right she had a glimpse of antlers raised alertly from behind a twisted tree trunk. But she was not afraid. She knew that although at certain seasons a stag might attack, it would only be if it sensed danger or was frightened. She went on quietly, and presently the beautiful sleek-coated animal turned and quietly moved away.

When she reached the pool below the track the sun glowed warm over the landscape, casting an aura of light on the water. Jaina pushed through the undergrowth, and seated herself on a clump of short grass edged by rushes. Then she unbuttoned her cape, threw it down beside her and took off her constricting boots and thick stockings. Laughter gurgled up in her; she thrust one foot into the water, splashing her toes to and fro so ripples flashed, sparkling with the myriad colours of rainbow light. The sensation was so sensually refreshing, she stood up, lifted her skirts, and waded in. Looking down she glimpsed the fleeting shapes of bright-winged insects and small fish darting through delicately feathered plants. Stones glittered up at her — rounded and shining, like the pebbles of some undersea world. She longed to fling off her clothes and bathe, letting the freshness of air and water enclose and caress her. The complete stillness was briefly broken by the brush of a faintly rising breeze against her face.

'Oh botheration!' she thought, and unbraided her tightly plaited hair so it fell in a silken dark cloud down her back, rippling with the shadowed brilliance of a moorland stream. It was then she heard twigs crackling. She looked round sharply and saw a face staring at her from the small thicket. The face was lean, dark, and curiously handsome. Jaina had seen him before, lingering in the vicinity of the lane, and had been forbidden, ever, to speak to him. But there was something about him that fascinated her — just as the wild creatures did — the animals of the moor, fox, badger, and the fleet stags. He was the son of the tinker woman, Mousha Sterne, and his name was Lucas. She knew that, because one of the maids had told her.

For a moment neither of them spoke; then wading out of the water, she said timidly, 'Hullo.'

'Why don't 'ee swim?' he asked bluntly. 'Warm th' water is.'

Jaina picked up her cape and drew it round her shoulders. Although she admired his looks, something about his manner intimidated her.

'Because I don't want to,' she answered bluntly.

'Frit are 'ee?'

'Frightened, do you mean? Why should I be?'

He grinned.

'A young wumman like you?' He shrugged, 'Meetin' one o' my kind. Most would be, I reckon. An' o' course — your stuck-up pa wouldn't like et.'

Realising Lucas meant Oliver she said curtly, 'He's my uncle. Not my father.'

'Oh yes?' The dark brows lifted. There was the flash of very white teeth. 'Who cares anyways? You do look a real beauty without them silly hair ribbons; an' wi' nuthen on at all, I reckon you'd be better still.'

She flushed.

'You shouldn't think of me like that.'

'Why not? Look here—' he stooped down and took a delicate water flower from the edge of the pool. 'That edn' all covered up an' dressed with frills and stuff to hide what glory 't was born with. An' them daffs we tek to houses an' towns shines brighter gold in the sun than in them stuffy rooms the rich folk have. Never thought that way have 'ee?'

Jaina shook her head.

'No.'

'Then you just start, see? 'Cos I know a few things. Our folks have the way of seein'. The true sight we do call et — us Sternes. An' there's sumthen different in 'ee from them down theer at th' big house. Sumthen that wants to spread its wings an' fly, an' dip an' dive, an' catch the magic o' the world to its own wild breast. Doan' you run away from the call. An' never be frit o' me, girl, 'cos I wouldn't hurt a true maid for all the wealth o' China.'

Quite suddenly he turned away, and pushing the undergrowth and constricting branches of bushes and trees aside strode upwards and out of her sight.

Jaina waited motionless for a moment or two until his strong figure had completely disappeared. Then in a kind of dream, she settled herself on the bank again, pulled on her boots and stockings, and presently made her way back to Carnack.

Questions were asked following her return, to which she replied, 'I've been walking, just walking. Is it wrong to go out on such a nice day?'

'Of course not,' Sabrina answered. 'And I understand. But

Lisette — well — you know she's different, and feels responsibility — which she doesn't enjoy — when Oliver — your uncle — isn't here. By the way, he's coming back quite soon.'

'Oh?' Jaina sounded uninterested.

If Sabrina had known about the girl's meeting with Lucas she would have been worried. Her surmise actually would have been quite wrong. Intrigued as Jaina had been by the tinker's knowledgeable observations concerning flowers and wild-life, it was not of Lucas she was thinking when she sat back, but of another quite different character — Frederick de Marchmont who had so stirred her imagination on that first day of their meeting. His polite air of gallantry, combined with an aptitude for 'understanding' beneath his fashionable exterior, had given her a queer yet romantic sense of security that still lingered. He was 'honourable' in more than just a name, she decided, and at moments she could visualise him fighting for her as knights in ancient times had fought for their ladies.

Of this, of course, Sabrina was quite unaware, having so much else on her mind. Her fondness for Jaina was deepening, but she was frequently irritated that she should have to be involved at all with the child's welfare. If it hadn't been for the girl's intermittent presence maybe Oliver could have been persuaded to take her on his latest jaunt abroad. She didn't want to be jealous or possessive, but the haunting memory of Lili Leblanc still troubled her. If only he'd said something on that angry night of their honeymoon — or even given a plausible word of explanation — made some attempt to set her fears at rest. But he hadn't. It was as though he took a pleasure in keeping her on tenterhooks, and was deliberately trying to punish her. She didn't really believe this; if she could have done, the situation might have been easier. The brutal truth, as she saw it, was that he didn't care sufficiently to consider her happiness. He wanted his marriage to remain completely intact and apart from his pleasures elsewhere. And life shouldn't be like that. It wasn't fair. Bitterness therefore increased in her, mingled with growing excitement as the hours and days passed.

Following two days of rain after Jaina's meeting with Lucas, the weather changed again, becoming warm and bright. Sabrina, making an effort to be optimistic and cheerful for Oliver's return, busied herself by contact with the guests, leaving Jaina free except for bored short periods with Lisette.

On an afternoon before Oliver's expected return, Jaina slipped out of the side door by the conservatory, and made another visit to the pool. Everything was sweet-smelling and dewy, gently warmed by the glittering spring sun. The shadows of yellow-green young leaves swaying danced across the path. From above, the drift of heather, gorse, and wild daffodils, was carried on the spring breeze. She wore no coat or restricting cape, and no stockings under her buttoned boots. Today, she thought, as she pushed through the willows and twisting elder, she was going to be her real self, and splash like one of the silver small fishes leaping from the water to catch flies. Only of course she wouldn't want to catch anything — just feel the tiny rippling waves on her bare skin, and the gentle brush of water lilies. Perhaps she would swim. She had been able to swim ever since she could remember. That would be lovely. Then she could lie on the bank and watch the rainbow-coloured light filter through the tracery of branches above. Perhaps a blue butterfly would fly on to her hand. She wouldn't move. She'd just wait and let it flutter its wings, tickling her a little, even brushing her bare skin where the rounded breasts every day seemed to become a little more full, tipped with rosy pink.

It was a wonderful feeling, growing up. She didn't believe what the nuns had told her about modesty any more. There was nothing wrong in having a pretty body, and what harm could there be in letting the sun play on it?

A little secret smile tilted her lips as she removed her boots, then the high-necked dress and calico underwear.

When she was quite naked she sat with her toes and ankles in the pool for a minute before slipping in.

As a spreading circle of water encompassed her pale form, a vole dived and passed to the opposite bank. She laughed. There was a stirring, a sighing of the air, a half-heard murmuring, and crackling of twigs. From her floating stream of dusky hair she lifted her head and looked up. He was there again. The tinker-man, Lucas, and he was standing by the glittering silver trunk of a young birch tree, watching.

Unthinkingly, she stood up, revealing the tender rounded stomach and breasts, her body licked to dappled rosy gold. A thousand iridescent drops of glittering water coursed from shoulders to thighs. His breathing quickened. He took a step towards her; then, instinctively, innocence was swamped by startled fear. She pulled her long black dripping hair over her shoulders, and placed one hand across her body; then she lifted the other arm and pointed to the bank where her clothes lay. 'Put them there—' she cried, 'and go away. Don't look. How *dare* you come sneaking round like that?'

Although she was not aware of it, his face coloured.

'I didn't mean nuthen—' he mumbled, trying to pull himself together. 'Beautiful you are − real lovely—'

Sensing his apology, tension eased from her and she started to cry. Desire for her died. He would have comforted her if he could, but he didn't dare. He turned away, picked up the tumbled garments and asked, 'Where do you want them? On that trunk there? It's dry.'

By then her body was once more shimmering under the surface of the pool. She nodded.

'Yes, yes. Only go. Someone will come. Please, Lucas.'

He was about to obey when something − a cry that was more of a loud gasp, startled them both. They jerked their heads round swiftly, and Jaina's rosy lips parted.

Sabrina.

A Sabrina who after the first shock looked very angry indeed. Jaina scrambled out of the pool, reached for her cloak and covered herself.

'What are you doing here?' Sabrina demanded of Lucas. 'And how could you, Jaina? What will Lisette say? And Oliver—'

Reaction made Jaina cry shrilly, 'What do I care? And you needn't say anything − not anything, because there's nothing to tell. I was only bathing, and Lucas is a friend.' She turned her back to them, and hastily dressed.

'That's right, Missis,' the man said coolly. 'D'you think I'd harm a chile? A young flower like that one? Is your mind so full o' muck you can't recognise the buds an' lilies o' th' fields − or they daffies up theer growin' so cool an straight an' flashin' gold—?'

'Muck? To talk like that to me!'

'It's my own way o' talkin',' the man said with quiet stubbornness. 'Simple folk we may be, but able to see deeper than some—'

There was a prolonged pause during which each stared at the other, as though probing for the truth.

Then Sabrina pulled her gaze away and gripped Jaina's hand.

'Come along,' she said quietly, 'we must get back.'

The man watched the young girl urged through the trees down the overgrown path. Jaina glanced back once, and he was still a static form against the background of moors and sky. The glint of water was suddenly taken into shadow. Jaina jerked her hand free.

'You needn't pull. I'm coming. I can walk on my own.' Her eyes were veiled, her lips mutinously set.

'Jaina—' Sabrina began helplessly.

'Don't lecture,' came the swift interruption. 'I'm tired of being watched and told what to do—'

'But you must realise it was wrong to let that — that gipsy see you naked?'

'Why?'

'Because it's not done. Because your Aunt Lisette and Uncle Oliver would be ashamed for you. I know you didn't mean anything. But—'

Jaina suddenly stopped walking and stood quite still.

'Not done!' she thought, 'how smug. What a stuffy thing to say.' Her dark eyes held a fiery contemptuous look.

'And suppose I did? What then?'

Sabrina paused before saying, 'Then I should have to tell Lisette, I'm afraid.'

'But you will anyhow, won't you? That's what you mean to do, to get Lucas into trouble, and make a row with Uncle Oliver?'

'It depends,' Sabrina said more coldly. 'If you go on behaving like this I shall feel it's my—'

'Duty.' There was a short angry pause before Jaina continued, 'I think duty's one of the nastiest words I know. At first I believed you thought the same; but you don't — you *don't* — you're just the same as them—'

She made a violent movement and started running, letting the protruding thorns and brambles tear her hands and clothing. She rushed on, heedless of Sabrina's protesting voice. When she reached Carnack she plunged through the side door, running down the hall and up the stairs towards her own room. On the main landing she passed Lisette, who having heard something of the confusion stared in shocked surprise at Jaina's wet hair and distressed face. Tears were streaming from the girl's eyes. Water dripped from the hem of her skirts and cape. Sabrina followed, and from the hall a housemaid stared.

Lisette caught her daughter-in-law's arm, as Jaina's door snapped to.

'Whatever's the matter? What's been happening?'

'Oh I don't think—' Sabrina hesitated.

'You must tell me. Of course you must.'

Later, rather reluctantly, Sabrina gave as mild a version as possible of events at the pool.

'But I'm sure no harm was done,' she concluded, 'and I think it would be best to let things rest now. If Oliver heard, there'd be trouble—'

'Oliver has to know,' Lisette's tones were firm. 'I shall certainly inform him — it won't be easy, but Jaina will have to be sent to some stricter boarding school where she has proper supervision. I'm sorry, Sabrina, in a way I'm very fond of the child. But my heart won't stand such scenes. And in view of her background — her parentage—' her voice trailed off. She took smelling salts from her reticule and sniffed the bottle several times.

'Do you mind telling me more of her parentage?' Sabrina asked pointedly. 'Her father, for instance. Surely you've an idea who he was, or is?'

For a moment Lisette looked startled.

'I don't know,' she said coldly. 'Oliver's the only one who could possibly say. And I doubt very much that even he's certain. Ask him if you must. But I advise you not to. There's enough to worry him about the child without fretting over her ancestors.'

With this observation, Sabrina for the time being had to be content.

10

Oliver appeared the next morning at Castle Carnack. Sabrina's excitement at seeing him again temporarily dispelled any niggling apprehension and fears she had concerning the possibility of a scene with Jaina, when Lisette informed him of the incident by the pool. She had done her best to make her mother-in-law promise to keep silent. But over this one matter Lisette, generally so easygoing over 'surburban morality' was surprisingly stubborn; partly, Sabrina guessed, because she resented the peaceful elegant routine of life being so disrupted. Jaina was no longer a little girl doing what she was told without argument. One disruptive influence in the household — Sabrina — was more than sufficient for Lisette. To have also an adolescent girl about the place, and a developing young beauty at that — was intolerable.

So once Oliver's passionate reunion with his wife was over, she made it her business to impart the news to her son, graphically, but with reasoning sympathy and a plea for him not to be too harsh with his niece.

Sabrina was upstairs, and Oliver and Lisette were taking sherry in the drawing room.

'It isn't that Jaina has any wickedness in her—' Lisette said, after the first impact of her story had registered. 'As I've suggested before — she's a child obviously destined for some more spectacular environment than we can give her here. She needs occupation, Oliver. I'm not sure the Convent was the right school for her. A stricter establishment offering a wider education and training of the graces would have provided a far better launching for the future.' She waved a delicate ringed hand commandingly. 'No, my dear. Don't interrupt. Wait and hear what I have to say first, then you can — blow your head off if you like—' she gave an artificial little laugh.

'Thanks.'

'I didn't mean that of course. But really! since that naked scene with the gipsy, I've been so distracted my old migraine's come on.' She paused, closing her eyes briefly with a half-swooning gesture that didn't deceive him for one moment. He thought he had never seen her look so well in her life.

'Continue,' he remarked coldly.

'What more is there to tell?' She shrugged. 'You're surely not going to allow things to go on in this way?'

'I haven't decided yet. It's odd—' He gave her a shrewd glance —'Sabrina didn't speak to me about it.'

'My dear Oliver, your young wife is half on the child's side.'

'Rot.'

'Oh no. She's an extremely wayward character herself, as well you know. I don't blame her for it — if she wasn't you wouldn't have married her. All the same she can hardly be the best influence on Jaina; or vice versa. If you weren't away so much, it would be easier. But I will not be responsible for either, under the circumstances.'

'No one expects you to be,' he said brusquely. 'All right, I'll think about it. In the meantime send Jaina down to the study. I'll see what she has to say for herself.'

Five minutes later an unhappy Jaina confronted Oliver defiantly in the rather dark room that was his own particular sanctum. The sun had not yet penetrated the lofty window which faced the west; the atmosphere was forbidding and chilly.

'I didn't do anything wrong,' she said in answer to his first direct question. 'Yes, I bathed, but it was nice in the water. And there were little fish swimming—' she broke off breathlessly.

'I'm not concerned with fish. My mother tells me you flaunted yourself naked in front of that disreputable tinker? Is it true?' His chin was set. The condemnation in his dark eyes confused and frightened her.

'No. I didn't flaunt − I − I − I didn't even know he was there, Uncle Oliver. And when I saw him—'

'Yes? What happened?'

She shook her head, 'Nothing − nothing—'

Oliver took her arm firmly and forced her face upwards towards his.

'Is that true?'

'Of course it is. And if you do anything to Lucas I'll never forgive you, *never*. He was nice. He talked about daffodils — flowers and things, and how — how—'

He suddenly released her.

'I've no intention of doing anything to Lucas, as you put it. There'll be no need. Because in future, Jaina, you won't be here—'

Her eyes, brilliant now with unshed tears, stared at him, shocked and unbelieving.

'What do you mean?'

'I shall send you away — to some establishment or seminary for young ladies where you will be taught good manners and how to behave with considerably more discipline than the nuns have shown. Do you understand?'

Her lips quivered.

'You couldn't. You mean — I won't see you, or Sabrina, or anyone I know? I'll be a — a sort of prisoner—?'

'If you look at it like that, yes. But only until you've learned what to do and what not. It's for your own good. I can assure you, Jaina, I've no intention whatever of allowing my own — niece — to develop into a strumpet.'

Suddenly she flew at him, and beat with her two hands on his chest.

'I won't, I *won't*. Whatever you say I'm not going to any nasty prison place. If you make me, I'll kill myself—' she was kicking wildly.

His arm tightened round her waist, while one hand went to her mouth. After a few moments her struggling ceased.

'Now listen to me, young lady. You'll do just what I say — even if I have to spank you into it, which is what you deserve. I'm not joking, and this is no game. Just as soon as things can be arranged you'll leave Carnack. And in the meantime you'll stay in your room and not dare to try and leave. I shall see you're safely locked in myself, then hand responsibility to Mrs Drew. Just thank your stars I'm being more lenient than you deserve. Well?'

He waited for her answer, but she said nothing. Her mouth was mutinous, her eyes half-blind with misery.

When Oliver realised there'd be no compromise on her part, he conducted her himself from the study to her bedroom.

There was the click of the lock, followed by the turning of a key and the sound of his footsteps receding down the landing towards the stairs.

Jaina moved lifelessly to the window. Clouds were already rising from the south, dimming the sun's rays. In the distance, beyond the stables and paddock, the moors stretched brown and gold streaked with purple beneath the changing sky. At one moment, shadows raced fitfully over humped boulders and twisted wind-blown trees; the next, the distant mine-stacks loomed as forbidding dark sentinels over a brooding landscape until the sun once more reclaimed it.

Instinctively the girl shivered. She couldn't stay here any more. She couldn't. Uncle Oliver no longer loved her, Sabrina had told tales and let her down, and the thought of being cooped up in some strict place where she was watched all the time by some dragon of a schoolmistress who punished her every time she disobeyed, was sheer torture. She'd heard of some places where girls were still tied face down over chairs, and whipped.

She was terrified.

She endured the rest of the morning mechanically, and somehow managed to eat lunch, which was brought up to her by Sabrina.

'They wanted Mary to bring it,' Sabrina said, 'but I thought—' she broke off, shocked by Jaina's fixed stare, continuing almost instantly, 'you must understand, Jaina, I said nothing to your – to Oliver; Lisette knew something and pressed me. I did my best, but—'

'Did you?' The icy question held contempt. 'You let it out anyway. And now I'm not even being sent back to the convent – I'm going to *prison*.' The last word came out with the hissing quality of some captured wild thing.

Sabrina ran forward and took Jaina by the shoulders. She gave an unconvincing laugh. 'Don't be melodramatic. You're imagining things. Prison! the idea. Oliver was simply angry. I'm sure he said nothing like it.'

'Oh yes he did. And don't treat me like a child, because I'm not. And don't try and be nice either. You're not nice at all.'

She tore herself away, turned her back to Sabrina and moved to the window again.

'Go away,' she said coldly and clearly. 'I don't want you.'

Sabrina's lips tightened.

'After a meal you may feel better. All right. I'll go. But see you eat your food. Please, Jaina.'

There was no reply.

Sabrina left. She had meant to leave the door unlocked, but at that same minute Oliver appeared at the bend of the landing. He waited until she turned the key, then came towards her.

'How is she?' he asked, as they went to their own room.

'Upset,' Sabrina answered. 'I don't think you should keep her shut up there. You've had a scene – you've told her what you thought; why can't you try and overlook it all now? What harm did she do after all? There's no shame in a young girl's body—' She broke off in a rush of indignation.

'Of course not. But as my niece, Jaina has no right to let all and sundry see it.'

'Your niece?' Sabrina had not meant the question to slip out, but something impelled her to continue recklessly, 'Is she, Oliver? *Is* she only your niece? Or something more?'

At first he was too taken aback to reply. Then he said coldly, 'Just what do you mean by that?'

Sabrina smiled, although a trifle wryly. 'I'm not quite sure. You're always so very mysterious about her. So is Lisette. And I expect Jaina's noticed. She must have. I know secrets are sometimes necessary, and you've made it quite clear more than once that you mean to keep your own intact. But why, Oliver? Why can't we all be honest with each other?'

Her sincerity touched him briefly. But his voice was stern when he said, 'I've warned you before not to pry into my affairs. As a business man I can't afford anyone – even you – to know intimate details either of my past, or plans for the future. There are some areas that have to remain strictly private, and can't possibly concern or affect you in any way. Try and accept it, Sabrina. And about Jaina too. I know what's best for her, and you, my love, have no right whatever to make wild inferences which have no basis in fact.' He moved closer, and took her into his arms. 'Do you understand? Do try.'

'No,' Sabrina told him. 'I don't honestly understand much about you at all, Oliver, but—'

He silenced her with a kiss. 'Then forget it. Understanding

doesn't always help. But this—' He lifted her up, lowered his head, so his lips rested on the gentle hollow of her neck above the breasts, 'this is all we need. I love you, Sabrina. I want you. God, how I've longed for you all these weeks—'

'Even through your business dinners, and — and — functions — and meetings—'

'Functions? Conferences? To hell to them,' he said. He carried her to the bed, and slowly, sensuously, disrobed her. His hands, as they travelled her body, were fire to her need and desire. Presently all niggling memories of Jaina and even Lili Leblanc were submerged by the passion that encompassed and drowned them in its welling tide of forgetfulness and dark sexual appeasement.

Only when it was over did she realise that he had won again, and that not a single one of her questions had been answered.

By mid-afternoon the wind had died unpredictably, leaving a stillness and gently spreading mist from the sea. The sky lowered, taking the landscape into merging uniformity. Promptly at four o'clock Jaina's door was unlocked and tea was brought in, not by Sabrina this time, but by Mary the housemaid. Jaina regarded her dumbly. Her eyes were so stricken Mary's kind heart responded.

'Don't you fret, miss,' she said, 'something will happen to end all this, you mark my words. I don't know what the trouble's about, but you'll get through et.' She glanced round furtively at the door, before putting the tray down. 'I have to lock it behind me,' she said, 'or Mrs Drew'll be on to me. But—' she put her hand in a pocket and drew out another slightly rusted replica. 'Take it,' she whispered. 'I found it in th' dairy. It'll fit most doors. No one knows I got it — mebbe they've forgot about it.' She paused then added, 'If it works you jus' dress yourself up and appear at dinner like the young lady you are and I reckon they'll be so dumbfounded everythin'll be forgiven. If it doesn't though, then there's nuthen more I can do.'

Jaina took the key automatically, staring at it for a few seconds. When she glanced at Mary, her face had completely changed, become radiant, though apprehension still lingered in her eyes.

'But won't you get into trouble, Mary?'

'Sh — sh! no one'll know about me unless you tell them. Mrs Drew'll have the proper one. Just see you throw that other right away somewhere where it'll never be found again.' Hearing footsteps approaching down the corridor, she coughed, cleared her throat, and said clearly and loudly, 'If you want more hot water, ring, miss, and I'll be up with some.'

She lifted her head, went to the door, closed it and after the familiar click of the lock walked sharply down the landing towards the servants' stairs.

The other footsteps paused for a minute outside, while Jaina stood very erect, steeling herself to face whoever it was — Sabrina perhaps, or even Uncle Oliver. But no one made any attempt to enter, and a moment later the footsteps passed on. They were obviously those of a man — the footman's or Oliver's. Jaina sighed with relief. She was still clutching the old key. She stared at it briefly, then slipped it into her pocket carefully, under her handkerchief. In a few minutes, when all was quiet, she'd try it in the lock to see if it worked; if it did she'd know what to do.

Five minutes later she had her answer. There was a stiffness, a slight rough jarring sound when she inserted the metal into the lock. Then, slowly it turned.

Excitement and a wild recklessness rose in her. 'Go down to dinner,' Mary had said. But that was too risky. She would probably be sent up to bed again. She had the most precious instrument of all in her possession now, 'a master key' — that's the kind the Mother-Superior had at the convent — a key to open all doors. And this one was hers. So she would escape. She wouldn't go to prison after all.

She would run away. Further than that she made no plan. Somewhere, somehow, she'd find work to do. Everything would be all right, and one day she'd see Freddie again.

11

The air was thick when Jaina left Carnack, wearing her serge dress under her cape, and a black shawl covering her hair. She had managed to creep down the back stairs carrying her shoes and a bag under one arm, when the servants were in the kitchen at tea. There was a door leading out to the vegetable gardens below the paddock which was seldom used. Moses, the gardener, she knew, would probably be having a snooze in the coach house, and once she was on the track to the moor no one would see her. Mist was already turning into fog. Later, when the moon came up it would probably lift a little. But except for the chill dampness, the darkness was a comfort. Her thickly-stockinged feet were soon wet; so she sat presently on a rock and pulled on her shoes.

Her plans were not yet clear in her mind, except to get away. She had been careful though to take all her pocket money, and some spare cash that was kept in a wooden box for servants' use on a shelf near the side entrance. It was stealing of course, she thought with a pang. But when they found out she'd gone, they'd know who'd taken it. And anyway, it wasn't really stealing. She'd pay it back somehow when she got to her destination. But where was that? She didn't know. She just had to get away — this was all that mattered, right away from Uncle Oliver's bullying and threats of sending her to that seminary place, the prison.

By the time she neared the high point of the moor, by the lane, her limbs were already aching, and her skirts were torn and dripping round her ankles. Everything suddenly seemed very lonely. She paused and looked back. No light or glow of lamp shone from Castle Carnack below. The outline of the building was completely swallowed up by the waves of milky thickening fog. Only nearby boulders and bushes were vaguely visible, stretching claw-like contorted branches towards her.

The thicket loomed as a huddled mass of threatening blackness. When she forced herself on again she took a wrong path, and found herself suddenly confronted by the stark misted shape of an ancient menhir. She put her head down, peering at the ground, and pushed her way in the opposite direction.

At last she came to the lane.

It was a little clearer there. But even if the fog lifted she knew it would soon be deepening twilight. Once more she put the bag down, and rested by the trunk of a tree, to ease her aching arm.

Presently, still without any concrete plan, she crossed the lane and took the trodden path to the tinkers' shack. Even through the wet scents of earth and dripping leaves, the faint perfume of daffodils lingered. And as a curling coil of mist momentarily disintegrated, a glimmer of pale gold shone fitfully from the thousands of sleeping buds crowding the small field and copse.

There was a ray of light, too, from the rough dwelling place.

She went up to the door. A lean face framed by strands of straggling grey hair, looked out.

'What d'ye want? What you wan 'ere. Eh?' The small eyes, black as sloes, peered suspiciously from the wizened countenance.

Unthinkingly Jaina answered, 'Could I stay here? Just for a time – I'm cold. I'm – I'm – I can pay – I've got money. But I've got to get to Bodmin. I—'

The woman shook her head.

'I've seen 'ee before. From the big place edn' 'ee? Then be off chile – go back where you do belong. My son an' I wants no truck nor trouble with them Cavannaghs—'

'But I'm—' Jaina swallowed with difficulty.

'You're runnin' away. Ais? Well, I doan blame 'ee for that. But you jus' run somewhere else, see?' The woman's voice grew strident, harsh. 'Lucas an' I wants no trouble. An' ef he wus here he'd say the same. So off with 'ee—'

The door snapped to sharply in the girl's face. At the same moment the mist thickened again. Overhead a lone gull screamed. Dejectedly Jaina walked back to the lane. She did not know quite how far Bodmin was, but obviously she had to get there somehow and find a station where a night train might be able to take her to Plymouth or London. So presently she started off again, still emotionally shocked, realising gradually as the minutes passed how reckless she'd been — as reckless as Sabrina when she'd left Freddie at the altar; only for Sabrina everything had been easier, because people were concerned about her — *really* concerned. Her father, even her stepmother. She was beautiful, well-born, and knew who she was — something Jaina had never known about herself. And she'd had Freddie. Freddie, so kind and handsome and understanding. Why, even after the awful way Sabrina had treated him he would obviously have forgiven her if she'd wanted. But instead Sabrina had preferred Uncle Oliver and stolen him too.

A small flame of indignation stirred Jaina's heart as she remembered. In a way everything was Sabrina's fault. However nice she'd seemed, and friendly, she'd disrupted everything at Carnack, and made even Lisette cross and schoolmarmish.

Before Sabrina's appearance, Oliver's mother had been so kind and placid; a romantic reclusive figure in her draperies, always willing to relate stories of her past experiences on the stage, and how young gallants had drunk champagne from her slipper. She'd even danced with King Edward when she was young, and had implied that if she'd responded to his advances she could have had a marvellous establishment of her own — grander even than Carnack, with all the jewellery and fine clothes she wanted. Of course she lacked for nothing now; — but to be mistress of the King — a kind of second Lillie Langtry, — that would have been far more marvellous, wouldn't it?

She wasn't quite sure what a mistress had to do to become so honoured, except to show her body without clothes, and be kissed all over, but truth was gradually registering in a mysterious way, and if two people could feel as she did about Freddie — well, the thing that happened wouldn't be unpleasant at all. In fact she could imagine rather liking it. Is that what her mother had done with her father? Liked it? And is that why no one would ever tell her anything? Because it had made her mother wicked?

There were so many questions to be answered; so much dimly suggested, but withheld. Why couldn't people be honest with each other? Why did she long so deeply and passionately to know every little bit about herself, and her background? In a ceaseless refrain such thoughts chased over and over through her brain, becoming more confused and uncertain the further she walked. The fog was clearing, but thin rain was blowing on a rising wind. She pulled the shawl further over her forehead, half shading her eyes. Her feet were heavy and wet. Without realising it her pace became slower and slower. Was she going in the right direction? She hoped so. Even if she didn't reach Bodmin there were other towns. She must sometime find a station.

At intervals she felt in her pocket to make sure the money in her purse was safe. Then she went on, keeping her eyes averted from the grim shapes of the rain-swept moor — the granite builders, strange dolmens and circles and in the distance the looming shape of Brown Willy. All, now, seemed to hold an elemental life of their own. With each sigh and moan of the wind, creaking gorse and undergrowth sent clawing fingers towards her. Her eyelids smarted not only from the rain but from unconscious tears flooding her eyes. If only Lucas had come to the door of the tinkers' hut, she thought miserably, everything would have been so different. Lucas would have made his horrible mother take her in for a time, then, when he set off for Launceston or whatever place he went to with the daffodils the next day, he could have taken her with him. He would have done, she was sure of it. Lucas liked her. He wouldn't have told anyone at Castle Carnack.

She was thinking about him, when a distant sound quickened her senses suddenly. Not wind or the swish of rain this time — but a grating noise accompanied by the hollow clippetty-clop of horses' hooves. She drew herself to her full height, looked round, pushed the drenched hair from her forehead and stared. Through the blurred air a cart was approaching, pulled by a single horse. Without intending to she swayed into the roadway. There was a 'whoa', a 'hello there', as the vehicle pulled up, followed by a man's voice calling, 'Blimey! what the hec's a woman doin' by herself on a night like this un?'

He held a small lamp out and peered into her face. 'A bloody girl,' he muttered. 'Streuth.'

Out came an arm and before she knew it he'd pulled her closer. 'Want a lift?' he asked. 'Goin' anywhere partickler? Escaped have ye? A serving maid? Or a thief? Are y' a thief, girl?'

She shook her head wildly. 'No, no. I've got to get a train.' She pulled out her purse. 'I've got money. I wanted to walk — to

Bodmin. You see my mother's ill—' The lie on her lips sounded sweet in her own ears, simply because of that one word, 'mother'. 'I work on a — a farm you see.' The false explanation once started, fell glibly from her lips. 'And they wouldn't — they don't know I've gone. I've got to get there—' There was no doubting her desperation. The man looked uncertain for a moment.

'You mean she lives in Bodmin?'

Jaina shook her head.

'Plymouth.'

'Whew! that's a helluva long way.'

'Yes, but if I can get a train—' She hesitated and thought quickly. 'I've got friends in Bodmin.'

'Oh well then—' He didn't believe she was telling the whole truth, but something about her impressed him. So pale and earnest, and wild she appeared, in her black bedraggled shawl with the rain running down her face. 'Up with you then. I'm headin' Bodmin way myself, Jake my name is — Jake Brewsten. Carrier of goods, and pedlar in a small way.'

When she was seated, and with a crack of the whip the cart was off again, she stole a look at him. There was an awning over their heads, and as her lashes dried she saw that the man was quite old. Well, perhaps not old, but middle-aged, pink-faced, wearing a bowler hat from which tufts of red hair straggled over the collar of his coat. A check scarf reached to his chin. He looked a bit rough, she thought, but kind. His features were not clear through the greyness, but he did not look Cornish.

For some time no word was said. Then he remarked casually, 'Cornish girl, are you?'

'Partly,' she told him, huddling her face deeper into her shawl.

'Hm. Me — I'm a real furriner to your kind then, though I've known these parts many years — more years than you've bin' born. Lunnon way I come from, ever bin to Lunnon?'

'No.'

'No one's proper bin born till they've seen th' city.'

She didn't ask him why he'd left. She didn't really care. Curiosity, with all other emotions, had died in her. She was so tired. The chill in her bones was easing, the warmth of the man's large body so close to her had a steamy comforting feeling.

Sleep began to claim her. Time faded. The moor, and the rain, and the rhythmic sound of horses' hooves and wheels clattering lulled her to semi-forgetfulness. Occasionally the driver paused to light his pipe. Once he stopped the cart at a wayside inn, bought a pint of beer for himself, and came back with one for her. 'Drink what you want,' he said. 'I'll tek the rest.'

She obeyed, and didn't like the taste, but it made her feel better. He got the lamp of the cart alight, and they started off again, up hill and down, round corners and along secluded valleys, passing huddled tiny hamlets of only a few stone cottages, then out into the lonely wilderness of the moor once more. A stray sheep occasionally baahed and crossed directly from one side of the lane to the other, its form briefly clear in the swinging rosy glow of the lantern. Shadows from boulders and undergrowth swayed and danced before disappearing again into the encompassing gloom.

When they reached Bodmin, the rain had stopped, leaving only a faint mist behind.

The man drew the cart to a halt near some cross-roads.

'If you want the station,' he said, pointing to his right, 'you tek that way. There'll be a train some time, an' I hope your ma's better.'

She thanked him, took out her money and tried to pay him. But he refused, with a wave of his hand.

'You kip what you want, girl. Mebbe you'll need it. Comp'ny's cost me nothing.'

She felt suddenly bereft as the cumbrous vehicle moved away. She was alone again, with the queer feeling deepening in her that she was in some strange dream from which she must wake soon and find herself back in the familiar bedroom at Castle Carnack. Yet all the time she knew, deep down, everything that was happening was real — frighteningly so.

She forced herself to move, following the directions given.

The station was not far, and there was only a sleepy old man waiting to provide tickets. She paid, and after being told a train for Plymouth was soon due, went through the barrier to the platform and into the waiting room. One or two passengers were about, but due to the bad light, lingering mist and general air of desolation, no one seemed to notice or bother about her. Why should they? A mere working girl obviously, in a draggled looking cape and shawl, carrying a bag or parcel under her arm? The train puffed in, about ten minutes after her arrival. Jaina found a carriage to herself, and presently there was a whistle, followed by the chugging motion of wheels, as the engine started up, puffing billowing coils of steam into the night air. She slept most of the way, only stirring when the train halted at small stations.

At last they reached Plymouth. Jaina pulled herself together, with a start. There was so much noise and sudden rushing and confusion — figures darting along platforms, luggage being unloaded, whistles and shouts, and porters pushing trolleys along.

When she stepped down from the carriage, she stood for a minute dazedly wondering what to do and where to go. A man glanced at her curiously as her shawl fell back. She pulled it quickly over her head again, shielding her face, and pushed forward following the main stream of passengers. At the barrier she gave up her ticket and went through. The air was fresher outside the station, but still odorous and thick with the smell of smoke and steam. She walked on mechanically, knowing she must find somewhere to sleep for the rest of the night, but with no idea what to look for. A hotel perhaps? if she had enough money. She thought she had. Her pocket was still quite heavy from the coins she'd taken. But what sort of hotels were there in Plymouth? And would anyone take her in, looking as she did? Round a street corner she paused, took the shawl from her head, and in the reflected light of a small window straightened her hair, pinning it on top with the one comb she had. Then she smoothed her cape, and shook her skirts as free as possible, from their wetness. After that she glanced round and walked on uncertainly.

How far and for how long she walked she couldn't guess. The houses seemed to grow smaller. From somewhere not far away the tang of sea was carried on a thin wind. The mist was gradually lifting. Through the lamplight people — mostly men — eyed her strangely as she passed. Some of them were foreign-looking — Bretons or Spaniards, even Indian. Other were obviously gentlemen in tall hats, and at certain points a carriage or landau stopped to allow rich looking male passengers to dismount.

The crowds troubled her. Occasionally taller buildings appeared, but they looked unfriendly and rather frightening. So when she reached a narrow quieter street — more of a wide alley really, with cobblestones underfoot, and only occasional lights twinkling, she took it. One or two sailors lounged about, and an old man pushing a barrow. She wondered if he'd know of a quiet hotel, but one glimpse of his face put her off. It was mean looking and narrow, dirty, and shifty-eyed, with a hooked nose curving over his nut-cracker mouth. Long grey hair straggled over his coat collar. He frightened her.

She went on, hurried too quickly round a corner, and bumped into a figure. Hands gripped her shoulders. Jaina jerked her head up. She saw a woman's face staring down at her; at least — she thought it was a woman. She had watery but shrewd eyes under something dark that could have been a hat or veiling. Yet her voice was harsh, like that of a man's, when she spoke, and she smelt of gin.

'Lost are you, dearie?' she asked.

Jaina shook her head. 'No. I'm — I'm looking for someone, for somewhere—' Her voice and face quivered. Under the pale beam of a gas lamp her dark eyes shone brilliant with alarm and exhaustion. She looked far older than her years at that moment, and had she but known it — beautiful, with a flower-like ethereal quality that could not have failed to attract attention.

The woman, who was not as old as Jaina had at first thought, smiled. Jaina was revolted, although she tried to believe that only kindness was intended.

'You shouldn't be wandering about on your own at this time,' the strange voice continued. 'Wanting a place to stay, are you?'

Dumbly Jaina nodded, trying to free herself, but unable to do so.

'Then you come with me, my pretty darling. There's a place I know where you'll be very welcome and cared for. Not mine, my dear, but folks I know.'

'I don't think I—'

The smile died.

'You do as I say or I'll have to get the law, won't I, darling? Young girls roaming the streets can be sent to prison. Now you wouldn't like that, would you?'

Prison? Jaina shuddered.

If she could she would still have escaped. But she had no choice. Against her will, with one hard hand gripping her arm she found herself being propelled down the street and into another. There was a building with a sign hanging outside, and the words were clear under its red swinging lamp. 'THE GOLDEN ROSE.'

The woman pushed Jaina up two steps and through a door. They entered a corridor with an opening on one side leading into a beer shop. Shouts and laughter came from inside, and the smell of spirits was strong; but Jaina was hurried past, with her wrist tightly clutched in the rough palm. The light became dimmer until they reached the end of the passage, where the flagstones were overlaid by thick rugs. Curtains draped a facing door. The woman tapped, pushed, and it immediately opened, leading into a comfortable-looking room with other doors leading from it. Chandeliers threw a comforting muted glow round the walls which were papered in dullish gold. Although it was spring, a fire burned in the grate. The furniture was of mahogany, with a round table in the centre. A woman with piled-up yellow hair was seated there, before an assortment of papers a bottle and two glasses. Behind her was a desk.

She looked up sharply as Jaina and her 'jailer' entered. She was stout, pink-cheeked, and after a moment smiled welcomingly, although the sharpened glance of shrewd eyes belied the gesture. But Jaina didn't notice how hard and veiled they were — only their colour. They were so very blue. As blue as the sparkling glass beads on her ample bosom — bright as the diamonds on her fingers and in her ears.

She sat up abruptly. 'Well?' she said, 'and who's this? A guest at this time of night?' The smile died; she turned to the other woman and asked sharply, 'Where did find her, Aggie? And who is she? She looks very young.'

'Yes, young and lost,' came the answer. 'That's true, isn't it, darling?' Turning to Jaina.

The faint fear, mingled with a sense of gratitude for the warmth and escape from the busy street, prompted Jaina to answer, 'Yes, I — I was looking for somewhere to sleep. I—'

'I see.' The stout woman, obviously the owner of the premises, closed an open book with a snap. 'And where were you going? Why? Haven't you any family? Eh?'

Jaina shook her head.

'They're dead. I was just—'

'Just looking for a home,' the woman who'd brought her interrupted slily. 'That's it, isn't it, my dear?'

Jaina nodded.

'And what's your name?'

For some deep, inexplicable reason, Jaina said, 'Petal', only recalling later that it was the name of a doll she'd had when she was a tiny child.

'Petal. Hm.' The large woman at the table thought for a moment or two, then remarked, 'Petal – well it's a pretty name, as good as any other, I suppose.' She paused before heaving herself to her feet. Upright she was far more stout than Jaina had thought, and extremely tall. Beside her Jaina felt like a midget.

'Very well, Petal,' the strong voice continued, 'you can stay here for a few days if you like. This is quite a large boarding house, and all our rooms are nice—'

'I've got money—' Jaina interrupted eagerly.

'Sh sh! you keep it for the time being. Later we'll see. I don't like to think of young girls walking the streets of Plymouth. There's one thing though—'

'Yes?'

'You'll be a good girl and stay put while you're in my charge. I want no trouble; and if you start wandering off again I shall have to inform the police.'

The police!

Jaina shuddered.

'Do you mean stay here for ever?' she demanded. 'Do you mean I'm a prisoner? Oh no. Not that. I *couldn't*.'

The rather unpleasant smile returned to the woman's lips.

'No, no. Of course not. What a strange word to use. Prisoner.' Her eyes narrowed. 'Only for the present,' she said, 'until you're better fed, and fattened up a little.' Involuntarily Jaina backed away, 'fattened up'. It sounded so awful, just as though she was a pig or something.

At that point she might have turned and made an effort to escape, if there hadn't been a sudden rap followed by the opening of a door.

Three heads turned.

The figure standing in the entrance appeared to Jaina the most beautiful she had ever seen — even lovelier than Sabrina. She was tall, fair-haired, and slender, clad in blue silk, with jewellery and beads twinkling everywhere. She was carrying a fan, and the buckles on her pointed satin shoes glittered under the lacy hem of her gown.

'Ah! Janetta!' the large woman said. She eyed her critically. 'Yes, you look quite chic, my dear. Your friend should be charmed. But first of all, will you take our young friend to a bedroom — the small single blue. It's vacant, I know. Tell Lollie or Lydia to look after her. She'll be staying here for a time.'

The exquisite creature offered a mittened hand to Jaina. 'Come along,' she said, 'the blue room's a pretty one. You'll like being one of us.' Although she spoke correctly, her voice had a rough edge to it that was not quite in keeping with her appearance.

Dazedly, as though in a dream, Jaina allowed herself to be conducted from the parlour.

There was muttered conversation behind the closed door for a few moments, the clink of coins, followed by the shuffling sound of heavy footsteps and click of a lock.

Outside the rain had started again. But the old hag Jaina had so lucklessly met, wore an avaricious, pleased look on her hard face. It had been a good night. She had plenty in her pocket now for as much gin as she wanted, and more besides.

What did it matter that another young lamb had gone to slaughter, as they put it? Pity there weren't more of her kind about — and anyway she could've done the simple little thing a good turn in the end. Men were always on the look-out. Rich men. And ships were always sailing to foreign parts. She could just imagine some lusting sheik drooling and ravishing her virginity.

Men? Muck!

Contempt almost spat the word out. Then she went on, half swaying through the night, to be taken at last into a world of drunken shadows.

12

In spite of the excitement, loneliness, and worrying experience of being forced to the inn by the unpleasant old woman, Jaina slept well. She had been given a tempting meal, followed by a draught that had soon induced forgetfulness.

It was quite late when she woke, already ten o'clock, with sunlight piercing chinks in the curtains. Sounds of footsteps from outside, intermittent passing of traffic, and the rattle of a milk cart jerked her suddenly wide awake. Where was she? The room was strange, luxurious, thickly carpeted, with gilt and glass shining, and hangings of velvet and brocade.

She sat up quickly as memory registered. Of course. It was the place — the inn, boarding house or hotel — where the big fair-haired woman had welcomed her and told her she must rest for a time until she was better and had been 'fattened up' — weren't those the words she'd used? But she hadn't been ill, Jaina thought, puzzled, she was just tired after running away from Carnack.

Carnack!

A shadow clouded her mind as one by one memories fell into place — Uncle Oliver's anger, being locked in her room and told she was a prisoner. Then she'd escaped with the help of Mary, and started walking through the fog across the moor. There'd been a kind man driving a cart, and he'd let her ride with him until they reached Bodmin.

A little shiver of dread filled her.

It had been so dismal on the dreary platform. The station had been so cold and strange. But a train had soon come, and after a long time she'd reached Plymouth.

That's where she was, Plymouth. There had been the smell of sea last night; and sailors wandering about the streets, speaking in strange tongues. That's why she'd found the dark cobble-stoned byway leading to the hotel. Like nightmare figures, memories of the bent old man pushing the barrow and the grinning ugly face of the crone who'd grasped her wrist, sprang to life again. She jumped out of bed, and hurried to the window, pulling a curtain aside. There was a blind behind it. She jerked it up with a rattle, and looked out on to the street. It appeared quite ordinary; rather bleak and narrow, but there was nothing frightening about it at all; just flat-fronted houses huddled together with entries branching off at intervals. A poor looking sort of street she thought, for such a rich kind of hotel. The lady who owned it must indeed be rich. Well − she wouldn't have worn all those diamonds if she hadn't been. The diamonds reminded Jaina of the other one − the younger woman who'd been so beautiful in her pale blue silk dress and who'd brought her to this lovely bedroom.

Awed, feeling again as though she was still in some strange kind of dream, Jaina turned and walked back towards the great bed. The carpet was like velvet under her feet. When she glanced down at her toes, she became aware, for the first time, of the lace-bordered satin nightdress − the slippers, trimmed with swansdown put ready for her, and the silk wrap lying over a chair.

She put it on, and gazed at herself through the long cheval mirror. The sunlight cut sideways across her face, accentuating its fine bone-structure, luminous tilted eyes, and lustrous quality of the unbound dark hair. Her youthful breasts were subtly obvious beneath the expensive nightwear − the trim waist, and gently curved slim thighs. She gasped. Just for a moment she imagined herself a princess in a fairy tale.

Her musings were disturbed by a light knock, and the entrance of a young woman carrying a breakfast tray. She didn't look like a real maid. She was young and pretty, but not so pretty as the one who'd accompanied her to bed the night before.

'Here you are,' she said, 'I'm Lydia. Madam said you were to eat it all up—' she smiled '—and no nonsense.' She paused before adding, 'My! you *are* young, aren't you? What's your name?'

Remembering in time what she'd chosen to call herself, Jaina said, 'Petal.'

'Petal!' the girl laughed. 'That's a nice one, that is. That'll suit her ladyship fine. And the others.'

'What do you mean, ladyship? And what others?'

The young woman's expression changed. 'Her ladyship is what we call Madam between ourselves, and that's what you must do from now on. Never forget. Madam she is and must always be to her − guests.'

'Are you a guest?' Jaina asked pointedly.

'What else?' The voice was sharp. 'Now you just get on and eat your breakfast. Then probably Madam will come up to see you.'

'After I've dressed?'

There was no answer. Jaina looked round. 'Where are my clothes?'

The woman shrugged and went to the door. 'Those old things? In the bin prob'ly. You won't be needing them any more.'

'What do you mean?' Jaina ran forward staring up at the strange face fiercely. She noticed what she had not before, that the features weren't really so very young after all. There was something hard about her expression, and her mouth was painted.

'They're mine. My own,' Jaina said. 'I want them.'

'Fiddlesticks,' the woman shrugged. 'I'll tell Madam; maybe she'll be glad to get rid of them − *and* you.'

The door slammed. There was the horrible sound of a key being turned, and Jaina realised she was once more a prisoner.

When she saw 'Madam' later, however, her fears were mostly allayed. 'You've no need at all to be frightened, my dear,' she was told soothingly. 'Not now you've been taken into our establishment. In trouble, weren't you? That's what made you run away from − wherever it was you were. Well − *I* knew trouble too, when I was your age, and—'

'It wasn't exactly—' Jaina began, but her attempted explanation was interrupted.

'Sh − I don't want to know about it. You keep everything to yourself, *everything*; and try and forget the past. What's done is done. Here you'll be looked after and have every comfort − pretty clothes and good food, and later we can decide about your future.'

Jaina was bewildered. 'What future? I've got the money I brought, but that's all. I—'

The wide smile silenced her. Probably it was meant to be kind, she thought, but all the same she was discomforted.

'There's no need for us to talk of money — yet. In the end, my love, you'll earn enough, and more — than any girl could dream of.'

'But how?'

Madam patted her shoulder. 'By looking beautiful, and being yourself, by helping about the premises. This is quite a smart boarding house you know. Fashionable people stay here. We have visitors, personages of importance, high class, you could say. Those you saw in the tap room when you came in last night were nothing. A different sort of trade altogether. The two sections are run separately. You won't be required to mix at all with any riff-raff.' She paused, adding a little more sharply, 'Do you understand?'

Jaina shook her head. 'No, not quite. Not really.'

Mild impatience appeared momentarily on the bland face. In those few seconds before she spoke again Madam's china blue eyes observed shrewdly every detail of the girl's nymph-like form outlined subtly through the thin wrap, the tempting allure of delicately pointed breasts, slim waist and gently swelling thighs, the potentials of sexual allure emphasised by her extreme innocence.

'How old are you?' she asked abruptly.

'Fourteen,' Jaina told her.

The smile returned.

'Quite a young woman.'

'Yes,' Jaina agreed, thinking of Freddie. 'But they don't think so at — at home. And the nuns said—'

'Nuns?' the interruption was a shrill one. 'Mother of God!' Two hands flew up expressively. 'Is that where they kept you? A convent?'

'I went to school there.'

'Hm. No wonder you ran off.'

Jaina looked away. 'It wasn't only them. It was — something else.' She felt the warm colour staining her cheeks. Madam relaxed.

'Ah. A man. Was that it? A lover, my dear?'

'I don't want to talk about it,' Jaina said.

'Neither do I want you to,' Madam said placatingly. 'As I told you, the less I hear of your past, the better. But I think I understand more now.'

Again the pat on Jaina's shoulder, then on one hand. Rings twinkled on the plump fingers. Black silk rustled when the large figure drew herself erect again and once more stared down into the girl's face. 'So it's understood,' she said, 'we're friends, and I'll take care of you until you're quite strong and ready to help in some kind of way with our — guests. Of course you must give your solemn promise not to go out or be seen below stairs—'

'But—'

The mouth hardened. 'That is very important, Petal. You're young, and my responsibility. If any harm came to you I should be to blame. We don't want that do we? You wouldn't want me — your — protector — to get into trouble?'

Jaina shook her head.

'Of course not.'

'So we mustn't take risks. I shall see your door is kept locked for the moment, but if you want anything you have only to touch a bell, and one of my girls will answer. Anything you wish for in reason, you may have. Celeste, my dress-maker, will visit you this afternoon to take your measurements and suggest dress styles so that you may be properly equipped for your new role.'

Jaina gasped.

'Dresses?'

'Oh yes.'

'Satin, do you mean? Or silk? And lace?'

'Whichever you wish. All if you like. I am not a poor woman my dear, and all my young ladies have a right to the very best. I can assure you—' The prominent blue eyes narrowed slightly, becoming cold as the glass baubles round her plump neck, '—in a week, two, three perhaps, you will not recognise yourself as the young beauty I'm going to make you.'

Jaina's spirits rose, with a strange excitement quickening her heart.

'Beautiful enough to be an actress?' she demanded breathlessly.

'An actress? Is that what you want?'

Jaina nodded. At that moment it was true. If she made a name on the stage, she thought wildly, Freddie would be sure to hear of her sooner or later.

'I'm sure we shall be able to arrange it then — in time,' Madam told her. 'Providing you are a good girl and do what I say in the meantime.'

Jaina promised.

In this way she became ensconsed at Plymouth's most secretive and well-established brothel, while dreaming of a glamorous future and having her fairy tale knight Frederick de Marchmont one day as her admirer and true love.

It was a strange life.

Madam's girls, if not all beauties, were every one picturesque and exciting. At times Jaina, though awed by the luxury of her life, was slightly apprehensive. During the daytime everything in the establishment, except for her being so confined, seemed quiet and well ordered. But at nights the soft tread of furtive footsteps along the landing, accompanied frequently by the murmur of voices from adjoining bedrooms, strange little squeaks and giggles, and muted laughter, followed by the creaking, of wood and tiny groans, roused deepening suspicion in her that she could not entirely erase.

What were they doing? And why did so many gentlemen call when the inn below was locked up for the night? She knew they did. She'd peeped from the window occasionally, and seen a top-hatted figure slip from a cab that immediately drove away. Mostly the callers came on foot though, hurrying along the alley keeping close to the wall in the shadows. And soon after there was the sound of doors closing quietly, followed by footsteps tip-toeing upstairs and presently a lot of whispering.

One of the girls, Mirabelle, was nicer than all the rest, and made a point of befriending Jaina. She seemed different somehow — gentler than the other young ladies, and her soft brown eyes held a pitying look sometimes when she was talking to the younger girl.

'Don't you think you ought to let your family know where you are?' she whispered one day. 'They must be worrying.'

'Oh no.' Jaina was startled. 'They don't want me. No. I couldn't.'

'A friend then,' Mirabelle suggested. 'Surely you must have someone you're fond of? Aren't you lonely?'

An idea began to form in Jaina's head.

'Sometimes I am,' she admitted. 'And there *is* someone — but I couldn't possibly tell him. You see—'

'I think you should,' Mirabelle persisted.

'Why? And how? I promised Madam to keep everything secret.'

'It will be secret with me, Petal,' Mirabelle assured her. 'This place isn't really right for you. No—' raising a hand. 'I can't explain. There'd be great trouble — for me — if I did. And anyway, it's too late where I'm concerned. But if you write a note to your friend I'll see it's posted. Will you do that? And will you promise not to tell anyone — anyone at all of our conversation?'

In the end Jaina promised.

The following day she wrote to Frederick de Marchmont.

13

Oliver's first reaction was extreme irritation rather than worry when Jaina's disappearance was revealed. A search was quickly put into action, the police were informed, and every practical source questioned, including Mousha and her son, who firmly denied any knowledge of the girl's flight.

The following morning when there was still no news he became uneasy, venting his temper on both Sabrina and Mrs Drew.

'It seems completely irresponsible,' he insisted, 'that a household of women can be outwitted by a mere child.'

'I did point out to you that Jaina was growing up quickly,' Sabrina reminded him, trying to retain a veneer of calmness. 'I'm sorry to disagree with you, Oliver, but I'm sure it was wrong to lock her in. There's a claustrophobic streak in her — a fear of being shut up, if you like—'

'Strange you should profess such a deeply intimate knowledge of my own niece,' he said sharply, 'when you've spent such a short time in her company.'

Sabrina faced him challengingly. 'You haven't seen much of her yourself lately, have you?'

The colour in his face rose a little. 'You'd better send Mrs Drew in again,' he remarked. 'The key was put in her charge. If we can discover who was so careless with it it will help.'

Mrs Drew appeared extremely indignant at being hauled before the master a second time.

'I've told you all I know,' she answered belligerently, omitting the 'sir'. 'I handed the key to Mary when she took the tea tray up, and I saw her myself take it in and lock the door again when she came out. I was at the linen cupboard only two doors down, and when she passed I took it from her and put it on my ring.'

Her eyes glowed fiercely. 'That's all I know, and if you doubt my word, Mr Cavannagh, then all I can say is that I've no wish to stay at Carnack any more—' Her breathing had quickened. There was something about the sturdy squat figure that carried conviction.

Oliver raised his hand in negation. 'No, no. It's not a question of doubting your word — I simply wanted to make sure there wasn't any small thing — a clue, however slight, that could concern any one of the servants.'

'I know of none. I'm not God,' the woman said coldly, with a thrust forward of her chin, which was a considerable one.

'And you couldn't find the old key — the spare?'

'If I could you'd have had it. So far as I know it hasn't been used for years. Why should it? This is an ordered household, Mr Cavannagh, and I've always made it my business to see servants know their proper place, and keep things where they should be. One of the gardeners might've seen it, but I doubt it. And now, if you've finished, I'll be getting on with my duties.'

For once feeling himself at a disadvantage, Oliver was relieved to give in, and allow the woman to leave.

He went through the tedious business next of interviewing each employee personally, ending with gardeners, all to no avail.

Mary gave no hint of duplicity, and eventually Oliver had to concede temporary defeat.

To add to his chagrin, Lisette sided with Sabrina.

'Locking up any young thing is odious,' she said. 'And I never agreed with the convent in the first place. If we had been a religious breed it would have been different. But Jaina should have been allowed greater freedom of thought with more normal discipline, without all those "Hail Marys" and dreadful penances. No wonder she's run away. I should have done in her place.'

'Running away seems to be an unfortunate characteristic of our family,' Oliver observed ironically. At that point Sabrina entered the lounge. She had obviously overheard her husband's last remark. Lisette tactfully withdrew.

'Were you referring to me?' Sabrina asked. 'About running away, I mean?'

'Hardly,' Oliver said brusquely, eyeing her with a quickening of his senses and the sudden stiffening of his loins her beauty so frequently aroused in him at inopportune times. 'Try it, if you care to,' he continued, with apparent lazy indifference that was belied by the look in his eyes and slight sensuous thrust of his underlip, 'I should then take considerable pleasure in bringing you to your senses.'

Sabrina, though stirred sexually, was also annoyed and irritated by his overt manner and possessive assurance.

She desired him at times as much, perhaps more, than ever. But their marriage was not going entirely well. His assumption that he owned her, both physically and mentally, frequently put her on edge. There were even moments when she found herself unwittingly comparing her present life with how it would have been had she married Freddie. Although she had tried to ignore Oliver's spasmodic absences, sometimes for a night, occasionally a weekend, resentment and suspicion still gnawed at her. Why should there be one rule for a woman, and one for a man, she thought rebelliously? And why wouldn't Oliver make an attempt to explain her unpleasant experience in France? True, she had married him with the knowledge he'd had other women, but she'd expected this to end when she became his wife. Instead he retained his independence apart from his life with her at Carnack, giving up no fraction of social or business commitments — even expanding them, because now there was this new involvement with politics.

Her mood was dark, therefore, when three days following Jaina's disappearance, he said without any warning, 'Tomorrow I have to leave for a night or two, darling. So you'll have to deal in my absence with any events concerning Jaina. I shall be at the one address so you'll be able to contact me if anything arises—'

They were getting ready for bed at the time, and Sabrina, who was brushing her long hair before the mirror, jumped up suddenly, knocking a crystal bottle to the floor.

'What do you mean, going away again? You've only just got back. And with your own — with Jaina lost—' She stared at him angrily, the hair brush still in her hand.

He smiled nonchalantly.

'No melodrama, please love. I'm not in the mood for it.'

'And me? What about *me*? What about *my* mood for once?'

He caught her close and held her, while she struggled for a few moments against him.

'Your moods, darling, are atrocious these days,' he told her. 'And drop that hair brush before I'm tempted to use it.' Lifelessly it fell from her hand. 'Now listen, Sabrina,' he said, with his temper and blood flaming from the close contact, but with his eyes cold, 'I've had an invitation from Lord Frayle to visit him at Penlevick, and it's very important to me. Not that we're of the same ilk exactly or likely to become bosom friends. But he happens to be in need of something I can give—'

'I see,' Sabrina interrupted sharply. 'Money. And in return I suppose you take a step up the social ladder?'

'Exactly. And under the circumstances I think you can hardly blame me since I came so willingly to your rescue after your insulting behaviour to de Marchmont.'

'Freddie!' her voice rose indignantly, 'what has he got to do with it?'

'Oh, quite a lot. Society didn't exactly thank me for my part in it. In fact on several occasions I've sensed a distinct — chill in the air — whenever my wife's name was mentioned. I've put up with it, because I've had to. But here's a chance to help redeem myself, and you. Frayle is anxious to open an abandoned copper mine on his estate. It was closed years ago in the old folks' time because of sterile lodes and lack of finance to explore new levels and sink fresh shafts. The venture will take considerable capital, far beyond Frayle's pocket. That's where I come in. In return for my part in forming the new company and acquiring the larger portion of shares, I think it's highly likely our aristocratic neighbour will be induced without difficulty to support me in any bid to sit as Liberal candidate for the constituency at the next election. He tends to Liberalism himself, and has an eye not only commercially, but in the power-game, for future—'

Sabrina was aghast.

'Politics! you put politics before seeing Jaina safely home?'

'Jaina's return will not be affected in any way. But I don't want too much of a scene and fuss made of her disappearance. I've done all I can already. The authorities set up to deal with such matters already have it in hand. Do you expect me to go searching the moors for days, perhaps weeks on end, with a stick and my dog?'

His apparent coldness infuriated her.

'I don't think you've a scrap of sympathy in you,' she said. 'You've deliberately kept publicity to a minimum simply because of your own ambitions to get on — be accepted. I'm sorry,' she turned away. 'I don't understand you at all. Women, hotels, politics and lords. How far do you intend to go, Oliver?'

'To the top,' he told her abruptly. 'And nothing, not even you, my dear, is going to stop me.'

Her bitterness increased. 'You made that very clear at the beginning of our marriage. On our honeymoon in fact.' She flung the jibe at him, uncaring of any angry forthcoming response. 'When you had to leave me in that elegant hotel so you could go visiting your obliging — your — your—'

He smiled, but not pleasantly. 'Say it, Sabrina, say what you *think* — mistress isn't an ugly word.'

He waited. She didn't continue, she couldn't. Obviously he was even beyond caring how he humiliated her. So she merely remarked after a drawn-out pause, 'There's no point in arguing. It's just a waste of time.'

'Exactly.'

'All right,' she removed her flimsy wrap and went to the great bed; so elegant, so rich, so suddenly heartlessly symbolic of life's trickery. Was it for this — the power of wealth and an idle life that she'd sacrificed the affection of a 'good' man — the esteem of society, and a place in her true environment?

She felt powerless; a pawn; forgetting in her frustration, that she had, after all, used Oliver more than he had her. He'd not promised her faithfulness or to be forever at her side. It was only when her temper cooled and she allowed herself to slip between the fine sheets that a sense of proportion registered. By then Oliver was in the dressing room. When he returned he was wearing a brocaded silk garment that gave him, for a moment, an absurdly theatrical air. He could have been a figure in a French drama, or from one of Shakespeare's tragedies. Yet as always, he appeared compellingly, excitingly male. She closed her eyes, and turned her head away. When he took her in his arms he was naked. Shivering, she allowed him once more to explore her body, and push the lacy nightdress gently from thighs and breasts, and over her head.

Then his hands slipped sensuously beneath her, and she could feel herself submitting.

His lips on her cool flesh were fire; her pulses and all that was physical in her responded with an urgency that temporarily dispelled doubt.

When union was over, and they lay side by side sensuously appeased, the memory of Jaina's plight returned.

It seemed inconceivable to her that Oliver really meant to leave on a mercenary matter of business, during such distressing circumstances. Why — and fear mounted in her as she considered the possibility — the child could be still wandering the moor somewhere, completely lost. She could have fallen and hurt herself, twisted or broken an ankle. More terrible still — one of the dreaded bog-pools could have claimed her and sucked her in, or she could have fallen to her death down one of those evil abandoned mine-shafts. There was exhaustion too. Even in summer the moor was a hungry, frightening area.

Tentatively she reached out a hand and touched her husband's chest.

'Oliver—' she whispered.

He was almost asleep, but sufficiently conscious to say, 'Yes? What — is it—?' His voice was drowsy. She shook him gently.

'Jaina. What are we going to do about her?'

He opened his eyes, glanced at her for a moment, then closed them again. 'Go to sleep, Sabrina. I've work to do tomorrow.'

Work? Work? And his own niece missing? But then it was worse than that, much worse. In a flash of instinctive knowledge Sabrina accepted that what she'd guessed from almost the first days of her marriage was true.

Jaina was Oliver's own child. And Jaina, she suspected, might even have a shrewd idea herself.

'I hate you, Oliver Cavannagh,' Sabrina told herself fiercely, lying wide awake later as he slept. 'You're cruel and heartless, without a shred of sympathy in you—'

Over and over again, the assertion echoed through her mind until she was too tired to think any more.

Gradually rebellion died in her. Tomorrow might be different. In the morning they might wake refreshed and be able to find peace. Jaina was the first consideration. She must be.

When the time came, however, everything was the same. Oliver's mood remained unshaken, and shortly after breakfast he left for Lord Frayle's establishment near the coast in the vicinity of Truro.

He kissed Sabrina hastily in the hall, before hurrying from Carnack's front door, down the steps to the waiting landau. His manner was casual, practical, and from his words she had no inkling of the effort it cost him to leave her in so cavalier a fashion. However much she taunted and irritated him, she meant more to him, basically, than any other woman ever had, or could. His pride in possessing her had not flagged one iota. But she had to learn that being her husband had in no way tied him to her apron strings. Rather the reverse.

As for Jaina! Though he hadn't shown it, he was shaken. So much so that for the sake of his forthcoming sessions with Frayle he determinedly closed his mind to any eventuality that might have befallen her. He did not wish to think of her at all.

So he did not.

14

Jaina's letter to de Marchmont reached him, by a strange coincidence, on the very morning he was to set off for Plymouth. A business meeting dealing with a shipping company of which he was on the Board of Directors had been scheduled for the following day, and he had arranged to stay at his flat there for the night. This consisted of just two rooms, comfortably furnished, and a kitchen. He employed a respectable elderly woman to look after the premises during his absence, which was for the greater part of the year. She looked in twice each week, to see everything was dusted and kept clean, and always had a meal ready for him whenever he informed her of his impending arrival.

The carriage was already waiting to take him to the station when the childishly written envelope arrived. He stared at it for a moment puzzled. It was not even addressed properly, but with his family being so well known there had been, of course, no difficulty in its delivery.

He slipped it into his pocket before getting into the landau, and although curious he did not attempt to read it until he was settled into a first class carriage of the train.

Then he slit the envelope and perused its contents.

'Dear Mr de Marchmont,' it read, 'or ought I to say dear Honourable Frederick, or just Freddie?

I would like it to be Freddie, because that is how I think of you. My name is Jaina Lee. Do you remember me? I am Uncle Oliver's niece, Oliver Cavannagh's, and I met you by the pool above Castle Carnack. Uncle found us and sent me away. I was so sorry, really I was. He can be so rude sometimes.

Anyway I got into trouble later — I expect you may have heard. I was bathing in the pool and someone saw me. Then Sabrina came along and told Oliver, which I think was mean.

He locked me in my room and threatened to send me to some awful place, like a prison. So I ran away. A man with a cart took me to Bodmin, he was rough, but kind, and then I got a train to Plymouth.

Please *please* don't say anything to anyone. I expect they're worried, and I'm sorry about that, but perhaps you'll find a way to let them know I'm all right without giving an address.

If you do that — tell them where I am I mean — I know I'll die. I expect you think it awful of me to write to you. But you're the only friend I have now. Do you feel at all the same about me, Freddie? Oh, I hope so because I'm sure you must be lonely and suffer sometimes about Sabrina. Please forgive me if I'm being 'forward' — that's the word the nuns use — in writing to you. Of course they are very good and saintly, but I'm not, and that's the trouble.

What I wonder is, could you come and see me one day? This is a lovely place in a way. There are gorgeous ladies living here. It's a kind of boarding house. I have had so many pretty clothes given to me by Madam — she's the owner — and I don't have to do any work at all. That seems rather funny, doesn't it? And I'm not a prisoner. Oh no. Still, Mirabelle — she's so pretty and nice — told me I ought to let some friend or one of my family know where I am.

I really don't think I have a proper family any more. I never did have, except Uncle Oliver, and I can't trust Sabrina. You're different though. I think you care, just as I do about you, and I know I can trust you. So will you please come Freddie? I'm not quite sure about everything here. Specially why I have to keep so much secret.

    Your devoted friend
    Jaina.

P.S. No one knows my real name. They call me Petal. Petal was the name of a doll I had when I was a child, and when Madam asked me who I was I told her that. I don't know why. I think I must have been a bit frightened or something.'

Frederick sat for a moment or two staring at the pathetic note. The emotional impact of the appeal shook him. He noticed that the address at the top of the paper bore no indication of any street — just 'The Golden Rose' which was familiar to him. It was not one of his haunts, but he knew vaguely it was situated in dockland, and had an unsavoury reputation for prostitution. Nothing had been proved in law against the hostelry — perhaps because the police had never investigated; or if they had, had turned a blind eye to the shadier side of its trade. Brothels, after all, existed in every important sea-port, and could keep many off the streets who would otherwise have been troublemakers.

However, the thought of any fourteen-year-old girl — especially Jaina — being held for such filthy purposes, horrified him. She was the perfect material for white-slave trafficking — innocent yet alluring, with already a subtle unconscious quality for setting male senses alight, that would prove invaluable to any unscrupulous trader.

Through the rhythmic rattle of the train's wheels, and motion, her face constantly invaded his mind like that of some appealing elf-maiden, haunting, ethereal, yet at moments so real he found it hard to dispel the image. He attempted to read his newspaper, telling himself he must be bewitched, obsessed. At every opportunity he went along to the restaurant carriage and tried to fortify himself with refreshment.

It was simply no use.

He decided that when he'd arrived and seen Mrs Cooke, his caretaker, he'd set off and locate the inn. Jaina, or Petal — whatever she cared to call herself — was in trouble. Somehow he had to get her out of that damned place, though heaven alone knew what he'd do with her when he did.

It was late afternoon when he reached his destination, and as he'd anticipated, Mrs Cooke had a meal waiting. In spite of being tired and worried, he was hungry, and sat down to enjoy the food, quite unaware during the two hours before setting off for the 'Golden Rose' of what was happening there.

Jaina had been told, after a light supper, to take a bath, and to be careful to look beautiful and charming when Lydia had dressed her, because something very important was going to happen to her. She was going to meet a most influential gentleman — a theatrical producer who would probably allow her to appear in one of his plays if she behaved well, and with discretion.

'Act, do you mean?' Jaina had demanded with her eyes and cheeks glowing brilliantly. 'Do you mean on the stage?'

Madam smiled in her characteristically humourless fashion. 'Of course, child. Why do you think I've gone to all this trouble in keeping you here, and paying for all your new pretty clothes?'

'I didn't—'

Madam waved a hand. 'I know, I know. There's no need for explanations or gratitude, except your promise to try and please, and do as you're told — without telling any other of my young ladies, even Mirabelle.' Her expression hardened as she spoke the last name. 'Mirabelle can be thoughtless on occasion. And if she betrays the little secret between us there could be trouble.'

'Why?' Jaina demanded. 'There's nothing wrong in being an actress, is there?'

'No dear, of course not. But you are not the only beautiful girl here, and women can be very jealous. So please don't argue, just obey me and be a good girl.'

'All right.'

'Lydia will help bathe you and dress you afterwards,' Madam continued. She bent forward saying in hushed tones, 'I have a surprise for you, Petal—' She drew herself up, went to the bedroom door and motioned mysteriously to someone who must have been waiting down the landing. Almost instantly she returned, closed the door, and said to Jaina, who had moved to the window, 'Come here, dear. Look at this.'

Jaina turned and moved slowly across the soft carpet. Madam had placed a cardboard box on the bed, and was unpacking it. From between layers and layers of tissue paper she took something shimmering and voluminous, sparkling with tiny sequins — a most beautiful dress of palest pink, carrying with it a faint drift of exotic perfume. Jaina stared entranced. She had become used to pretty clothes while staying at the establishment. But this was something exquisite, far lovelier than the rest — a gown such as a princess might wear in a fairy tale — or a real queen for some important function.

Madam held it up. It was low cut on the shoulders, shimmering with diamanté and lace.

Jaina gasped.

'But is that — for me?'

'Who else, my dear? Who else could wear it but someone as young and charming and talented as you?'

After the first shock of delight, a thought struck Jaina.

'How do you know I have talent, Madam?'

Just for a second Madam was taken aback. Then she answered patronisingly, 'Tut-tut! what a childish question. You really must try and be less naive, Petal. Gentlemen don't always like it, especially the friend, the great producer you're going to meet. Besides — you told me you wanted to be an actress; that means you must believe you have some aptitude for it—' she broke off in exasperation. When Jaina made no further comment she laid the dress on the bed, went to the door and said more brusquely, 'I'm leaving you now. I have business to attend to. Get ready for your bath. Lydia will be with you in a minute.'

'Couldn't I have Mirabelle?' Jaina's small mouth had a stubborn set to it.

'No, you can't. Mirabelle's otherwise occupied, and Lydia is far more proficient in make-up.'

'Make-up? Do you mean I've got to have my face painted?'

Madam's face became suddenly disagreeable.

'What do you think? A beautiful gown like that one is only suited to a stylish young woman. It would look quite ridiculous on a pasty-faced child.' She drew a deep breath. 'You have potential, Petal, but only that. To succeed on the stage, or with men, you have to be ravishing.'

Jaina wanted to cry, 'I don't want men, I only want Freddie.' But she held her tongue, and the next moment the door had closed, taking Madam with it.

When Lydia appeared Jaina was feeling distinctly uneasy. Although ignorant herself of the seamy side of life, she wasn't stupid. One of the girls at the convent had a book that she secreted under her pillow at night which told of young women being captured and sent abroad to live in the harems and palaces of rich princes. Only snippets of the forbidden book had been revealed to Jaina, and at the time she had frequently been secretly envious — especially during dreary penances — of the 'stolen brides' — that's what her older schoolmates had called the unfortunate captives — who had ended up in such glamorous, if wicked circumstances.

Now there was no envy in her.

She wished desperately that Madam had not treated her quite so lavishly, or insisted on keeping her presence such a secret.

There was something distinctly odd about it. Still — what she'd said about acting was most probably true. No great producer would be the slightest interested in a pale-faced girl with no looks to attract his attention.

Madam had said she had potential.

What exactly did that mean?

When Jaina had slipped into the dress and saw her reflection in the mirror, she knew.

She didn't really appear pasty-faced and plain any more. Her eyes held the quality of glowing jewels in contrast to her delicate complexion, her hair fell in a dusky silky cloud about her shoulders. She lifted both arms, and let it ripple through her fingers. At that moment Lydia came in.

'Whatever are you wearing it now for?' she demanded. 'You're supposed to be in the bath, for God's sake. Take it off quick, and undress properly. We haven't much time.'

Jaina felt a quick rush of temper.

'Don't order me about like that. If you do, I won't have a bath at all, and I'll tell Madam why.'

This seemed to quieten Lydia.

'Come along now,' she urged more appeasingly, 'this is a big night for you isn't it? Most girls would give their eyes to meet Joseph King—'

'King — is that his name?'

'Of course. Didn't you know?' Lydia paused, regarding Jaina speculatively. 'No, I s'pose not. I thought Madam—'

'Madam only called him a great dramatic producer,' Jaina said innocently. 'If he likes me he's going to put me in one of his plays — as an actress, I mean.'

Lydia laughed shortly, although the laugh sounded, derisive, more of a cough. 'Oh, he'll like you all right.'

'What do you mean? How do you know?'

'Use your loaf.' The remark held contempt. 'Surely you're not that innocent.' Realising she might have revealed too much of the true situation, Lydia continued quickly after a brief pause, 'What I meant was, Petal, is that if you make the most of yourself, and we're going to do that, aren't we? — you'll be the perfect type for getting a start on the stage, just what Mr King wants.'

'I see.'

Jaina was partly satisfied, but not entirely.

However after undressing, when she'd been bathed in perfumed water, with sweet smelling soaps, dried and powdered all over her delicately slim body, excitement filled her, and she temporarily forgot all niggling fears.

It was only when Lydia slipped the pink dress over her shoulders and said, 'You'd better put your wrap on while I do your hair,' that Jaina experienced real shock.

'But you can see everything,' she exclaimed, with another quick glance at her reflection, 'I haven't got my bodice on, or anything. Look!'

Lydia looked.

The gently rounded breasts and pink nipples were subtly and enticingly visible through the sheer, flimsy material. From the trim slender waist, the youthfully swelling thighs and stomach were sensually enhanced beneath the transparency of diaphanous chiffon. There was an enchanting quality about her — the allure of some seductive nymph about to entrap a lover.

Jaina simply stared.

Then she heard Lydia say, 'Well?'

'But I can't meet anyone like that,' Jaina protested at last, 'it would be better to have nothing on at all. What would Madam say? And Mr King? No. You don't mean it, do you?'

Lydia sighed. Her manner once more became irritable. 'Of course I mean it. Don't be ridiculous. You're not living with nuns here, you know. Joseph King will wish to see you from every angle. It's like an artist painting a model. Models don't wear clothes — except of course something like you have on now. Oh Petal, for pity's sake stop arguing. Just sit on the stool and let me get on with your coiffure.'

Automatically, in a kind of daze, the girl agreed, and after her hair had been swept off her face to an elegant bunch of curls on top, Lydia, not allowing her to see herself, turned the stool round, placed a white star-shaped flower here and there in the lustrous mass and commenced on the make-up process. Dusky rouge, pink lip-salve, a faint pencilling of brows, and kohl for the eyes, were supplemented by a dusting of fine powder on the high cheek-bones.

When she once more saw herself, Jaina was so astonished a fit of trembling seized her. It couldn't be she — it simply couldn't — not that elegant grown-up sophisticated looking beauty who could have been a young queen if she was only wearing underclothes. The silence seemed interminable as the moments ticked away; then Lydia said, 'What do you think of yourself now?'

'I — I—' Jaina struggled to find the right words, but only remarked lamely, 'wouldn't it be better if I wore a chemise — or knickers? Those lacy ones?'

Lydia laughed.

'You little goose. Knickers! That would be unheard of — in Mr King's circle of society. Now we'll just tidy up the bedroom, and then Madam will come in to inspect things.'

Five minutes later Madam appeared very gratified indeed.

'Perfect,' she said. 'And don't be nervous, Petal. A very important and new phase of your life is about to begin. I'm sure Mr King will be more than pleased. You'll make a great conquest.'

Those words proved to be prophetic, although not quite in the way Jaina had hoped and anticipated.

From the moment he was presented to her by Madam, in the bedroom, she did not like or entirely trust him. He was a large man of middle-age, impeccably dressed, with a rose in the lapel of his smartly-cut tailed coat. Most women of that period would have thought him good looking. When Madam took his top hat and silver-headed cane from him at the door before leaving them together, Jaina noticed that his hair was curling and of a rich chestnut shade. His complexion was fresh — inclined to be florid — his features boldly carved, though the nose was rather large. The lips, beneath the twirled moustache, were smilingly sensual. The eyes — Jaina tried not to look directly into them, they held such obvious desire; shrewd quickly moving eyes that seemed to bear down upon her, assessing every line and detail of her youthful figure through the revealing gauzy garment.

She had an instinctive wish to cover herself, and backed away from him, with one hand across her breasts.

He offered his hand. There was the flash of a bland smile when he said.

'My dear Petal, don't be afraid — sit down please, so we can talk. I'm not here to eat you.'

But that was just what he looked like, she thought, with a jerking of her pulse. He reminded her of the Big Bad Wolf in Red Riding Hood which had so frightened her when she was small.

Still — she wasn't a child, neither was he a wolf. He was there to discuss allowing her to appear on the stage in one of his plays; Madam had promised her, and it was the one — the only thing she wanted just then — except of course to have Freddie beside her — to escape Uncle Oliver's threat of 'prison' or a spanking, and to prove she was already a young woman with an identity of her own.

So she let the powerful Mr Joseph King touch her hand for a moment, holding her breath until he let it go.

'There!' he said with a sigh of relief that made his large stomach appear suddenly larger under the white waistcoat. 'Now we must have a little refreshment while we talk.' He seated himself on a chair. She did the same. But after a moment he got up, went to the chest where Madam had left wine with two glasses, uncorked the bottle, and after filling both, handed one to Jaina.

She took it, guessing it was champagne; there was such a plop as the fizzy stuff bubbled up. She'd had some before at Lisette's last birthday party; but this time the taste of it seemed headier somehow, and more potent.

Joseph King watched her, lifting his hand first to 'celebrate' — though she didn't know what. Then, before she'd finished her own, he filled it again.

'Well now,' he said, in throaty tones, rather like a great cat purring. 'Madam, my good friend, tells me you have aspirations for acting. Have you had any experience?'

'Not really.' Jaina swallowed nervously. 'Except — I was the Madonna once in a Nativity play. Then, at a party at Carnack I had to be a boy. It was a sort of pantomime you see.'

'Carnack?' Mr King looked startled for a moment, 'I've heard of the place—' He didn't look pleased. 'Is that where you come from?'

'Oh no,' Jaina lied. 'No, no. I was staying with my aunt at Merlyn's Gate you see – that's a village near, and she knew the — the maid there. They wanted someone at the Castle for the part, and she got it for me. But I haven't been for ages. She's dead now, my aunt I mean—'

She broke off, shamed that she could have thought up an explanation so glibly. The nuns would have thought her very wicked, and they would have been right. But defiance and the necessity gave her sufficient courage to continue lying, and when her supposed sponsor asked abruptly, 'Have you no friends or relatives, Petal?' she shook her head, stating with surprisingly nonchalant bravado, 'I'm a bastard, I think. Someone told me at the mission who didn't like me. She was older than me with yellow hair, and very proud because she was English. But that was a long time ago.'

'I see. Well—' the bland smile returned again to the thick lips. 'You're no worse for that. And you certainly have — potential.' He got to his feet, and laid a stout hand upon her shoulder. She tried not to wince. 'I think you will make a quite charming actress — after tuition,' he continued with a thickening in his voice. Then with a sudden note of command, 'Get up Petal, let me see you properly.'

Trembling, but trying to disguise it, she got to her feet. He observed, hungrily, the youthful luscious lines of pale flesh, thighs and breasts shimmering seductively beneath the flimsy material. Desire mounted in him. He touched her waist. 'Turn round, Petal.'

She stared at him.

'Why?'

'Because I say so. Because from now on, my dear, we're going to see a great deal of each other, are we not? And I wish to know every inch of you—' Large fingers stroked her skin suggestively.

The warmth of him, the pressure of his hot palms caressing her back and buttocks, revolted her. She tried to escape; but against him her strength was puny. With his hot mouth fleshy and firm against her mouth, then travelling downwards to her most secret private places, he carried her to the bed and flung her on it. She started to scream. A palm silenced her. She turned her head helplessly, trying not to see him unbuttoning himself, or the hard projecting part of his body that so filled her with terror.

As he mounted her, her arms flailed for a moment. Then she felt a jab, a terrible searing pain that despite her struggles, persisted, until at last there was a moan followed by a loathsome grunt of satisfaction.

He rolled away from her, leaving her to cry soundlessly into the pillows. She felt drained and spent; torn apart, and ready for death. Something in her that she knew should have remained intact and precious until given willingly, in love, had gone for ever, spoiled and degraded.

At last the session of fitful crying ceased. When she opened her eyes and looked up, he was staring down at her with a kind of contempt on his large face. She wondered however she could have thought him in the least handsome. He was a big bully, no more. Horrible.

'You weren't worth it,' he said, sneeringly, straightening his tie automatically, below the heavy chin. 'I could have found better value for my money from any street-woman. As for acting — you haven't the looks or talent. If you'd had a shred of either you'd certainly have put on a better show just now. Pretence, my dear, is the first essential of any successful whore.'

She sat up. 'I'm not a whore — I'm not, I'm not—' her voice was choked and thick with tears again.

He shrugged, laughed, and went to the door, saying, 'Well then, you should be grateful for your first lesson.'

Madam must have heard something of what was going on. She entered before he went out, almost bumping into him.

'What's the matter, Mr King?' she asked, casting a brief condemnatory look towards the bed. 'Didn't the young lady please you?'

'Rather to the contrary, I'm afraid,' King answered coldly. 'In future, Madam, I'd be obliged if you'd show more discretion in your introductions, otherwise I shall have to take my patronage elsewhere.'

Madam's face flushed a dark ugly crimson. She held the door open and followed him out. Jaina, still terrified and shocked from pain, heard their footsteps gradually fade along the landing. For a minute or two she lay rigidly clutching the bedclothes to her chin. Then she made her way to the basin on the washstand, and vomited violently.

She was shivering when Madam returned.

'A fine thing you've done,' the woman said, 'after all my kindness, and Mr King one of my richest clients.' She pushed her large face close to Jaina's and glared. 'Now what do you think I'm going to do with you?'

Jaina didn't reply. After a moment the hard voice continued, 'Get that thing off immediately, and cover yourself. It was expensive let me tell you, a complete waste. It will have to go into the bin now.'

Automatically Jaina pulled off the flimsy ripped garment, noting, with horror, that there were spots of blood on it.

Madam grabbed it, rolled it up, and marched out with it under her arm. The door banged. There was a sharp sound of the key turning, and Jaina realised that she was once again a prisoner. She was shaking when she managed to fling a wrap round her shoulders and go to the window. The street below was by then very dark with only small dots of light sprinkling the night sky and cobbled alley.

No tree climbed against the wall; there was no possible way of escape, unless she jumped and probably killed herself. And what good would that do, when it would mean she'd never see Freddie again.

Freddie.

Thinking of him brought on a return of the sickness. He'd never want to be her friend again, not after what had happened; and she wanted and needed him so.

Still in a kind of nightmare she went back to bed and flung herself upon it.

How long she lay there she never knew. The shivering, accompanied by sudden bouts of weakness persisted, taking her at last into numb semi-consciousness.

She was disturbed to quick alertness by raised voices and a scuffling on the landing. Above the rest, Madam's shrill tones echoed intermittently in protestation. A man shouted, a girl screamed.

Then Jaina's bedroom door flew open.

At first she couldn't believe what she saw.

Freddie, looking dishevelled, his tie loose and straggling over his high white collar, hatless, and with his usually benign and handsome countenance doggedly set into fierce determination, just stood there shaking his shoulder free of an immensely strong and bucolic-looking man's grip. Madam waited a little behind him, but clearly visible in the yellow stream of lamplight. Her face resembled a cold dead mask, with only her hard blue eyes darting sparks of angry life. From the shadows at the far end of the landing a door opened. Two heads, a man's and a woman's appeared for a moment, then disappeared discreetly. There was the muffled whisper of 'police', followed by Madam saying in urgent low tones, 'Leave him alone, Caleb. I can deal with this.' The rough looking man who could have been an ex-boxer, but was obviously now Madam's bodyguard, retreated a few steps to watch, as Freddie pushed into the bedroom.

Madam followed.

'Get her out of here then,' she said, 'and be sharp about it. This is a decent place, properly run. There's been no trouble here — ever — until that — that wanton run-away wheedled herself in. She had me fooled, as fooled as you are now—'

Freddie turned, giving her a long cold stare.

What she saw on his face momentarily quelled her outburst of vituperation.

'She's a child,' he said. 'A schoolgirl. You could be jailed for abduction and soliciting—'

Madam's large mouth curled sneeringly. 'What proof have you? See the boot's not on the other foot — for your sake, mister, sir, or whatever you are. Breaking into others' premises — that's an offence isn't it?'

She broke off, breathing heavily. Her protector stepped into the doorway with his fist raised.

She waved him back.

'It's all right, Caleb. I told you. I can manage—'

Jaina meanwhile was hurriedly pulling on a pair of slippers at random. Freddie turned.

'Where are your clothes, Jaina?'

'Jaina!' Madam echoed. 'So that's her name. She was Petal when she came here begging for shelter. Does that tell you anything?'

'Her clothes, I said,' Freddie repeated, still with the controlled deadly determination.

Madam shrugged. 'She hasn't any. Rags they were. Nothing but tattered old-fashioned things worse than any tinker woman's—' An uncontrollable burst of anger sent her reeling towards the frightened girl with her hand raised. 'Slut, vagabond—'

Instantly Freddie had both hands on the plump shoulders, and with all his force pushed her into the corridor. Caleb came forward and lunged a fist at de Marchmont's cheek catching him with a heavy blow. Freddie staggered, then managed to slam the door in both their faces. He took off his light overcoat, threw it round the girl's shivering form and lifted her into his arms. She was crying again by then, moaning fitfully with the pain of a young animal wounded beyond healing.

'Hush,' he said, 'it's all right. We'll soon be out of this. Please darling, please, don't you believe me? You must trust me, Jaina, it's all right, all right—'

Her hands reached to his shoulders and clutched them frenziedly. 'Oh Freddie — Freddie — I thought I'd die. That man who came. He — he—'

'What man? Caleb? That brute?—'

'No, no. It was a rich man—' Between her sobs small gasps of explanation emerged, incoherently, but sufficiently revealing to tell him what he so dreaded to hear.

He quietened her briefly, and only seconds later was plunging with her still in his arms down the landing and thickly carpeted stairs.

Jaina, though only half aware of what was happening, saw through the blur of tears Madam's threatening outraged stare as they passed out into the street.

It was very dark. The summer night sky had clouded, and no stars or moon shone. When they'd crossed to the other side of the street, Freddie waited under the swaying light of a street lamp, peering first one way then another. A cab passed. He hailed it, but it didn't stop. Opposite, the lights of the Golden Rose had disappeared one by one from the windows, like candles snuffed out. A sailor and his girl, arms linked, and drunk, nudged them as they passed. Freddie's arms tightened round Jaina's slim form. Abruptly he started hurrying, half running, towards a main street. When he reached a corner it seemed they were confronting another world. A normal comparatively busy district of passing cabs and pedestrians, of cafés and night bars; and beyond the darker silhouettes of buildings, the distant glimmer of ships' lanterns pin-pointing the activity of Dock-land at night. Voices were raised intermittently — laughter, a man's shout, followed by brief silences except for the echo of horses' hooves. Small groups of seamen with bundles over their shoulders jostled towards lodgings or in search of feminine company.

Freddie managed to stop a cab driven by a seedy-looking

elderly man who paused suspiciously for a moment before agreeing to accept such an ill-matched-looking couple; but when he heard the address — that of a 'toff', obviously, he agreed, and after half-payment in advance started off again, leaving Freddie trying to comfort Jaina in the back seat.

He said little, just held her hand, as she rested against his other arm with her head drooping on his shoulder. She tried to speak, but the words no longer formed properly on her lips. She felt tired — so completely exhausted that nothing properly registered but pain and a shuddering sense of revulsion.

When they reached the flat and Freddie had paid the man, giving an extra bonus for obliging, he carried her up the steps to the door, unlocked it, turning the key again as soon as they were in the hall. Then he deposited her on a couch in the sitting room, poked the fire that had been well stoked up by his caretaker before leaving, and fetched her a small glass of brandy from the cabinet. He put it to her lips, and as she drank it once more placed a hand over one of her small ones. It felt very cold.

'Poor Jaina,' he said, when the shuddering had ceased. 'I could kill that brute — the whole lot of them—'

She opened her eyes, staring at him for some moments without saying anything at all, simply trying to believe it was true — she was safe, and Freddie was there. Frederick de Marchmont, wonderful Freddie who had come to rescue her from that awful place. Then, slowly, she forced a smile.

'What's going to happen now?' she asked.

'When you're warm and have had food — I suggest bread-and-milk or something, isn't that supposed to be good for sickness?'

'I'm not sick, Freddie,' she told him, 'I'm only — only—'

'I know. Don't think of it. Still,' — he forced optimism into his voice, 'I'm sure bread and milk's the answer. There's enough milk in the kitchen. Then you'll go to bed — I shall camp down here, and in the morning we'll decide what to do. You'll have to have clothes—' Still trying to concentrate on the lighter side of events, he resumed after a brief pause, 'I think Helen's would rather swamp you — she's decidedly of the large, sporty type—'

'Helen?'

'My sister. She puts up here for a night or two when it suits her and never fails to leave something behind. There's a cape and a dress, I know, and something quite unmentionable—' he grinned. 'I've often cursed her for her carelessness, but maybe it's going to pay off for once.'

Jaina nodded but didn't speak, and presently, when a little of the shock had receded, Freddie insisted on carrying her into the bedroom, which was at the back.

It was small, ordinary, and conventionally equipped with the minimum of furniture. A typically male interior possessing no pretension to beauty or luxury. But it was spotlessly clean, and the bed was comfortable.

With a sigh Jaina relaxed between the clean sheets, and for a minute or two was satisfied to stay there with her eyes closed, knowing that Freddie was nearby.

He was about to tip-toe out, thinking she was asleep. She instantly roused, opened her eyes and said, 'Where are you going?'

'To get your milk,' he told her.

'Not out?'

'Not yet. Later perhaps, just for a few minutes, to—'

'No.' Terror sharpened her voice. 'You mustn't. Promise me. Don't leave me, Freddie, not even for a second—'

'But you'll be quite safe. I—'

'You mustn't, you mustn't. Don't leave me—' Tears sprang to her eyes. 'You can't, I couldn't bear it. Oh Freddie, I'm sorry. But I'm frightened. Please – please don't leave me.' In the end, distressed, yet deeply touched by her need of him, he agreed to stay. He'd meant to report the incident immediately to the police, but after all, he thought, in self-justification – possibly it was wiser to think things over for a bit.

All that night, when she'd drifted into fitful sleep following liberally sweetened bread-and-milk, he sat on a chair near her bed, dozing off occasionally, yet always alert to her slightest request or any sign of distress. For half an hour at a time, her small hand lay in his, while compassion flooded him, a desire at all costs somehow to protect this fragile, infinitely lovely young creature from further abuse. For the whole of that long period he found it hard to review things objectively. During bouts of wakefulness he realised he should have insisted on reporting the assault first to the proper authorities – the police, her family, and that a doctor should have been called. But except for her impassioned hysterical appeal to him, she seemed to be recovering remarkably well. The shock to her of an immediate medical examination might prove too much for her and do irretrievable damage.

Above all things, he wished peace for her — to restore her faith in someone — a friend who would give understanding, and help in obliterating the horror she'd endured. He was aware in a dim way of his own folly — that he was behaving irrationally. But hang the conventions. Whatever anyone might think if the news leaked out — as was bound to happen later — she was only a schoolgirl. In the morning he'd do what was right and proper. Tonight she was a child in his care.

A child.

But was she?

Looking at her from time to time when she was sleeping, a lump churned in his throat. In spite of her pallor she was so lovely, so infinitely desirable — even following her dreadful experience. He had never before remotely thought of himself as being a romantic. His love for Sabrina — or what he had accepted as love — had been of the normal earthy kind. Her rejection of him at the marriage ceremony had hurt and humiliated him. Apart from the loss of a lovely wife-to-be, he had been made to appear a 'bit of an ass' in the eyes of his friends and current society. The wounds for a time had cut deep. But this — this extraordinary longing and devotion for Jaina was something quite different — tender and overwhelming. Child she might be, but woman also.

During those hours of revelation he had to accept depths within himself that he knew now could never be entirely dispelled. He loved her; incredible as it seemed, he was prepared to dedicate his life to her welfare, sacrificing the dictates of his family, social status — even his considerable sexual needs — which were those of any healthy young man, until she was old enough, and willing — please God — to reciprocate.

And he would not betray her.

Unless her heart strayed elsewhere during the next few years, two at least, he would be faithful. There were practical things — things demanding his energy in the meantime — shipping concerns, involvement with management of the estate — riding, shooting, the Hunt — although he had a shrewd idea that Jaina would disapprove of the latter, and if things went according to plan would eventually get him to abandon it.

Curiously he wasn't perturbed by the thought. Her sensitivity, subtle awareness and sympathy to nature and wild things which he'd sensed on their first meeting — had opened doors in his mind and imagination that he hadn't previously known existed. A man besotted, he told himself whimsically, during the hours of early morning, that's what he was. Besotted by trust, and above all by her innocence which remained intact, he was sure — despite the ravages of brutal rape which could so easily have destroyed her.

She woke about nine. For a few moments her expression changed suddenly from peace to terror. Then, when she recognised Freddie standing by the bed with a breakfast tray already prepared, she gave a sigh of relief. She smoothed her hair from her forehead, and sat up, while a tentative smile curved her lips. Her eyes widened. They were shining and brilliant with gratitude — and something else; something that quickened his tired senses, but which he resolutely controlled.

'So here we are,' he said over-brightly. 'A tray prepared for you, Mademoiselle, and all by mine own hands.' He gave a mock bow that made her giggle. 'Not up to hotel standards, I'm afraid. Just an egg, marmalade, and toast that luckily has escaped being a burnt offering.' He put the tray before her, then asked more seriously after a brief pause, 'How do you feel? You look better now.'

She reached for his hand. His palm enclosed her slim fingers comfortingly for a second. 'Oh I am,' she told him. 'Now you're here. I—' a shadow crossed her face. 'Last night, I—'

'Forget it,' he interrupted. 'It's over. Done with. Nothing will ever happen to you like that again, darling, I swear it—'

'Darling? Did you say darling?' Her voice had become hushed, incredulous. 'Do you really—?'

He shook his head and took two steps away, towards the door. 'I shouldn't have said it. It slipped out.'

'But you should — you *should*—'

'No, Jaina. Not yet.'

'What do you mean not yet? Tell me, Freddie.'

'No.' The denial was firm.

She looked towards her plate. 'All right. But all the same—' the smile was on her lips when she looked up again '—you meant it. If it slipped out it was real, wasn't it?'

'Jaina, eat your breakfast, and while you're doing it I must nip out—'

There was the rattle of a spoon as she dropped it in her saucer.

'What do you mean out? No — you mustn't, I can't be alone—'

'It will only be a few minutes,' he told her, 'I have to report what happened, you realise that, don't you? You were hurt — and so was I,' he rubbed his cheek ruefully, trying to make light of things.

'But if you say anything they'll know — *everyone*,' Jaina protested.

He returned and seated himself on the side of the bed again.

'I'm afraid a few people will have to,' he said. 'The police, and your family — Uncle Oliver — I'll have to wire Castle Carnack—'

'No, no no. I couldn't bear it. What good would it do?'

He took her hand and stared at it — the small pink nails, delicately boned fingers and satin smooth skin.

'It won't be easy for you at first, Jaina,' he said quietly, 'or for me. But when I've explained I think you'll find your uncle and Sabrina warm and understanding to you. And the police will be on your side—'

'I don't believe it. No one understands, ever. Except you.'

He withdrew his hand, got up again, and said seriously, managing not to look at her, 'Jaina, you're only fourteen. Whatever you feel now, or I, we must be sensible and not take advantage of — of circumstance. Until you're older you must try and behave as Oliver expects you to. I must admit he's not my type, but you're in his charge, legally as well as by blood—'

'What do you mean?'

'He's your guardian. He may not be ideal, but I do happen to know that he's done everything possible to find you. I expect he's even sorry for any trouble there was between you—'

'You're talking to me like a child now,' she said dully. 'Uncle Oliver's never really sorry for anyone except for himself when he doesn't get his own way.'

Inwardly Freddie agreed, but he did his best not to show it.

He had to do the right thing, dammit; whatever his personal feelings were.

He'd no illusions about Cavannagh. He was a hard nut all right, a climber, and a bit of a rascal if all he'd heard about him was true. But he had to be put in the picture, and as quickly as possible. There was no possible way of secreting Jaina in some ivory tower where he couldn't locate her. She was under-age and had been kidnapped by evil means for that shady whorehouse — or worse. Rape had occurred. Justice had to be done, and Cavannagh was the one in authority. The trouble was that he, Frederick de Marchmont, would have to testify in court, drag this young beloved creature through the mud. There would be endless strain for her, and gossip. The thought of it tortured him. Inevitably it would be a dragged-out affair that would have to be proved before the full truth was established; and this might be difficult. There would only be his word, Jaina's, and medical evidence. Here again the evidence in question would not alone suffice.

The Golden Rose was merely one of several brothels in the district. Pinning down such a serious charge on villains of Madam's cunning calibre would be more than tricky — especially when the Law so far had been content to turn a blind eye to unsavoury rumours and speculation.

He was recalled from such distressing conjectures by hearing Jaina saying, 'It's true what I've said. You believe me, don't you, Freddie?'

'I don't know your uncle very well, Jaina,' he said, 'in fact hardly at all. But he's looked after you all these years. And darling — we have to be fair to him, you and I, he must be told.'

The 'you and I' comforted her a little.

'I suppose so,' she agreed grudgingly. 'But not yet—'

'Of course not,' he said, with false confidence. 'The first thing is for you to eat.'

'Are you going to have breakfast with me?'

'If you like,' he answered, smiling, 'although it will be a second one. I've already had something.'

He made a pretence of enjoying a few more pieces of toast while perched at the foot of the bed. Then he got up suddenly, lifted a forefinger in mock-fatherly fashion and said, 'I'll be back in ten minutes. I shall lock the door behind me, so you'll be quite safe. Be a good girl now—'

She lifted her face, 'Please kiss me, Freddie.'

He paused, staring at her with bewildered emotions of apprehension and longing throwing him momentarily off balance. He bent his head, felt her hands reach his shoulders, and the touch of her soft sweet lips under his. The pressure of his mouth deepened. Child, was she? Or woman? This tantalising exquisite creature so completely at his mercy? With an effort he pulled himself under control. The impulses stirring him during that brief interlude couldn't be justified — not by any man with a shred of decency left. He wasn't that kind of cad, dammit. So he jerked himself away, patted her cheek, saying in tones that shook slightly, 'Just look what you've done, young lady — plastered my face with marmalade.' He went to the mirror, drew a finger across his underlip, tightened his tie, and resolutely strode to the door. Before leaving he said, 'When I get back we can have a rummage through the wardrobe and see if anything of Helen's is any earthly good.'

After he'd gone Jaina pushed the tray away, jumped out of bed and went to the window. The early sun had dimmed behind cloud, and the vista was a dull one of grey rooftops, houses and small gardens. A quiet area, empty just then of traffic. Now Freddie had gone, fear once more began to engulf her. She'd heard him lock the front door when he left. So she was a prisoner again until he returned, and when he did he'd have wired Carnack, and worst of all perhaps, have told the police.

She couldn't face that; she just couldn't. When it was known where she was Uncle Oliver would come storming to collect her, she'd be punished and the police would blame her for running away in the first place. They'd somehow prevent Freddie coming near her. She might never see him again.

The realisation of that was the most terrible thought of all to bear.

She ran through to the kitchen. There was no door leading outside, but a window was open a fraction. That decided her. On quick light feet she returned to the bedroom, and pulled open the heavy mahogany wardrobe. The clothes there, as Freddie had implied, were dull and far too large for her, but included the dark cape that would cover any too obvious discrepancies.

She flung on what she needed, including a pair of oversized

boots, then rushed back to the window. Pushing with all her strength she managed to force it higher. Then, after making sure no one was about the quiet street, she crawled through, landed on the pavement without mishap, and with head bent forward under the dark hood of the cape, started walking towards a main thoroughfare, guided by the sound of traffic from the distance.

It was quite by chance that she haphazardly bumped into someone in a crowd, and nearly fell from the impact. When she looked up, startled, she saw to her astonishment, Mirabelle staring down at her. Mirabelle — the one person at the Golden Rose she had been able to trust.

The meeting was not only opportune, but one destined to have a significant bearing on Jaina's future. After a brief cup of coffee in a seedy-looking café, Mirabelle supplied sufficient money, in cash, to cover a train journey to London, also the address of a contact in the city when she got there.

'Mike Lawson,' she said. 'He's a good friend of mine, and won't take advantage of you. He's the sort you need — runs a kind of theatre, not high class of course, but when you mention me he'll see you get going—'

'Do you mean—?'

'A part, darling, show-business. You've got the looks, everything, youth too. And don't make the mistake I did of believing in any good looking man who sets your heart fluttering and promises the earth. You've had one rotten deal already, but you'll recover, so long as you keep yourself to yourself. Men — they're swine mostly. Just remember that. And now, bye-bye, love — I must be off.'

So it was, with money in her pocket, and an address for the other end of her journey, that Jaina set off for her new life.

When de Marchmont returned to find Jaina gone, he was distracted. No clue left, except the open window, no note, no word for him — nothing but an overturned glass on the bed-side table and the wardrobe door yawning, empty. The long nightshirt he'd lent her lay on the floor, with the slippers she'd worn, and a few pins and odds-and-ends.

Shock and desolation encompassed him for only a few minutes. He pulled himself together decisively, and hatless, went out again to a nearby post office. From there he sent a brief telegram to Cavannagh, saying, 'Have news of Jaina. Important you come here immediately.' He gave the address of his rooms, and signed it 'F. de Marchmont.' Then he hurried to a corner of the road and took a bend which he knew led to an area police station. He didn't notice a large male figure standing in a doorway — was quite unaware that for the whole of the night his rooms had been watched, and that he had been cunningly followed when he left them that morning. How he'd been located he'd never know. Dock-land had its own freemasonry which was quick to spread news when the necessity arose. The Golden Rose was certainly not prepared for unwelcome police investigation, or for a man of de Marchmont's status to be called as witness in court.

So the blow, when it came, was quick, well-aimed, and sufficient to knock Freddie out. He fell, cutting his head on the pavement, and by the time an unsuspecting pedestrian rounded the turn, there was no sign of the unknown attacker — only the recumbent figure liberally smelling of rum from a broken bottle lying in the gutter.

The Law, when called, found a card in his pocket bearing the Bristol address and the key. He was taken there, and carried to the bedroom, where after a brief examination, he was left to recover.

Obviously there was nothing seriously wrong with the 'gent' — merely suffering from bruises following too lively a night on the tiles. The constables were grinning when they left. Freddie had recovered by then and was trying to explain. But his words were garbled, quite natural, they assumed, after the drink he'd taken; the cut was superficial and headquarters would certainly not wish to make a case out of a mere gentlemanly celebration. So Freddie's mishap was conveniently overlooked, and when he finally came to himself and events fully registered, he realised the futility of making any attempt to justify his plight.

He had a thorough wash, made himself a pot of strong tea, took a draught to soothe his aching head, and after realising he was in no state to attend the planned business meeting, decided to stay put until he heard something from Carnack. Obviously Cavannagh would not receive the wire for some hours. During that time Jaina might return. He hoped to God she would.

The mere memory of her was torment. Why the devil couldn't she have trusted and waited for him? He flung himself on to the bed, but couldn't rest.

He got up again, and a sudden revival of pain from the cut jaw sent him reeling back. He sat there for a time with his head in his hands then got up to take a good look at himself through the mirror.

There was no blood there any more, but on one side of his face was a lump the size of an egg.

What a sight!

Cursing himself for not having been more wary and suspecting someone might have been on his trail, he wandered backwards and forwards through the small interior, peering at intervals through the kitchen window, up and down the road. It was still comparatively deserted, and there was no sign at all of Jaina.

The clouded summer day gradually passed.

As twilight brought a sullen pall of summer mist to the grey streets, there was a knocking at the door. Freddie, with a lurch of his heart rushed to open it, and had a shock.

No Jaina stood outside, or even Oliver.

There, pale-faced and anxious-looking under the blurred light of the hall lamp, was Sabrina.

She stood a moment, just staring, then passed by him into the hall.

'I came as soon as I could,' she said. 'Oh Freddie, what's happened?'

He ushered her into the sitting room.

'Where's Oliver?' he asked, before attempting to explain.

'Oliver, as usual, is away,' she said bitterly. 'A habit of his nowadays.'

'You'd better sit down,' he said mechanically. 'A drink?'

'Thanks.'

He poured her a sherry, then grudgingly, and still not entirely coherently, did his best to put her in the picture.

15

Oliver faced Lisette accusingly. She had been in bed for three hours. It had turned twelve o'clock, and Oliver had returned unexpectedly at this 'ridiculously late hour' — her own words — expecting to find the household peaceful, with Sabrina dutifully waiting for him when he arrived upstairs ready for the connubial welcome.

'You should have let us know,' Lisette complained fretfully, putting a hand to her head. 'If you had, your wife would no doubt have stayed until you arrived. But when that telegram came she insisted on leaving immediately. I did suggest postponing things a little. But you know, Sabrina, or should by now—'

Oliver waved the official slip of paper at her angrily.

'It wasn't even addressed to her, was it?' he said in cold condemning tones. 'Why did you allow her to open it when you knew very well it was for me?'

'Oliver!' his mother's voice sharpened. 'I will not be disturbed by you in this distressing manner. Remember my heart!' She lay back, fanning her face with one white hand. 'I couldn't have prevented her. She guessed — she knew it concerned Jaina—'

'Did she? I wonder.' Cavannagh's tones were grim. 'How do you know that? How do I? Was it planned?'

'Oh, don't be ridiculous.'

'She was going to marry this "most honourable" swain of hers, wasn't she? Don't you think it just a little odd that at the first opportunity, in my absence, she dashes off at the crook of his finger for a jaunt to meet her ex-lover in Plymouth?'

Lisette's startled gaze turned to wonder.

'You're jealous,' she commented. '*You*.' Her tiredness appeared to vanish like magic. She began to laugh softly. 'Oh, Oliver! I'd never have expected it.'

He turned on his heel abruptly.

'I'm just damned annoyed. And when I bring her back I'll see she learns to behave in future. No woman makes a cuckold of me — certainly not Sabrina.'

Lisette became serious again. 'Cuckold! Really, Oliver, you're being very stupid, and if I were you—'

'You're not me. And it's a bit late to start giving me motherly advice. So shut up! I'm sorry, hold your tongue for God's sake, before I properly lose my temper.'

'You've lost it already, Oliver. And I find it extremely — exhausting. Please go now. Do whatever you like. But don't entirely forget Jaina. She should be your first consideration.'

Without another word he left her, slamming the door smartly behind him. He returned five minutes later to say he was off again, driving himself to the nearest station where he hoped he'd find some night train for Plymouth. By then he was looking smart, composed, but extremely determined, with a certain fierce gleam in his eyes that made Lisette sorry for Sabrina should he find her at Freddie's flat.

The journey, for Cavannagh, was prolonged and irritating. The train service was bad, with various stops en route, and no restaurant car or any opportunity for refreshment.

By the time he reached Plymouth, it was almost four in the morning, not yet dawn, but with a fading washed-out moon receding behind a belt of mist.

He took a cab from the station, reflecting moodily on the waywardness of women, his ill-temper increased by his own frustration and thwarted ego.

The monotonous jolting along badly-lit streets seemed to take an unnecessary time. When at last the cab drew up outside de Marchmont's rooms he was already prepared for a scene.

He paid the cabby, dismounted, and as the vehicle jerked off again with the echo of horses' hooves and carriage wheels grating, he stood for a few seconds staring up at the building. A light glowed behind the blind of a downstairs room. As he watched he saw the blurred shapes of two figures silhouetted from inside. His muscles tensed. There was no mistaking the delicate lines of profile, high piled hair, or subtle curves of breasts to waist. He recognised that handsome devil of a man too, blast them both. For quite a minute he remained on the pavement, as though petrified, watching a feminine arm and hand reach up to the male face and linger there, with a gentle stroking motion. The blood churned through his veins. An ugly sense of betrayal intensified in him. So she'd been there all night!

My God, Madam, he thought, you'll suffer for this.

He jerked himself to life suddenly, and ran up the few steps to the front door. He pulled the bell, feeling a savage satisfaction in its noisy, insistent clanging.

The two shadows receded from the window. Seconds later the door opened, revealing Frederick de Marchmont fully clad in a lounge jacket and drain-pipe trousers, but showing unmistakable signs of strain and exhaustion in his expression and posture.

'Thank heaven you've come,' he said.

Oliver, wishing to strike him, but refraining, said coldly, 'Where's Sabrina?'

'Sabrina! Oh, she's here. She—'

'Get out of my way.' Oliver unceremoniously pushed by and strode into the sitting room.

Sabrina, also dressed — but then she'd had time to pull on a gown Oliver told himself ruthlessly — was standing by the table, eyes wide, her cheeks very pale, and with intriguing strands of hair escaped from the piled curls to her shoulders.

She moved towards him, trembling, but managing to smile. 'Oh, Oliver, I'm so glad to see you. I shouldn't have opened the telegram, but—' her words came out in a number of little gasps '—it was Jaina you see. I—'

Oliver slapped her face sharply. 'Put your cape on immediately, Sabrina, do you hear?'

Freddie, who had entered the room too late to see the incident, stared in dismay at the couple facing each other so belligerently, she with stubborn chin and one hand to her cheek, Cavannagh towering over her in the attitude of some schoolmaster about to administer corporal punishment.

'I say,' he protested, coming forward to push between them, 'don't get things wrong, Cavannagh. This happens to be my flat, and your wife has come, in your absence, to learn distressing news about your—'

'My daughter,' Oliver said very coldly and clearly, 'my bastard daughter who has so inconsiderately landed me in this most unpleasant situation. You may as well hear it from my own lips — no doubt the news will soon leak out. But—' he jerked Freddie's hand away and lifted a finger warningly, 'don't you dare spread any unsavoury news about her, de Marchmont, or you'll rue it. I'll denounce you, not only as her seducer, but as my wife's lover as well. So keep your mouth shut, understand—'

Freddie's lip curled. Instinctively he raised his fist. 'Why! you jumped-up mountebank — for two pins I'd—'

'If it wasn't for that cut and swollen face, you'd be on the floor first,' Oliver said sneeringly. 'But I don't kick a dog when it's down!'

Freddie sprang forward again, but Sabrina was there between them first.

'Stop,' she cried. 'You're behaving like — like—'

'Two ill-bred males fighting over a she-cat,' Oliver interposed. 'Exactly.'

He flung the cape at her. 'I told you to put it on. Later we'll discuss this.'

Freddie did his best to get matters under control, and as Cavannagh, grasping Sabrina by a wrist, jerked her towards the hall, made a last effort at interception.

'Jaina's slipped off again,' he shouted. 'Can you take that in? She was here when I contacted Carnack. Now, blast you, thanks to your neglect and time-wasting, she's on the run. Well, Cavannagh, if *you* don't report this business, I shall. You say Jaina's your daughter. If that's right, you should know she was in a brothel last night. She'd been raped. I found her and brought her here — not without trouble, I can assure you—' he rubbed a temple significantly. 'So don't blame your wife—'

'For caressing you? I'm not blind,' Oliver snapped. 'I saw what was happening. If you want *amours* with other men's wives you should keep away from lighted windows. Damn you, de Marchmont—'

'Don't be a fool,' Freddie said, trying to control his temper. 'Sabrina was merely rubbing something on this cut. There it is — on the table — that bottle. Read it; see what it says — for cuts and bruises.'

Cavannagh grudgingly turned and observed the lotion. 'How convenient for you,' he remarked. 'I'm sure such lengthy administrations must have been beneficial. Let's see—' he scrutinised his Hunter watch. 'How many hours—?'

'Enough,' Freddie replied for him. 'And during that time Jaina, your child, has been wandering about the streets, God knows where, shocked, and frightened and needing care. Did you get what I said? — She'd been raped, man. *Raped*.'

Oliver appeared temporarily stunned.

'What did you say?'

Freddie repeated the unsavoury statement.

'How do you know? And since when were you a doctor?' Oliver's lip curled.

'Oh, Oliver, please!' Sabrina caught his arm. 'Can't we sit down and talk?'

'No. First of all I'm getting you back where you belong.' His hand was on her arm again, hurting her. 'As for you, de Marchmont, just you keep your mouth shut. Any reporting concerning my little slut of an offspring will be done by me, and myself alone. If you try to make a case of it, I'll have you in court; with such filthy publicity proved, the mud will stick for a lifetime. Understand? So watch your step.'

Sabrina tried to free herself. Cavannagh held her mercilessly. Freddie stood watching them as he pushed her through the door down the passage to the entrance. She turned her head once, whispering, 'I'm sorry—'

Freddie shrugged, and went back into the sitting room. A further scene, at that point, would have been useless, he thought wearily. Cavannagh obviously intended to shrug off Jaina's desperate plight as quietly and unobtrusively as possible. If he, de Marchmont, took the case up on his own, only more trouble would fall upon Sabrina, which wouldn't help Jaina in the slightest; rather the reverse.

Overcome suddenly by the ordeal he'd been through, lack of sleep, and a tormenting vision of the child-woman who'd so touched his heart, he waited for the slam of the door followed by the sound of hurried footsteps and a cab starting off, then he returned to the room, poured himself a drink, and flung himself moodily into a chair. He sat there for a time, until he found himself dropping into a doze. With an effort he got up, slipped on a light overcoat and went out into the chill of early dawn. Thin rain was falling. The few pedestrians about registered only as dreary shadows through his mind, the sparse traffic seemed unreal — ghost-like.

Where had she gone, he wondered, and what direction should he take? It was like looking — in the words of the old adage — for a needle in a haystack. But find her he would, somehow, some day.

Even Freddie had not the remotest idea of how long it would take, or the shape of events to come.

Lisette was still in bed the following day when Oliver and Sabrina arrived back at Carnack. She waited for both to come into her room to see her. But all she heard were footsteps mounting the stairs and taking a turn to their own quarters, the slam of a door, then, for some time, silence.

She lay rigidly alert, expecting at any moment for both, or at least her son, to appear. Something was wrong, she told herself at last. Very wrong indeed.

Eventually, when she could bear the suspense no longer, she slipped on a negligée, pushed her feet into furry mules and made her way to their bedroom. She tapped at the door. There was no response.

'Oliver,' she called sharply. 'What's happened? Aren't you going to let me in?'

After a few seconds there was the click of a key turning; the door opened a fraction, but she could see nothing except her son's large form blocking a sight of the interior.

Oliver's face was cold, set, and enigmatic.

'Yes, Mama?' he queried in dangerously polite tones, 'is there anything you require?'

Involuntarily she flinched. 'Of course not. I only — naturally I want to know what's happened.'

He smiled.

'No doubt you will learn all in good time, Mater. At the moment both my wife and myself require rest to recover from our — ordeal.'

'What do you mean? What ordeal? How is Sabrina?'

'Sabrina is in robust good health, I can assure you. Just a little put out, shall we say, by having to learn a somewhat undignified lesson. Take a look at her if you wish—'

He opened the door wider. Lisette pushed her head through.

Sabrina was lying in the ornate great bed with the silk quilt pulled up close under her chin. Her eyes, through the wan rain-swept light from the window, though slightly puffed — through tiredness, Lisette hoped — blazed brilliantly. Her cheeks appeared a rosy child-like pink. She didn't smile, and said nothing to her mother-in-law's greeting.

'I hope you're satisfied,' Oliver said. 'Later, at dinner, we shall no doubt meet.'

'And what about Jaina?'

Oliver gave her no satisfaction.

'I said later,' he answered more coldly.

Lisette retreated, worried, yet in a strange way titillated. What had happened, she wondered uneasily, as she made her way back to her bedroom.

As Oliver had said, there'd appeared to be nothing wrong with Sabrina but a touch of sullen temper.

Sabrina, still smarting both mentally and physically from Cavannagh's undignified treatment of her person, thought completely otherwise. This time Oliver had gone too far. She was not a child or chattel, and had no intention whatever of going through life in such a ridiculously submissive role.

Cavannagh's explanation to Lisette before dinner that evening was brief, practical, and decidedly unsatisfactory. Sabrina listened stony-faced as he told how the Honourable — with emphasis on the 'honourable' — Frederick de Marchmont — had discovered Jaina in unsavoury circumstances and taken her to his own rooms where he had doubtless enjoyed himself at her expense before contacting Carnack. An extremely pathetic and plausible story had been concocted between them and in the meantime she'd conveniently disappeared again.

'Oh dear. And Sabrina?' Lisette's glance turned fleetingly to her daughter-in-law.

'What Sabrina did is her affair and mine only,' Oliver said, still with a certain dead-pan expression on his handsome countenance. 'But you can be assured, Mater dear, it will not happen again.'

Sabrina still said nothing, but her mind was seething. She was looking proud, beautiful, and as cold as an ice-queen in palest green chiffon and white. Jewels twinkled on her fingers, in her ears, and at her breasts. But it would be the last time, she told herself resolutely. Tomorrow she would be gone, leaving all that hated finery behind — not in flight to nowhere as Jaina had, but to her family; her own father at Fern Hill.

Her stepmother would be dismayed, tongues would start wagging all over again, but it wouldn't matter. She would be safe at her old home, and somehow, in the end, would be able to start life afresh.

16

Henrietta was more than dismayed. She was chagrined and bitterly annoyed at her step-daughter's unexpected return to the Penderrick home. Sir Martin, to the contrary, glowed with satisfaction. Although life at Fern Hill had run on a comparatively even keel since Sabrina's marriage, there had been a gap in his existence that he'd felt more than he admitted. His wife, certainly, ran the house remarkably efficiently; what entertaining they could afford was done with subtle expertise and good taste. But the truth was he found her company and feminine 'small-talk' at times extremely boring. When his daughter had lived with them there had been frequent fireworks. No day had been completely predictable. Of recent months, he had begun to feel his age and more. Sabrina's presence, therefore, would bring a touch of brightness back again. Tongues would get wagging once more, naturally. Well, it wouldn't bother him; in fact he'd probably discover a touch of humour in the situation, although not for the world would he let Henrietta suspect it. There was another thing too. He loved his daughter, and Cavannagh hadn't been right for her. The worldly type — like so many jumped-up magnates; a brigand of the most dangerous kind — ruthless and clever enough to get to the top even if he destroyed others by climbing on their shoulders to do so.

'Blast the fellow,' he said to Henrietta on the first night of Sabrina's flight when she was unpacking her valise in the bedroom. 'Deserves a good horse-whipping for treating my girl that way.'

'What way, Martin?' Henrietta sounded slightly belligerent, and felt it.

'Well—' He shrugged vaguely. As usual Henrietta had caught him out. 'I haven't questioned her too closely, but mark my words, he's a bully and a scoundrel. She'd never have left him otherwise. Sabrina isn't the kind to run away.'

'Isn't she? What about Freddie?'

'That was different, Henny. Nerves — just nerves. Girls get 'em sometimes at the last minute. If he'd run after her and held her close it'd have passed over. They'd have been back again in no time.'

'Rubbish. She was simply playing fast and loose with the poor boy. Dramatics. Melodrama. And please, Martin—'

'Yes m'dear?' His voice was mild.

'Don't call me Henny. I dislike it immensely. It's — it's vulgar somehow. Bourgeois.'

A hint of amusement lit his eyes.

'That's the very last description that could be applied to you, Henrietta.'

And indeed it was true.

In her high-necked grey silk gown, frilled with lace, and boned under her decisive chin, Henrietta, Lady Penderrick was a handsome, quite formidable figure. Magnificent, her husband liked to consider her, tall and well proportioned, with a small waist emphasising her swelling hips and well rounded bosom. Her hair, as always, was impecably dressed, taken severely from her forehead in a roll, and pinned on top in a knot carefully primed by curling tongs.

Shortly after the brief conversation, Sabrina came downstairs, looking, despite the dark rims under her eyes, youthful and vulnerable in pale green muslin.

Henrietta was about to leave father and daughter together, when Sir Martin, who'd already had his chat with Sabrina, got to his feet.

'Time you two made friends again,' he said. 'I'm off for a smoke. If Harry arrives' — Harry was an old retainer, who had once been head gardener '—tell him I'm in the billiard room. Maybe he'll fancy a game of snooker.'

Henrietta inwardly tut-tutted. How very characteristic of her husband to be on such close terms with a servant. For that's all the old man had been after all — a servant, of however superior a calibre. She turned suddenly to Sabrina, and in spite of herself felt a stab of sympathy. The child really did look tired.

'Well, Sabrina,' she heard herself saying automatically, 'I suppose for your father's sake we must make the best of things and try and get on together. But — sit down for heaven's sake. You make one feel edgy, just standing there.' Sabrina did so reluctantly, feeling immediately at a disadvantage.

'I hope you're not going to lecture,' she said. 'I've been through enough. Oh, I know some of it's my own fault, but this part isn't. What I did was to go looking for Jaina when Oliver was away. She'd disappeared, you see—'

'Yes, I'd heard. I should think the whole district's aware of it. But why did you go on your own? And where?'

'Plymouth. I told you, Oliver was away, and a telegram came telling him there was news.'

'For you?'

'No. Oliver. But I guessed — I knew somehow it was about Jaina. I opened it.'

'I see. And what did it say? Who was it from?'

Sabrina paused before answering. Then she said defiantly and very clearly, 'Freddie!'

Henrietta gasped. 'De Marchmont? Frederick de Marchmont?'

Sabrina nodded.

'And you actually went? To Plymouth?'

Sabrina nodded.

'Then you deserved a — a — you should have been soundly spanked.'

'I was,' Sabrina said coldly. 'When we got back. And that, if you must know, was the reason, partly, that made me leave Carnack. But not all. The fact is, whether you believe it or not — Oliver is the most callous, cold-blooded man I've ever met. About Jaina, I mean. I could have treated the rest as a game. A rough and tumble doesn't hurt anyone — but that poor girl! — he just doesn't care. He really seems to have turned against her.'

'As I know so little about the situation it's not for me to make judgement there,' Henrietta said self-righteously. 'But, as you well know, Sabrina, I would not care to mix with that type of family unless forced to. Gentlemanly conduct can scarcely be expected from a man of his origins and ruthless ambition. The girl, too, is no longer the mystery she once was, is she? The whole countryside knows now of the relationship between them, whereas before it was merely surmise. Still, one must be fair I suppose. She'd led him a pretty dance; you both have, between you.'

Sabrina's under-lip tightened. 'If you don't mind,' she said rather curtly, 'I'd rather not be lectured, or reminded of the past. It's over.'

'Is it?' Henrietta sounded sceptical.

'Yes. All I'm worried about is Jaina.'

'Whilst you remain here, Sabrina, it would be better for all concerned for you to put her out of your mind. She has mixed blood in her; anyone could see that. I realised it last year when we bumped into each other by chance, at a provision merchant's in Truro. She had that tired, starchy-looking woman with her, a governess or servant of some kind acting as chaperone, I suppose. Those slant eyes were unmistakable. To be concerned on her behalf is quite ridiculous — especially when she happens to have such a wealthy father.'

The barb went home. Sabrina paled, pulled herself together and went to the window. She would have liked a breath of fresh air, but a fog was rising, and it would soon be dark. There would be nothing to see, and no one was likely to be about. Not even Cavannagh. He'd been in Penzance when she'd left Carnack earlier, but probably he'd be back now and already knew of her flight. Lisette, who'd tried to dissuade her from leaving, would have dramatically added colour to the affair, but Sabrina guessed she'd touchingly have tried to comfort him, pointing out that 'everything had probably happened for the best', or that 'life was a pattern', or some other equally ridiculous platitude. There would almost certainly be a sharp reaction of temper from Oliver enlivened by a few curses, or else a retreat to his sanctum with a whisky bottle. He might even take it into his head to summon a swift business meeting with one of his numerous company directors where he could vent his feelings on some innocent colleague.

Actually none of these eventualities occurred.

Oliver simply braced himself to accept the news with false equanimity, retreating into sullen silence when his mother had finished.

'You do understand, don't you?' Lisette couldn't help enquiring when no visible impact registered. 'Your wife has left you.'

'You make yourself quite clear, Mater. Well, the world hasn't come to an end. We just have to accept it, don't we?'

Lisette was aghast. 'But aren't you going to do anything about it? Bring her back?'

Oliver smiled enigmatically.

'We shall see. In the meantime I have some papers to attend to.'

Lisette, in the end, had to accept that Oliver would go his own way whatever she might say, and that there was no point at all in fretting herself unnecessarily over Jaina's disappearance or Sabrina's desertion. Nevertheless anxiety had cast a lingering shadow over her mind, and had she but known it, Oliver was not nearly so unconcerned as he appeared. Feeling it his duty, and with an unpleasant sense of guilt in not seeing that his wayward child had been more carefully supervised, he reported Freddie's unsavoury story of the Plymouth incident. The reply was that Mr de Marchmont had already contacted headquarters, but that as there was no concrete evidence she'd been molested – no factual proof even of her ever having been at the Golden Rose, and that as she was still missing, his statement had not really helped matters. Jaina could be anywhere. They were still making every effort to find her, and could not do more.

Morose and embittered, Cavannagh told himself Jaina had reverted to type, and turned out after all to be merely a replica of her mother who had been a dancing girl in Ceylon when he'd first set eyes on her and rescued her from an inevitable future of prostitution. At the same time, he knew, uncomfortably, he was not being strictly fair. Solanges Lee, half French, half Chinese, had possessed a rare quality of beauty and innocence that had set her apart at that time from others of her profession – a certain exotic purity that had inflamed his desire to possess her. Her mother had been dead for a year, her father was unknown when he'd found her and given protection – including a bungalow for their mutual pleasure, with a garden containing a small pool framed by ornamental willows and flowering plants.

Had he loved her? To a certain extent, yes. She was young,

only sixteen, with a dewy fresh loveliness reflected in her limpid dark eyes, delicate features, small hands and feet, and glistening wealth of dusky dark hair. Her gestures had held the instinctive grace of some finely-bred princess. Her skin, though faintly golden, was pale and fragrant, reminding him of lily-buds opening sensually to the sunlight. She had been both woman and child to him — an expensive toy he'd treasured for more than a year, then, when business called, had abandoned.

He hadn't meant things to work out that way. After leaving her with adequate means to cover expenses until his expected return, circumstances and an ambitious deal had driven him to the other side of the world. There he'd stayed; stayed far longer than he'd meant, and had managed during the prolonged absence conveniently to disregard the human side of his commitment.

When at last he'd gone back she was dancing her life away in a flower-house. He'd been shocked by the ravages of time. The slender body was ill-nourished, the beautiful painted face strained with the avid desire to please; to please men. The limpid eyes had lost their innocence. She was a travesty of the child-like exquisite young creature who'd been so sweetly submissive and faithful during the months of their life together.

He'd done what he could for her, forced her to see a doctor, but she'd been bitter in her gentleness, and when the truth of her illness was revealed she'd smiled acquiescently, and he'd realised she'd known all along.

She'd died quite soon after their tragic reunion. The child, who'd been cared for adequately, but without personal love by an ex-prostitute who earned a livelihood as a baby minder, was put in the care of the mission. Cavannagh had never doubted Solanges' word that she was his, and since that time he'd contributed liberally to her welfare.

He'd done his best, dammit, he'd told himself, time after time. But what was in the blood couldn't entirely be erased. Later, when Jaina had come to England he'd seen as little of her as possible, not because there was anything unattractive about her, but because when the luminous strange eyes melted towards him with pride and love, he saw a ghost staring. When the flower-lips smiled it was as though Solanges returned from the grave.

So he'd been strict with her as she grew older, and sometimes hard. She had at first adored him as her mother had. He had not wanted such adoration from Solanges; marriage between them would have been unthinkable. Neither did he wish filial worship from Jaina.

The fact remained, she was his child, and he was now reaping the ill-reward of it.

As for Sabrina! He'd been cuckolded outrageously. There was no practical proof of course, but with a good lawyer he knew he could obtain a divorce with no trouble at all. She deserved it, by God. And it would very effectively smear the name of that snobbish de Marchmont family. The trouble was, he didn't at the moment wish for a smear campaign. Neither was he prepared to lose Sabrina in such a way.

So, what?

During the next few days he concerned himself exclusively with affairs of the estate — devoting more time than usual to the interests and welfare of the guests who were flattered by his courtesy, and the dominating brilliance of his personality. At opportune moments he flattered rich widows and the aspiring Mamas of eligible daughters, making them feel queens. He even attended a dance held in the ballroom of the guest-wing at Carnack, and partnered the plainest of the young women with such gallant chivalry, they blossomed from drooping wall-flowers to budding excited new life. Rumours that his marriage was an unhappy one, and that his wife had already left him, had already penetrated, from whispered conversation of the servants' quarters. Disapproval registered in a number of elderly bosoms, but was subdued gradually through speculative comments holding the query of whether actually there had ever really been a legal marriage? After all Miss Penderrick, as she had been at the time, had obviously been a wild erratic creature. In any case, divorce in current Edwardian times could be accepted under certain conditions. The dashing, handsome Mr Cavannagh had obviously been the injured party. One day — who knew? — he might emerge again as an eligible suitor needing a wife to share his lonely bed.

Oliver, ironically aware of his capacity to stir hearts and heads, used his gift to the full. At other times he threw surplus energy into physical activities of riding, and exercising the horses. He spent hours walking the terrain and supervising new projects including the site of a swimming pool already under construction.

In this way the irritating business of Sabrina and Jaina was forced to the dark recesses of his mind. But he never entirely abandoned the determination to have his wife back when the right moment arose.

One bright morning desire suddenly overcame discretion. He rode to Fern Hill, starting off early and taking a quick cross-country route over the moors.

He'd hoped to find her lingering about either in the grounds — cutting flowers perhaps — Sabrina had a love of flowers and was an adept at arranging them — or perhaps merely wandering aimlessly along the lanes. But there was no one to be seen when he reached the drive except a gardener poking about one of the untidy borders. So Oliver strode purposefully to the front door, pulled the bell, and when he gave his name, accompanied by a card, was admitted by a female servant who looked tired and over-worked, and was shown after a brief pause into the library.

'I don't know about Miss Sabrina,' the woman had said when he'd asked for Mrs Cavannagh, 'but the master's in.'

Oliver had nodded approval.

'He'll do.'

He found Sir Martin already rising from his place in an alcove by the fire. The room was a cool one, even in summer, and the old man liked the comfort of a blaze where he could retreat when he felt like it, from his wife's bustling presence.

'Come in, come in,' he said, frowning at the sight of Oliver's tall form. 'No need for ceremony. I can guess what you're here for.'

Oliver joined him by the fire, and after a gesture from Sir Martin's hand seated himself.

'Well?' The curt word was not encouraging, so Oliver came to the point with no hedging.

'Sabrina. My wife, and incidentally your daughter, I'd like a word with her if you don't mind.'

'And if I do?'

Oliver's bland smile was mechanical, giving nothing away.

'I shall think you're afraid, sir.'

'Afraid? Of you?'

Oliver shrugged. 'I shall think Sabrina is, unless you allow me to speak to her; and I can assure you she's no need to be. I'm neither a hardened wife-beater nor complete cad, though she may have persuaded you to think so.'

Sir Martin paused before saying in more conciliatory tones, 'There's been very little tale-telling from my daughter — I wish there'd been more, because she's generally honest. But I gather you had a disagreement over your—'

'My daughter's disappearance.'

'Hm! glad you admit it. Well, that's none of my affair, but in my family we have never resorted to physical retribution.'

A flash of white teeth momentarily lit Cavannagh's face turning its hard lines to humour.

'Perhaps if you had, sir, Sabrina would have learned how to behave with proper propriety as a wife, and later chastisement would have been unnecessary.'

Sir Martin's complexion took a deeper hue.

'How dare you have touched a hair of my child's head?'

'I didn't, sir. It was quite another area of her anatomy. And believe me, if she'd had less false pride and more sense of fun she'd have been tickled to death by the humour of it. As it was, she wasn't at all averse to a most exciting and passionate finale.'

For some seconds Sir Martin didn't answer, then he said, 'What exactly is it you want with her now?'

'My business I think, sir, and hers.'

'Very well — we'll see what she says. But don't count on any meeting.'

Following a touch of the nearby bell, a servant appeared. Sir Martin gave brief instructions to the maid to inform his daughter of Mr Cavannagh's arrival, with the request that if possible she come down to see him.

Minutes passed, during which time Cavannagh accepted a short drink, while Sir Martin got up and went to the window waiting for Sabrina's response, if any. She arrived looking particularly lovely in a dress of subdued rose-pink, pale-faced beneath the piled up tawny hair, but with a touch of salve on her lips. Her small head was held high on the slender neck.

Oliver stood rigidly waiting for her to come forward. Sir Martin coughed, and went to the door saying, 'Hm, well, I'll leave you two to talk. But—' he cast Sabrina a quick direct glance '—If you want me, m'dear, I'll be in the smoking room. Just touch the bell.'

He went out.

Oliver still waited motionless, with his hands linked behind his back. Then he said, steadily, but with his blood quickening, 'Come here, Sabrina.'

Mutely she obeyed.

He moved a step towards her, touched a shoulder tentatively, longing to crush her in his arms. Her only response was to draw away sharply.

'What do you want, Oliver?' she asked. 'Why are you here?'

A hot reply was on his lips, but he curbed it.

'Come back, Sabrina,' he urged more gently. 'I want you. There's no need for this stupid situation—'

Her face flamed.

'No? Then why have you forced it? You weren't invited.'

'A husband doesn't generally require an invitation from his own wife to visit her,' he told her coldly. 'Pull yourself together, for God's sake, and show sense for once—'

'Sense? You must be mad. I hate you, Oliver.'

Those few words so sharply spoken cut him with the ice edge of a knife thrust. He had no means of knowing how her own heart pounded, how her aloof proud manner betrayed the sensuous longings of her innermost being.

He had been on the point of pleading. But quick resentment and frustration rekindled a furious desire to bring her to heel.

'One day,' he heard himself saying harshly, 'you'll pay for this, Madam. Do you understand?'

Her lips curled.

'Don't threaten me,' she said. 'Just leave.'

'And you expect me to—'

'I expect nothing from you at all. And you can do nothing about it — *nothing*. Divorce me, if you like. For all I care you can go to hell.'

'When I do,' he said, 'I'll see you're with me. And that's not a threat, it's a promise.'

Her cheeks blanched. As he strode from the room he neither touched nor looked at her. When the front door slammed she was still standing motionless; with a feeling mounting in her of futility, and having finally set the seal of negation on any mutual future they might have shared.

17

During the following weeks Lisette abandoned any attempts at reconciliation between her son and his wife. Oliver had made a point, following his unsatisfactory interview with Sabrina, that he had no intention of discussing the affair, and that he was far too busily occupied business-wise and politically, to waste his energies in emotional combat. Actually his latter ambitions had met a rebuff. Lord Frayle had invited him to the stately home one day in July, for lunch. Oliver had gone, sensing something was in the air — something not entirely favourable to his own aspirations.

He had been right.

After an agreeable lunch, when the two men had retired to the smoking room for a chat over vintage brandy and cigars, Frayle, in a manner too tentative and soothing to be quite genuine, himself broached the matter of the forthcoming parliamentary election. There was a certain preliminary humming and ha-ing, complimentary phrases concerning Cavannagh's acute business sense calculated to put the other man into an equable mood, which did not however deceive Oliver for one moment.

'Out with it, sir,' he said abruptly, 'you're trying to tell me my capital and advice are still very much to be desired and appreciated, but that certain other matters are no longer on the table. Is that it?'

Looking a little embarrassed at the direct question, his Lordship had replied ambiguously, 'I would not put it quite like that, but the fact is, Cavannagh, during the past months things have changed a little.'

Oliver emptied his glass quickly. Frayle had obligingly

refilled it, and now the worst hurdle was over had continued, 'These stories that've got about — they say that girl who's disappeared was your daughter; of course to me it's of no importance — women's gossip — middle-class chit-chat — all bunkum and ballyhoo as far as I'm concerned. But my kind are in the minority, Cavannagh. And this other business concerning you and your wife. It's true, I suppose, that you've separated? That she's back at Fern Hill?'

'True enough. But what of it? Whose business is that but my own?'

Frayle's mouth took a gloomy twist. His eyes were cold. 'You must know very well. The Party may be go-ahead in some ways, but the moral image remains strong. Convention! you can't afford to ignore it—'

'Meaning you're not prepared to support me as a candidate?'

There had been an uncomfortable pause. Then, 'Do I have to spell it out, Cavannagh? Believe me I'm sorry.'

'I see.' Oliver braced himself. 'Well, at least we know where we stand now. I take it you already have an eye on a more worthy protégé?'

'Protégé?' The short laugh was derisive. 'Come now, I'd hardly put you in that category. You could buy me out — financially — any day.'

'That's true,' curtly. 'I could. And get your mine on its feet. But I suppose you have already an eye on capital from elsewhere.'

Frayle had looked briefly discomforted.

'I know of someone willing to invest, certainly.'

'Of far more honourable and deserving calibre than myself obviously.'

'Look here, Cavannagh, I'm sorry to have to say this, but your unsavoury marital situation combined with that girl running away, and then crossing swords with de Marchmont — why did you have to do such a tom-fool thing?'

'I see. De Marchmont! so he's been throwing the mud around? I might have expected it.'

'No. I've heard Freddie's kept curiously mum about the Bristol episode. But things get about. And when the police are drawn in—'

'You can't keep tongues from wagging or the dirt from flying. I quite see your point.'

'I hope so. And I hope you understand there's no personal animosity in my decision. I think if you'd been able to enter the House you could have been a valuable addition to the Government, and stirred things up a little. In any case you can go it alone, if it's really so important to you, and—'

'You mean put up against one of your already firmly entrenched colleagues? Oh no, sir. I'm not that kind of fool. When I put my mind to a thing it's with a ninety-nine-and-a-half percent chance of getting what I want. Otherwise it's out.'

'Yes. I can believe it.'

Oliver had extended a hand. 'No hard feelings; I never grudge a man backing the most likely winner. I wish you luck with your mine. From what I've heard it will need it.'

The interview had ended shortly, leaving Cavannagh soured by politics for the time being, angry and frustrated still by his wife, and determined to push both unpleasant topics from his mind. For the next four months he had visits abroad planned — even a trip later to Ceylon was on the cards.

Yes, he told himself with a certain dedicated purpose, he had plenty on his plate. Sabrina could be left to cool her heels for a time. He had no doubts at all — or if he had he would not admit them — that eventually she could be won back or forced to return. He would not consider divorce for one moment. She had brought discredit on them both, and deserved to stew in her own juice until she came to her senses. Jaina, of course, was a different matter. She was young, defenceless, and of his own flesh. Privately he did all he could to trace her, but so far his efforts and the considerable expense entailed had been to no avail. So time passed.

At odd moments the vague image of Jaina's mother floated through his mind like the blurred reflection of a flower through the constant ripple and changing light of a flowing stream.

Solanges. How compliant she had been — how sweet and trusting until circumstances had marred her. Sabrina at least would escape such savaging. She was tough. In spite of himself he couldn't help a quickening of his blood and senses whenever he remembered.

But his daughter?

These emotional lapses however were rare, and in the meantime he devoted his excess energies to a new scheme for his developing hotel empire. Politics might be out — for the time being — but an immediate project comparatively near at hand provided an outlet for his frustration.

He had acquired some acres of land in Devon, not far from Torquay, which he had scheduled for a new luxury establishment complete with a swimming pool, riding school, and casino. He was already envisaging a theatre to provide amusement for the sophisticated and rich. There would be, of course, a resident orchestra and palm-court.

Be damned then, to the arrogant Frayles and de Marchmonts. Their kind were already on the way out. The future belonged to men who could not only dream but build dreams into fact, and turn bricks and mortar into gold.

Defiance strengthened and fortified him. Edward's reign was kind and complacent to the wealthy well-bred. But Oliver possessed sufficient acumen to envisage a future society when the latter would be forced to bend a knee. Their select circles would crack then, giving access to the power-builders; and he, Oliver Cavannagh, meant to be among the first to benefit.

Charmed circle? Yes. He'd spread his own empire through Europe and across the world. From tea, he already saw a new society evolving; exotic, splendid, remembering what his father had said more than once. 'Purpose, looks, and the wherewithal, boy. You've got it all. Brains too. Remember that — and use them well. Never get swamped by ideologies or sentiment. Riches can buy anything — even romance. There's not a woman in the world hasn't a price. Aim high and play safe. In other words, keep control of your heart. Only a fool can afford to lose it.'

Well, he'd done his best to keep to the rules of the game; Sabrina, for a time, had almost foiled it. But not quite. He could well live without her if she stuck to her sterile path. There were other women in the world — warm, obliging, without the audacity or stupidity to deny him.

So after preliminary visits to the Devon site, he took off to France again, and made a visit to the Leblancs.

Lili, as he'd expected, was lavish and warm in her welcome.

'Ah!' she exclaimed, spreading her plump arms wide, 'but it is so kind and so veree generous, Oliver, *mon ami*, that you should trouble any more about Marie and myself. Come in — come in, and see how my child has blossomed. She is no longer an *enfant*, but a true woman—' She broke off smiling, and Cavannagh noticed with faint embarrassment that the wide high-boned face seemed to have thickened and slightly coarsened during the last year. She had put on weight, and was no longer the placidly pretty woman he had slept with in the past. Those occasions had been rare. There'd been no pretence of love between them. Her body had been his mostly through gratitude and a desire to please an English gentleman who in a moment of kindness, following her husband's death, had set her up in business, with the proviso she paid him an annual small sum from her profits. She'd regarded the arrangement as a strictly honourable one.

It had proved most successful. Lili, herself a good cook, was also a competent business manager, and as the child Marie grew older, she also had been an asset. Her father had been a seaman who had drowned off the coast of Brittany. His daughter had inherited his striking good looks, and though not so vivacious as Lili, outwardly, was admired and respected by customers, and had kept her virginity intact. Yet when she met Oliver on his brief visit she discomforted rather than pleased him. Lili was all warmth! Marie, though smiling, had a bright independence about her that he found somewhat chilly.

He'd called at the restaurant with an idea simmering that he'd share his bed with Lili that night. But he quite quickly discovered when they were alone, that he no longer wanted her. She showed no hurt or displeasure.

'I understand,' she said, politely adjusting the bodice of her blouse which she had been on the point of unbuttoning for a tempting glimpse of her full white breasts. 'We are friends now, yes? But no more lovers. Ah well, it is to be expected. I am no longer the *jeune fille*, and you, my friend, have a beautiful wife to warm your sheets.' She laughed merrily. 'No matter; Lili Leblanc will be always grateful and willing to please you in any way possible — if only over a glass of cognac. Yes? Or dinner. Now why not have dinner with Marie and me; I have—'

Before she had finished, Oliver quickly declined. 'Sorry, Lili,' he said. 'I already have an appointment, and now business is done with, I should leave.' He glanced at his watch.

She made a move. 'So soon? How sad! but—' She gave a

characteristic shrug. 'All things pass. And time is not always kind for a woman.'

Oliver conjured up his most charming smile. 'You give time itself warmth, Lili. The eternal, undefeated femme fatale.'

With inborn French cynicism, Lili remarked, 'I'm flattered you try and make me believe it, Oliver. But you know very well it isn't true, and that I'm no fool.' She wagged a finger with mock disapproval, 'but for all that, I still like you.'

He took her plump hand, kissed it, then her cheek lightly, near the temple.

Minutes later he had left, and was making his way back to his hotel.

The stimulus Paris generally afforded him was curiously lacking. A hint of boredom dulled his spirits. He was in no mood for the Folies Bergère, ballet, or more dubious places of enjoyment that had known his patronage in the past. The business he had to deal with in France this time was slight, and had been more of an excuse to get away from Carnack than of necessity.

The truth was, had he allowed himself to admit it, that he missed Sabrina. As it was, he set his mind firmly against the past and once more conjured wordly visions for the future. At moments his gall rose when a fleeting memory of de Marchmont shadowed his mind. He saw again blurred figures silhouetted against the blind of the Plymouth room — the affectionate gesture of his wife as her hand reached to her ex-swain's face. So familiar — so somehow — understanding. He doubted they'd ever been physical lovers. If they had he could have swallowed the situation more easily. He was no prude. He'd been no saint himself. But that tenderness, dammit, showed she still had feeling for the fellow — was playing the tease as she'd expected to play it with him, her husband — Oliver Cavannagh. And on top of it all de Marchmont had used Jaina as a foil — utilised the situation for getting Sabrina to himself. He was not even sure that he believed a word of Freddie's explanation. It was like a duel in the dark — neither could possibly know the full and factual truth. All Cavannagh could be certain of, was his own simmering resentment and dislike, almost hatred — of the other man, and a determination one day to make him pay.

Freddie, on the other hand, had managed to put Oliver practically out of mind. He was preoccupied only with Jaina.

Unknown to any official authorities or to Cavannagh, he had engaged a private investigator for the case, and also followed up his own enquiries. Nothing so far had come to light. He spent far more time than in the past at Plymouth, trying at the same time to show no neglect of the family estate. He was seen frequently on social occasions with Constance Penmorran, the sporting daughter of a neighbouring squire, which pleased his aristocratic parents.

'Constance comes of good stock — not bad looking either — the sort to make a good wife and breed strong sons. I'd like an heir, my boy. Why not think about things?' Lord de Marchmont, suggested. 'You could do worse.'

Freddie nodded. 'I know that. Plenty of time though. I like Con, but we just happen to be good friends, that's all.'

'Friendship can be a sound basis for marriage,' his lordship pointed out. 'Beauty — romance — all that stuff,' can be titillating in youth, but the years take their toll, Freddie, and when a man reaches my age he needs other things for his comfort. Remember this, too — you're not the only one on the scene where Constance is concerned. Plenty would jump at the chance of getting her.'

'I quite realise that,' Freddie agreed nonchalantly. 'I've got eyes in my head. But I don't intend getting pushed into something I'm not sure of. And—'

Detecting the rising warning note in his son's voice de Marchmont hurriedly interrupted appeasingly, 'Say no more, m'boy. I'm not trying to force anything. Wait a bit if you must, sow a few wild oats and then put your thinking cap on.'

Freddie being quite a normal product of his era and class had already sown a few, and enjoyed the fleeting experiences while they lasted, of which his father must surely be aware. However, to close the topic amicably he merely said, 'Don't worry, I'll remember what you've said. I'm hardly likely to bring the family name into disrepute.'

But was that quite true? he wondered lately. If he ever managed to locate Jaina and somehow take a hand in her life, wouldn't it inevitably cause considerable affront to the ancestral dignity?

Still, that was a problem for the future. His overwhelming concern at the moment was to find her. He could not get her out of his mind. She had become an obsession, a haunting dream, that would allow no emotional or mental rest until he knew what had happened to her.

The breakthrough came in the early autumn of 1905 when a private investigator called at his Plymouth rooms one day and informed him that he had managed to obtain a certain London address that might prove fruitful in the search. During discreet but cunning and apparently casual conversations among frequenters and inhabitants of Plymouth's underworld, he'd come into contact with a prostitute who refused to give her name or address, but who had clearly known Jaina, and shown a sympathy and understanding of the child's plight. Yes, she had said, she thought she had met the girl, and admitted, when pressed, following the detective's solemn oath not to reveal the source of any information divulged by her — she had herself given a helping hand to the runaway, by paying her rail fare to London, and providing the name of an acquaintance in the city who had dealings with the theatre there. Apparently, the investigator told de Marchmont, Jaina had stage ambitions, and the woman had known of someone who might help her.

'Nothing grand of course, and the address is in a bad area — East End,' he said. 'But this woman I was talking to seemed genuine — a bit above most of her class.'

'Give me the name,' Freddie interrupted, startled by his own excitement, 'and where to go. Come on, man. Anything could have happened in the meantime—'

'And probably has,' the man reminded him. 'Over a year — it's about that, isn't it? — is a long time for a young girl on the run and in poor company. When you find her — *if* — don't expect her to be the same.'

'I'm not a fool,' Freddie said abruptly. 'But there are two kinds of innocence. I know what you're implying — well, virginity isn't everything. After what's already happened I wouldn't expect physical faithfulness — besides, she's probably forgotten me already. But there was a quality about her that — that's worth fighting for and saving.' He paused, adding reflectively with the hint of a wry half-smile on his lips. 'You think me besotted — an adult suffering from calf-love out of his time — that's it, isn't it? I don't blame you. But just give me that scrap of paper and let me get on with things.'

He took the card from the man's hand and read the name of 'Mike Lawson, Theatrical Agent'. The address — a decidedly unsavoury one — had obviously been quickly scribbled.

He dismissed his informant with instructions still to make further enquiries at the Plymouth end, then with a small bag, and leaving a note for his caretaker, set off for the station.

Half an hour later he was seated in a first class carriage of a train bound for Paddington.

When he reached London fog was already descending upon the city, giving promise of a pea-souper. The air was moist and murky, overhung with an atmosphere of chilling unease. The endless stream of blurred forms crowding the platform — the swathed shapes and outlines of passing vehicles outside, held, for Freddie, an impersonal sense of another dimension in time. It was as though, for a period, he stood on the threshold of some strange other world into which the girl Jaina had been taken and hidden.

He'd never thought of himself as an imaginative individual — not Frederick de Marchmont, the practical good-humoured young country gentleman, heir to a noble estate — but for that first short period he felt himself trapped in some monstrous web of sterile commercialism. No warmth — nothing but the ghosts of men caught up in the endless queue of an industrial age.

The sensation was only brief. He pulled himself together sharply, hailed a cab, and headed for Brown's Hotel where he booked himself in, and after a bath and change of clothes had dinner, while pondering on exactly what time, and in what manner, to contact Mike Lawson.

Meanwhile the fog had so thickened he decided against making the journey that evening. It might, in any case, prove impossible. So he retired to the smoking room to study the newspaper over a brandy and a cigar.

He went to bed early, rested fitfully for a hour or two, then fell into a deep sleep from which he did not wake until past nine. He had breakfast brought to his room which he took with strong black coffee. He then shaved, dressed, and went downstairs.

An attendant called a cab for him. The man appeared slightly suspicious when de Marchmont gave him the East End address.

'Sure you've got it right, sir?' he enquired before they set off. 'A rum kind of neighbourhood for a gent—'

'Quite sure,' Freddie emphasised.

'Very well then, if you say so, sir.'

There was a 'gee-up', a flick of the man's whip, and the hackney-cab was on its journey through the city to Mike Lawson's. In an effort not to appear conspicuous, Freddie had taken care to dress casually, wearing a dark grey jacket, grey trousers and waistcoat, with a dark floppy tie at the neck of a cream shirt. The effect, rather than fashionable, was artistic. He looked well groomed, but not particularly wealthy. Instinct had prepared him for what could be a hostile reception. He hoped for co-operation, and realised that his slightly theatrical air would win more confidence from a man involved in stage affairs, than if he appeared as himself — the Honourable Frederick de Marchmont — poking his nose into business — possibly dubious — that did not concern him.

The thick fog had lifted, but mist hugged streets and buildings with its shivering film. Thoroughfares were already busy. At one point a group of suffragists were harrying a motor-car as it chugged slowly down a main street. Soon though, the sun would break through. Faint radiance already tipped the dome of St Paul's. The surface of the Thames shone dark through the plane trees, spotted with dots of light where the squat tugs lay. Freddie, who knew London well, never failed to be impressed by its ever-changing vista which could be mysteriously chilly one moment — the next a bustling scene of activity under clear skies.

As the cab jolted eastwards, restlessness rose and increased in him. He knew very well the driver was taking a longer than necessary route, spinning out time, he supposed, to make more for his pocket. But when he remonstrated the man merely shrugged, turned his head, and said, 'Got to take care. These new-fangled motors make horses jib. Can't go more direct than I am, sir, and that's the truth.'

Realising he was in the man's hands, and there was nothing more he could do about it, Freddie settled back in his seat, and said no more until after travelling a network of crowded narrow by-ways the cabby drew his horse to a halt, and said, 'There's an office over there — side of the road, see? "Lawson's" writ on the window, Mike Lawson.'

De Marchmont's pulses bounded. 'Good.' He got out. 'Now, what do I owe you?'

The dour expression on the man's face indicated that he deserved more, probably, than he'd get. He obviously hadn't enjoyed the journey; his long pale face with its downward tilt of mouth under the drooping moustache held a doom-like quality.

'Do you want me to wait?' he enquired. 'It's not a nice neighbourhood to keep my cab safe. If you want taking back I'll have to move to that corner by the square, see? Near that old theatre place—?' Unsmilingly, he cocked a thumb over the road to the left.

Freddie, elated that he'd obviously found the right area and address, generously handed a sovereign and some silver to his dreary escort.

'Do that,' he said. 'Wait for half an hour, and if I'm not there by then you can go.' He fumbled in his pocket, and handed further cash over. With mumbled thanks, the man took his vehicle to the appointed place, and de Marchmont quickly covered the few yards to Mike Lawson's office.

The room was level with the street, at the bottom of a tenement building. It was small, dusty, with a desk, chair and table hoarded untidily with papers of every description. The walls were plastered with photographs of beauties of the period — Lillie Langtry, Gladys Cooper, Ellaline Terriss — and more characteristically Marie Lloyd, whose exuberant rendering of 'Champagne Charlie' was causing riotous applause among audiences everywhere, whether in public houses providing comedy acts for men and women of the lower orders — or in more authentic theatres catering for music hall, and comic turns.

Mike Lawson turned out to be a shortish burly man, of florid complexion and with a cauliflower nose. His eyes were small and shrewd in mounds of wrinkled flesh; yet the smile was genial and friendly. The air stank of cigarette smoke. A mug of beer stood on the table at his right hand.

'Well?' he queried, when he'd read Freddie's card, "tisn't often a gent like you calls. Look more like Gattis or the "Old Mo" to me. What is it? Wanting a job are you? Professional?'

Freddie gave a short laugh.

'Lord no. I haven't the talent.'

The man frowned.

'What then? Not from the p'lice I hope — no underhand prying and poking?'

'I'm prying on my own account,' Freddie answered quickly, 'and if you can help — give any information, I'll pay you well.'

Lawson paused, sniffed, took a further appraising look at his caller, then asked abruptly, 'What is it? What do you want to know?'

'I'm anxious to find a girl — a very young girl who ran away from home some time ago, and eventually came, I believe, to London, in search of stage work — acting.'

'We get plenty of that kind here,' Lawson told him, 'mostly no use at all. Not a chance in the world. Pretty bits some of 'em, but without an ounce of talent. Could she be that sort?'

'No,' Freddie told him firmly. 'She's — or was — unique in every way; not like any other girl I've ever met—'

The broad face grinned.

'I see. Like that, is it? Turned your head — got a crush on her.'

'Finding her is very important to me,' Freddie said, successfully smothering any sense of anger.

'What's her name?' Lawson turned the pages of a ledger open. 'And what sent you to me?'

'A mutual — acquaintance,' de Marchmont answered. 'Mirabelle. That's all I can tell you.'

'Ah—' the exclamation was profound and long-drawn out. 'Now I understand.'

You don't, Freddie thought, not by a long chalk, but he did not say so.

'Mirabelle now—' the man resumed. 'Yes, of course I know her. We were good friends once. A real beauty. But then—' he broke off adding almost immediately, 'what was the girl's name — the one you want to track down?'

'Jaina. Jaina Lee.'

Lawson thumbed page after page, then with a shrug answered, 'Can't remember having Jaina on my books. What did she look like?'

'Dark-haired, winsome — small and slight with lovely eyes,' Freddie said. 'Quite enchanting really, only of course she could have changed her looks I suppose — to a certain extent — as she did with her name. Yes — of course! she called herself Petal.'

'*Petal!*' the other man's head jerked up abruptly; obviously the name had registered.

'Then why the devil didn't you say so, Mister? Of course I know Petal. Got her her first job. Not because she showed any particular talent, but because I felt kind of sorry for her, and because Mirabelle had sent her.'

Freddie's face became suddenly a hard pale mask of determination. Politeness and his usual air of savoir-faire were swamped by something ruthless — almost threatening — that told Mike Lawson this was no game he had been drawn into — no ordinary involvement of a wealthy man with a taste for young girls.

'Where is she? You tell me now, or I'll have the police—'

'You'll put no police on to me, Mister,' Lawson said with rising belligerence. 'And don't start the threatening lark. I only gave a helping hand to the poor kid, and there's been many a time since, I can tell you — when I've wished I hadn't. Brought a bagful of trouble she has, in one way or another — walked out of shows, insulted sponsors—'

'Sponsors.' The word made Freddie wince. 'What do you mean by that?'

Lawson laughed in de Marchmont's face. 'What do you think? A girl in the theatre game with no one to back her, no talent or experience, has got to have a friend in the background or she'd be out on her ear in no time. So don't try any moralising on me, Mister. Your girlfriend Petal had to find out what real life was — and she's learned all right.' He paused, then added, 'She's survived, and you should be grateful. Not often out of work now — knows how to make the best of herself and show a leg when necessary—'

De Marchmont's right fist rose a few inches, then suddenly the reality of the situation — the overwhelming urgency to see Jaina — drove all anger from him, leaving only a dull ache.

'Where is she?' he repeated.

Lawson went to the desk, fiddled among some papers and ledgers, and finally produced an address.

'She's got a room at the back of Todd's eating place,' he said, scribbling the number on a scrap of paper. 'That's a café at the corner of Lilac Street and Mount Lane. If you go now she may be there. I've got an act planned for her at Dan's tomorrow night. She may be rehearsing now, but you can try.'

'Dan's?'

'A pub, Mister, very popular. Always in need of some flash bit to catch the eye—'

Flash? Jaina? The thought was repulsive.

Freddie crossed the room, and at the door said, 'What do I owe you?'

The man shrugged, gave his price which de Marchmont promptly paid, with a little over.

'Keep the rest,' he said. 'But if I find you've tricked me I'll be back. There'll be trouble then.'

It took him only a few minutes to locate the eating place. It was crowded for the time of day, smelling of fat cooking, tobacco, human bodies and beer, mingled with cheap perfume and a faint aroma of salt and fish. The locality was obviously near docks. Seamen – including foreigners who appeared to be talking in Spanish – were eating voraciously at a corner table. The atmosphere was cosmopolitan, and de Marchmont guessed that a ship had just arrived in port.

He gave Petal's name to a black-haired girl who was serving, and asked exactly where her room was. The girl shrugged, paused for a moment, then answered grudgingly, 'You have to take the corner round Mount Lane, then up an entry. It's number one. But if you like you can go through here and out the back way. Part of our place it is reely, but Nick lets it out.'

'All right,' Freddie told her, 'thanks.'

She indicated a passage at the end of the room, and turned her back on him to join the sailors, leaving de Marchmont to find his own way through the house.

The odorous smell of cooking increased, with waves of steam when he passed the kitchens. A stout woman was frying at a stove, but owing to the continual burble of chatter, and rattle of utensils, appeared not to notice him. Freddie hurried by, found the door leading into the street, and went out. The frail sunlight had now climbed above the mist giving brief sordid clarity to untidy streets bordered by tenements, alleyways, and small huddled beer-shops. The blinds of No 1 were half-drawn. Freddie knocked on the door several times, and when there was no answer pushed his face against the glass and peered inside. It was impossible to discern details through the musty panes, but he was surprised to see flowers on the table, and got the impression that the furnishings were comfortable and far more tasteful than the interior of Todd's.

With a lurching in his stomach and a dull feeling of disappointment that Jaina appeared to be out, he returned to the door and thumped heavily. This time, from the background somewhere, he detected a slight but distant movement.

He waited.

After seconds, which seemed an eternity, there was a creaking, followed by footsteps, and remonstrances from a male voice. Freddie stood rigidly until the outline of a girl's form emerged from the shadows. The door opened. In two long strides Freddie had a foot on the step. Then his senses froze.

Undoubtedly it was Jaina standing before him, but a Jaina he had never seen before, with heavy rings under her eyes — her beautiful features still bearing traces of make-up. A hurried attempt had been made to tidy her hair. She wore a flowered wrap smelling of cheap perfume.

She said nothing at first, neither did he. They both just stared at each other as though searching the past for recognition. Then, suddenly, in clear crystal tones, Jaina said, 'What do you want?'

The abruptness of the question, the apparently callous indifference, charged Freddie with such emotional distress he reached for her hand, gripped it, and said in a rush, 'Oh Jaina! Jaina darling — after all this time, without a word or clue, and you can ask that? It's *you* of course — I want you — Jaina, I've come to take you home—'

For a moment he fancied the glimmer of tears clouded the luminous eyes. Then her lips tightened.

'No. It's no use — go away, Freddie—'

She started to close the door. De Marchmont pushed his foot inside. There were remonstrances from both, then a cultured but shrill male voice, holding nevertheless a faint twang in it, said from near at hand, 'You heard what the lady said — get out.'

Before the latch clanged in his face, Freddie had the impression of a half-naked large figure with a rubicund moustached face glaring. Then only the shabby outside door of No 1 remained — a static motionless barrier to all he'd hoped and searched for during the past months. Or was it years? It seemed in the sterile climax of so much effort and soul searching — an eternity.

He stood for a time irresolute, until the truth fully registered.

Then heavily he made his way back to the place where the cab was waiting. He should have known better than to imagine, or even hope that the childlike ethereal Jaina he had first known could still exist, he told himself honestly, when he reached his hotel room. An innocent young girl without means or protection — what chance could she possibly have had — especially after the first violation — of retaining the pristine quality that had first drawn him to her? Her very vulnerability must have invited desecration of her youth. A dull kind of hatred against Cavannagh rose in him. How could he have bred such an exquisite creature, only to abandon her when she most needed love? Yes — love; tenderness to nurture the subtle awakening of sexual and spiritual flowering?

And yet Jaina had been the first to snap the link between them. The overbearing tea merchant wasn't solely to blame, neither — thought Freddie — was the young girl entirely without guile. He recalled, during wakeful hours that night, the shy look of awareness in those glowing tilted eyes — the half-smile of longing that all unconsciously had first aroused desire in him. In some ways so naive — in others so secretly mature for her years. The fact remained whatever she was, he wanted her. That he could have become so deeply involved was difficult to accept logically, when he recalled the eligible string of attractive young women in his class just waiting to catch his eye. Girls of beauty and breeding, and sufficient brains to fill the role of wife with intelligence and charm. He knew he was acting without any regard for family or tradition. His parents would be shocked at the very idea of serious commitment to a girl of Jaina's background, and not merely because of Cavannagh's reputation, but because of her mother.

'A bastard' Jaina had called herself. Well? What of it? In the past kings and queens had been bred on the wrong side of the blanket. But the blood? That was different. The mysterious quality he'd found so intriguing had roots in unknown foreign genes. The tilted eyes — the pale goldenish skin and tremulous flower lips — her delicate gestures and soft, almost husky voice, that could be so expressive of both joy and sadness — these were qualities quite alien to his own race. An exquisite flower had been uprooted to bloom in foreign soil, and had been forced through lack of understanding and true affection to struggle like an unwanted weed on a scrapheap of vice.

Freddie was amazed at his own capacity for poetic imagery. It was strange, he thought ironically, that Sabrina's desertion should have left him so vulnerable to suffering. With Sabrina he'd have been content. No troublesome emotional problems would have risen to turn his life upside down. He would probably never have met Jaina, and if he had, it would have been a quite-by-chance brief encounter that would have been dismissed and forgotten except as a slightly titillating incident in the social and sporting routine of his normal existence.

Or would it?

Life was a chancy, odd sort of business. A trick of time, a sudden change of mood at a crucial moment − an unexpected gesture, or step in an unintended direction, could set off a whole new pattern in the course of a day's events. But perhaps it was all planned, he thought, with a slight surge of optimism. Perhaps after all, there was some reason, some pattern to explain things.

The snag was that he could hardly expect his parents to accept such argument. He wouldn't have himself, if he hadn't been the one concerned.

Frederick de Marchmont! Cheery, sporting, good-sort Freddie, who'd been born with a golden spoon in his mouth as heir to a vast estate. How his own crowd would gasp and wonder − and no doubt titter − to find him fretting and mooning over a sad-eyed waif of fate who was little more than a schoolgirl.

Well, dammit, he told himself when he managed to jerk himself from introspection, there was no time for mooning anyway. He had to pull himself together, get cracking, and somehow force Jaina from her sordid background even if it meant dragging her by the hair of her head. He hoped it wouldn't come to that but he could deal with her, even if it came to spitting and scratching, and he had a strong right fist with a good punch in it if any blackguard attacked. He didn't think the latter likely. The sort he'd glimpsed in Jaina's room behind her shoulder were generally cowards when it came to a confrontation, and the odds were that the next time he and Jaina met, the odious bull-headed invader wouldn't be there.

Getting facts into some sort of commonsense perspective helped. All through the day Freddie kept himself somehow occupied, idling about the West End, strolling along Cheyne Walk, and taking stock of riders in Hyde Park.

He had dinner in the evening at Brown's, and shortly afterwards set off once more by cab for the public-house named by Mike Lawson, and where, if he was lucky, he'd find Jaina.

The pub, as he'd expected, was a sleazy, raucous, flea-pit of a place, and when he arrived there was already a crowd there — a mixed breed of seafarers, artists, seedy looking working-men and women, and lascivious-eyed 'gents' who'd all gathered, presumably for a glance and maybe more — of 'Princess Petal' in her luscious, titillating state of promising half-nudity. There were coarsely depicted hand-coloured caricatures of her plastered round the walls. Freddie's heart lurched with a sense of revulsion when he saw them. Although so grossly interpreted, the face and figure were unmistakable travesties of Jaina. He had an impulse to protest, to sweep the whole lot of that raucous crowd into the street, to tear the vulgar hoardings down, and put a match to them. Justified arson, that's what it would be, he thought savagely.

Then self-control returned.

He settled himself into a corner with a mug of beer on a sidetable, trying to escape notice or comment from any customers who might be suspicious of a stranger. One half-drunken seaman came and perched himself nearby, gave a nudge and a wink, and muttered, 'Goin' to see somethin' worth looking at tonight. Eh mister? They say she's young. Ripe enough for the taking though — that's what they say. Not that I'm that sort. Got a wife I have, the moral sort—' For a moment his gross face sobered. 'Rum sort of world, ain't it? — When the good 'uns turn out to be such battleaxes, and the wicked little bits can so easily turn a man's head—' He pushed his face close to Freddie's ear and muttered some obscenity that drove de Marchmont to his feet. The man grabbed the mug, settled back to enjoy the half drained contents, while Freddie retreated to the shadows behind the door.

As hilarity grew the atmosphere became more cloying.

Then, quite suddenly the chatter and jokes faded into only a muttered murmuring. The landlord, bartender — whichever it was — had lifted his arm significantly and shouted, 'Now folks, here she is — Princess Petal.'

There were stirrings, coughs, little gasps of anticipation as the door at the back of the tap room opened, revealing a doll-like painted figure wearing a frill of feathers round her waist above a gleam of pale flesh where suspenders stretched enticingly to fish-net stockings. She had a spangled headpiece outlining the dark hair which had been grotesquely frizzed. The lovely eyes were smudged with kohl, the red lips set in a fixed smile. Her hips swayed from side to side as she moved forward on glittering high heeled shoes. Her shoulders were bare. Over her breasts she held a large feathered fan.

Stupefied, Freddie watched.

Despite the cheap make-up, the gaudy attire, and calculated sexual gestures, Freddie, through some strange instinct could glimpse a certain child-like quality — the very essence of which must create either lust or wonder from the audience.

As she slowly, suggestively, wove among the crowd, she paused at intervals, moving ahead quickly each time a male hand touched her thigh. The landlord frowned. She was being stand-offish. 'Mix, girl, mix,' he muttered, not knowing he spoke. He hadn't engaged her just to wander round in a few feathers and pair of pants, without letting them down. She was supposed to have another purpose in her act.

Then, very quietly at first, Jaina started to sing. Nothing like 'Champagne Charlie' or 'Daisy, Daisy', but something of her own — something nostalgically and magically revived from her far-away childhood — telling of rivers and flowers — of far-off pagodas, palaces and lakes — of longings too deep to express fully — tears — anguish, and the pain of loss.

Freddie endured it as long as he could, but when a large male hand tugged the fan from the gently rounded breasts leaving them naked and vulnerable, he sprang forward shouting, 'Jaina, I'm here—' There was a scuffle. He was forced back; two beefy-looking customers held him by the shoulders.

'Get out — gent,' one of them threatened. 'Or you won't recognise yourself when you c'n move agen. Out — you bloody nark.' Freddie's last glimpse of Jaina before being thrown into the street, was of her cold set face staring at him through the blurred crowd. Then the door snapped to, and he realised, bleakly, that he'd done her no good at all by his interruption, only harm. He should have been more subtle and kept his head. God! what was to happen now? There was no way he could contact her in that place. He'd have to wait until she left, and it wouldn't be by the front door. The back probably, and he'd first have to locate the street leading to it.

He smoothed his hair, straightened his tie, and started off immediately. The route wasn't hard to find, winding down a narrow street that took an abrupt turn at the end, changing gradually into more of a wide alley than a thoroughfare. Small buildings were hunched between taller tenements. A thin wheezy-looking old drunk with a bottle to his lips lurched from side to side of the cobbled byway, and bumped into de Marchmont as he passed. The bottle fell and shattered. There were curses, and for a second, under the lamplight, Freddie glimpsed a vacant face with a draggled beard and red-rimmed eyes staring up at him. The smell of methylated spirit mingled with gin was strong as the pathetic creature passed, tumbled to the ground, and somehow managed to pick himself up again. Freddie checked an impulse to help, shuddering inwardly. So this filthy area was where Jaina had landed herself! The realisation hit him with renewed disgust. From down the street came the strident notes of a woman's shrill laughter and a man's shout. There was rowdy singing in the distance. A window shot up, and a female voice rang stridently through the blurred air, laden with obscenities.

Here and there lights from windows sprinkled the darkness. But the main impression to Freddie's heightened senses was of furtive watchful evil — lurking like some monstrous furry creature, from every angle and corner greedy for prey.

'Tommy rot!' he said aloud, to fortify his courage. He went on, found the door to the public house, and huddled himself into the shadows of a recess. Faintly from the front of the building, the singing continued, accompanied by the echo of stamping and thumping of feet. There were intermittent pauses that gradually after a considerable time died into a longer silence. Freddie glanced at his watch and guessed it must be closing time. Or time, at least, for Jaina's act to end. Would she be alone? Or in company? If the latter he knew what kind, and prepared himself for a scene. So he kept alert, and waited.

At last there was a muted murmuring, and remonstrance from somewhere inside, followed by the hurried soft tap of footsteps approaching the door.

With heightened excitement, Freddie, a perfectly motionless shadow against all the other shadows of the night, still stood, rigidly watching.

The crack between door and wall opened, throwing a stream of wan light across the pavement. A figure with a dark cape pulled round her body, plunged into the street and hurried, head thrust forward, towards the corner. Freddie, in a moment, had caught up with her, placed both hands on her shoulders, and forced her face up to his. The soft black hair was tumbled over her forehead. Signs of paint still mottled her skin garishly. But her eyes — smudged dark with kohl — were unmistakable. Jaina's eyes.

'Oh Jaina—' he said, almost whispering her name, '— my love — my darling child—'

She pulled herself away.

'Leave me alone. I don't want you. I said so, didn't I? Go away.'

In spite of the defiance her voice was terrified.

He could sense the stiffening of her body. Knew she wasn't aware of what she said.

He caught her again, and put his arm round her waist. 'Look, Jaina,' he urged. 'I'm here to help, that's all. I'm your friend—'

She shook her head.

'No.'

'Yes,' he insisted firmly. 'And we've got to talk. Oh Lord!' He wiped the sweat from his forehead, and forced himself to continue firmly, 'Isn't there anywhere we can go, to be alone for a bit? Your room? Or will—'

'No. Not there, not ever there.' She started to shake.

'Very well then, some small café where we can be quiet and talk — we can't stay here, Jaina — any of your — acquaintances—' his tones became bitter '—might come upon us, and I've already played Sir Galahad sufficiently on your behalf not to want any more trouble—'

The touch of wry humour must have penetrated. After a

pause she said, 'All right. There's Ferrati's over the road there. It hasn't a bar, so—'

Without further argument he accompanied her over the cobbles to a small secret-looking place, low-roofed with only a suggestion of habitation from a light behind yellow curtains. It was set back between two narrow tall tenements, and appeared to Freddie to be already closed.

But when he pushed the door it opened.

On the left of the narrow hall a woman, stout and Italian-looking, was carrying a tray from the deserted eating room. She cast one grim look at them as they entered, then said sharply, 'We were just closing. What is it you want?'

'Coffee — black, and sandwiches,' Freddie answered promptly. 'Anything that's easiest for you. I'm sorry to worry you at this hour.'

'Hm!' Mollified by his manner, she agreed, 'Very well, just so long as — you're not on the run or anything are you? We have to be careful these times.'

When Freddie had reassured her, she retreated, leaving Jaina and himself together.

It was a sordid room, badly lit, with still the smell of food hanging about. But Freddie hardly noticed. His eyes were riveted on Jaina's face.

After they'd seated themselves at a small table with a none-too-clean cloth on it, he pushed the cape from her head, took out a clean handkerchief, and handed it to her. She shook her head. 'Leave me alone. I'm all right.'

'No, you're not.' His hand very gently wiped a smudge of rouge from one cheek, and drew the soft fabric over the painted lips. Then he took a comb from his pocket, handed it to her and said, 'Tidy your hair, darling. I want to see your forehead.'

'Why?'

'Because I love you, Jaina. You should know that by now.'

'*Me?*' she laughed. 'Don't be so potty, so soft. Do you know what I am?'

'Yes.' The word came out suddenly. 'But the present doesn't matter. I love you, Jaina. And you've felt the same, haven't you? All this time. Don't lie to me—'

'I'm not lying.' She spoke dully. 'I was a child then. But I'm not any more. I'm nearly sixteen, and things have happened—'

Her face paled, her expression was fierce, condemning. After a pause she continued, 'Because of *you*, Freddie. You did this to me, do you see?' She pulled the cape aside with one quick gesture, revealing the naked breasts above the cheap feathered finery. 'If you hadn't threatened to tell Uncle Oliver and send me back to Carnack I wouldn't be like this. You could have kept me in Plymouth and looked after me. That's what I wanted — I *dreamed* of you, of being with you for always. But of course that was just stupid, because you never wanted me at all — except to make me a prisoner again. So I hate you now. *Hate* — do you understand?'

His stricken face betrayed his own shock, but she didn't see.

'It's too late,' she said, suddenly drawing the cape round her again and getting up, 'Go home, Freddie de Marchmont. Go back where you belong. You're nothing to me now, just nothing. Believe it, will you?'

'No.'

'You fool!' The contempt on her lips stunned him. He did not see the sudden rush of tears to her eyes, or trembling of the lips — was aware only of the blazing eyes — that a woman, indeed, stood confronting him, where before had been a defeated disillusioned girl.

She made an abrupt movement, and before he completely realised her intention, she had run from the room, almost colliding with the Italian proprietress who was bringing the food. The woman remonstrated; Freddie haphazardly threw a couple of sovereigns from his pocket, and raced off after Jaina.

Having to locate her retreating figure took moments of precious time. When at last he saw her cutting down an alley on the other side of the road, he made a dash across but was not quick enough.

The sound of an approaching cab had not registered. Horses' hooves caught him. There was a shout from the cabby, screams from a nearby witness, followed by a grating sound, and Freddie's body rolling into the gutter.

Jaina, hearing the commotion, turned back. She ran forward, but the quickly-gathered crowd ushered her away. Helplessly she stood watching while strong arms lifted him and carried him to a nearby tavern. She protested and screamed, and tried to enter the building but it was as though she didn't exist.

Presently the police arrived. Jaina watched numbly as Freddie's body was put into a van and taken away.

Her eyes and throat were choked with tears.

All she wanted at that moment, was to die.

18

For the rest of that night, Jaina, fearful and terrified, wondering if Freddie was dead or alive, wandered the streets. At last, unable to bear the tension and anxiety any longer, she found a police station and went in to enquire.

'Freddie?' she asked the sergeant at the desk. 'Mr de Marchmont? Is he going to be all right? Tell me — please *tell* me—'

Something about her, the urgency in her eyes which appeared enormous under the wan flare of gas-light, her youth, and above all, the genuine distress betrayed by every gesture, every word she uttered, impressed and moved him strangely.

'You mean the gent who was knocked down in that accident earlier on?'

She nodded wildly. 'Yes, yes—'

'Who are you?' the uniformed man said. 'What's your name? Did you know him?'

'He was a — a friend,' Jaina answered. 'I was with him when it happened. At least—' she broke off with a wretched feeling of futility sweeping over her.

The sergeant paused, and as he stared at her she unwittingly allowed the top of the tightly clutched cloak to ease at the neck, displaying a glimmer of pale skin above the tawdry spangles. The hem also parted slightly, and in one quick glance he glimpsed a suggestion of the cheap finery beneath the dark cloth.

'How well did you know the man?' The official tones had hardened perceptibly. 'And what did you say his name was? We looked everywhere on him, there wasn't a card, clue, or even a wallet — taken probably in a punch-up. Now try and think, girl. It's important we know because of getting hold of his family — if he has any.'

'Is he alive?' Jaina demanded, hardly daring to breathe. 'Just say where he is, please, please. And then—' she half choked, '—it won't matter any more, I'll tell you anything, everything. So long as—'

'Very well.' Somehow he believed her. 'He's going to be all right as far as we can tell — cuts and bruises, a broken rib probably where he hit the kerb. Wonder he wasn't killed, though. He was lucky.' He turned his keen eyes upon her, probingly. 'And now it's your turn. His name if you don't mind, and speak clear please. This is official.'

'De Marchmont. Freddie — Frederick. His father's Lord de Marchmont.'

The man stared.

'Is that true? Or are you trying one on me? I don't advise it—'

She shook her head vigorously.

'No, no, it's true. He was looking for me you see, because I — I — they didn't want me to be an actress, so I ran away. I—' she was suddenly aware of her surroundings, and felt a smothering sense of claustrophobia enfolding her.

The sergeant peered more closely at her.

'Good God!' he muttered. 'So you're the one—'

'What?'

He cocked a thumb towards a wall behind him, stared hard at it, while Jaina, with a shock that registered even through her fear, anxiety and exhaustion, recognised a placard bearing her photograph pinned up among other notices. She turned to run away, but this time there was no escape. The strong uniformed figure had darted back and held her firmly by both arms. Before she could quite take things in, he was ushering her into a small room at the back of the office. A fire was glowing there, and a second blue-clad figure — 'a bobby' — was brewing tea in a pot.

'You'll be all right here — Miss,' she heard her captor saying. 'Everything you want'll be brought to you until we can get hold of your — uncle. There's a wash-place here, food, and we'll find something better to cover you with than those fancy bits and pieces. But don't you go trying to hop it any more. Look after her, Alf. I'm off to the hospital to tell them what I know about the gentleman.'

The door shut with a snap.

The younger policeman drew a chair up to the fire, and told Jaina to sit there. She made no effort to resist. She felt numbed; once more a prisoner. Her surroundings made no real impact. She was so tired, so suddenly exhausted it was a relief just to sit back and try and forget everything — all the terrors and strain of the past months — the bawdiness and greedy hands, the lusts and laughter, and loathsome company. Above all — the longing — the longing beneath everything else for Freddie. If he'd died — she shivered. But Freddie wasn't dead after all. Freddie would go back to his family, and she would land up again at Carnack if Uncle Oliver ever wanted her back again. He might not. He might send her straight to that strict seminary place he'd threatened her with before. She smiled to herself bitterly. It would be stupid if he did, because nothing could erase what she'd experienced. Nothing could give her back her girlhood or make her good again.

There was something wicked in her. Something that went along with being a bastard.

The young constable handed a cup of steaming tea to her. The expression on her face disturbed him.

'What are you thinking about?' he asked solicitously. 'You must try and forget the accident now. Everything will be all right.'

She shook her head.

'It can't be. Nothing can be all right again. And don't look at me like that. I hate men.'

He was shaken by her sudden vituperation.

'You've been unfortunate, I expect,' he said. 'Most of us go through something unpleasant when we're young. It all passes in time.' He paused, then added, 'What's your name?'

'Jaina.'

'And the rest? Oh well, I can look it up—'

'You needn't bother. Uncle Oliver calls me Jaina Lee. But I'm not sure. You see, I'm a bastard. And bastards don't have proper names do they?'

Her companion laughed.

'Everyone has a name. And I like the sound of Jaina.'

'They called me Petal at that place.'

'What place?'

She stared him very straight in the eyes. Something cold and disillusioned far older than her years chilled him.

'A brothel,' she said. 'That's what it was. I didn't know at the beginning, but I did afterwards.'

'After what?'

'I was raped,' Jaina said in cold clear tones.

For a few seconds there was no sound in the room but the steady tick-tocking of the clock. Then the constable said, 'What were you doing there?'

'I was running away from home, because my guardian wanted to shut me up in a prison-school. I didn't know what sort of place Madam's was — I heard someone call it that — a brothel I mean — after it happened. Then I ran away from Freddie—'

'Hm! you seem to've got into quite a habit of running away, don't you? What was the name of the whore-house?'

Jaina thought quickly. The last thing she wanted was to get Mirabelle into trouble.

'I don't remember,' she lied. 'It was in Plymouth somewhere, or Bristol — I'm not sure. I just got a ride in a cart to Bodmin, and got on a train, and then all the rest happened — going to London — the dancing and singing in those places, and Freddie being knocked down. He will be all right, won't he?'

'Of course he will. He'll be fit and ready to see you in no time.'

Jaina shook her head.

'I shall never see him again if I can help it.'

'But I thought you were friends.'

Her strange eyes momentarily softened. Tenderness, affection, complete devotion, transfigured her once more by unsullied compassion; he saw no longer the wayward girl, but a young woman torn by her own overwhelming desires, yet at the same time ruthlessly determined to deny them.

'We were never just friends — not really,' she told him, in soft low tones. 'I always loved him, from the very beginning. And if things had been different, perhaps—' She hesitated then continued, reflectively '—but it's no use now. It's all spoiled. Me too. I shall probably be a nun. That's what Uncle Oliver will want now. Well — nuns are kinder than men, anyway—'

Her voice trailed off; and that last remark, the constable thought, was the saddest he'd heard from any girl in all his twenty-eight years of living.

'I'm sure they're very good women,' he managed to say after a pause, 'but cheer up, I can't see you shut up in that sort of place for the rest of your life. You'll get over this and have fun like other young girls when you've got over this mess.'

'No — I don't think so—'

Her tones were dreamier. He bent down and took a further hard look at her face. The lids of her eyes were half closed. She was at last, after the long ordeal, falling asleep.

He placed a rug gently over her slim legs.

Presently her head nodded.

Once or twice he fancied her lips moved, but her thoughts were very far away — she was drifting along in a cool stream, with the glint of butterflies' blue wings above her head. The water lapped against her body gently. There was the sound of music — tinkly music — in the distance, and the pale pink buds of water lilies brushed her softly as she passed. The air was fragrant with the scent of flowers, and soft lips touched her cheek, soft perfumed lips that far, far away in infancy had meant security, peace, and infinite love. The love of a mother.

Then the vision passed, and she was taken into a comforting well of darkness where she remained for some hours. Later, when she woke, she had to undergo the undignified procedure of being examined by a doctor. His verdict was concise and down to earth. There was nothing physically wrong with the young woman, except exhaustion and a certain amount of undernourishment. She could have been abused in the past, but was perfectly healthy.

So that was that.

Until Oliver's eventual arrival to collect her, she remained mutinously silent.

Nothing, for the time being, seemed to matter to her, any more.

19

'What are we going to do with her?' Oliver asked Lisette, after his return with Jaina to Carnack. 'She talks of becoming a nun — that was all I could get out of her. Not a word of apology — even during the train journey back. She just sat very stiffly and said I needn't worry any more. It was best to shut her away — she'd go back to the convent and stay there.'

'Oh dear.'

'Ridiculous. Can you imagine it?'

'No, Oliver. And I can't even believe they'd accept her. From what you say, she's led a very dubious existence in London. And if you take my advice you won't question her too closely. What you're not told you don't know. I really do think—'

'Yes?'

'You should allow me to contact someone, one of my old theatre friends. Having her at Carnack would be a great mistake. And—' Her vague eyes suddenly bright with condemnation slipped to her son's. 'Something's happened to her you know. I'm sure — I feel it here, Oliver.' She tapped her breast. 'Something, as her father, you should have managed to avert.'

'What the devil are you suggesting?'

Lisette's lips tightened. 'The nicest way of putting it, at least with gentlefolk is, I believe, a life of ill-repute.' She placed a cigarette into her long jade holder and allowed Oliver to light it for her. During the short interlude his complexion had darkened. Both hands were clenched at his sides.

'What do you mean? A fifteen-year-old child? It's—'

'She's sixteen. Really!' A gasp of derision escaped her, accompanied by a short cough. 'For a worldly, go-ahead businessman, with a series of amours behind you, you sound quite absurd. Oliver. Of course I wouldn't want to prove it — it would do no good; and I don't believe for one moment that Jaina will ever confide in us. The only one who might have a single clue is obviously Freddie de Marchmont, and I wouldn't advise questioning him.'

'Why not? Why the hell not?'

'Because if he was going to speak out, he'd have done it before — I think in some way he may be shielding Jaina.'

'Shielding her? That blackguard? If what you say is right, then he's the one responsible, and I'll see he smarts for it when he's fit enough.'

'Don't be a fool.'

Oliver stared at her, 'A fool? You expect me to accept your insinuations and do nothing about it?'

Lisette turned languidly away and seated herself against the cushions of the chaise-longue. 'I expect you to do what you've always done in a crisis, Oliver — take yourself off somewhere to France, or your Torquay project, and allow matters to simmer down for a bit. Whatever the rights and wrongs of this — this upheaval — Jaina's tired and needs rest. She'd certainly be better off without you. In the meantime she may learn to trust me again. I only wish Sabrina was here. I'm far too exhausted these days to face crisis after crisis without feeling some effect.'

'You'll manage, Mater,' he said drily. 'You're as strong as a horse beneath all the sighs and vapours. Now,' he held up a hand, took one quick stride towards her, bent and kissed her soft perfumed cheek, 'no frowns. You're quite a remarkable woman and well you know it, so don't try and fool me. What you suggest is probably commonsense. I'll leave tomorrow, when I'm sure Jaina's prepared to behave for a bit. Gossip will spread, of course. Give old Frayle no end of a kick won't it?' A hint of regret for his lost pipe-dream of political backing from that quarter soured him momentarily, then he shrugged it off with the comforting thought that, after all, the seat might still fall to the Tories when the time came. The months leading up to next year's election gave ample time for some trick to be played by the government. The mood of a country could change overnight. Better be on no side at all than to emerge as a loser. In any case he had more than a normal amount of business to attend to. Constructing, planning, manipulating circumstance always with an eye to the future — one step ahead of other men — this was his forte, and always had been. The de Marchmonts and Penderricks were small fry when it came to the area of power building. One day he'd have them all eating out of his palm when he felt like it — even that defiant young madam of a wife of his who needed a lesson if ever anyone ever did.

His blood boiled at the memory of her. Her haughty stare, insolent manner and cool way of walking out just when it suited her.

One day he'd teach her who was master and which side her bread was buttered, although heaven alone knew at that moment just how he'd accomplish it. In the meantime his mother was right. He'd get out of Carnack for a time, and cool his heels where he wasn't constantly reminded either of Sabrina, or his daughter's misdeeds.

He left the following morning, and was away for three weeks.

During that time Freddie was sufficiently recovered to return home.

His mother, who knew little of the truth — only that he had gone to town and had had an accident through recognising and trying to capture that wayward Cavannagh girl, was all sympathy and soft reproaches, mingled with tearful relief that he had escaped with such comparatively minor injuries when he could so easily have been killed.

His father was more perceptive.

He knew his son well, and sensed intuitively that something of Freddie's spirit, more than physical pains and bruises, was injured.

'Look here, son,' he said when they were together in the library following dinner one evening, the first time since the accident that Freddie had felt like taking a meal downstairs, 'what's on your mind? Out with it. You're brooding. And it's not only that sordid London business. Come on now, I was young myself once. What's fretting you? A girl, isn't it?'

'Very much a girl,' Freddie admitted.

'Well then?' The shrewd grey eyes under the older man's bushy brows stared keenly, unswervingly, into the anxious blue ones. 'In trouble, is she? A bit of a game gone further than it should?'

'She's in trouble,' Freddie answered, 'but not the kind you mean.'

'Ah!' there was a sigh of relief. 'That's something?'

When no reaction came to the remark, Lord de Marchmont

casually picked up his pipe, lit it, and continued, 'You're not referring by any chance to that young runaway are you? Cavannagh's ward — or whatever he likes to call her? Worrying over her kind is futile. You've done enough for her already, and more than she deserves. Wants a good spanking if you ask me. How you met in the first place beats me. What the devil got into you, Freddie?' De Marchmont broke off, shaking his head.

Freddie paused before delivering his bomb-shell.

'I'm going to marry her, Father.'

The silence between them following the short statement was electrified. Every small sound was intensified — the ticking of the grandfather clock in the corner, occasional spitting of a log, and the solitary crying of a bird as it passed the window.

Then, at last words came.

'*Marry?* Say that again will you? No — don't. I don't want to hear. You can't mean it. You're still shocked. Your head must've cracked harder than they said.' The old man got up, poured two stiff brandies, handed one to Freddie and kept the other for himself.

Freddie said nothing.

'Well?' The sharp voice became imperious, commanding, although anxiety underlay the irate tones. 'You're joking of course.'

Freddie gulped the brandy. It steadied him, enabling him to answer firmly, 'No I'm not. I'm sorry Jaina isn't your idea of a wife for me. I couldn't have expected it. And we shall try for Cavannagh's permission, of course. If we don't get it I shall marry her without it.'

'Cavannagh! — that — that jumped-up tea trader! And you a de Marchmont. *My heir!* Have you thought of that? And they say the girl's a—'

'Bastard. Cavannagh's, yes, so I've heard. It makes no difference.'

'But she's barely sixteen. A schoolgirl — a child.'

'If you knew what she'd been through you'd hardly call her that.'

'I won't have it!' His Lordship drew himself up rigidly, fleetingly in the manner of his military days. 'And with dubious blood in her too—' He broke off, and continued after an outraged pause, 'You should've had a stable career as I wanted when you left Oxford. But your mother thought differently, and I was soft with her. It's not too late though. Not for you to learn a bit of sense. If you go ahead with this tom-fool notion, Freddie — I'll — I'll damn well disinherit you—' De Marchmont drew a hand over his forehead wearily, and began again, 'For God's sake, boy—'

Freddie stood up. 'Do you mind, Father, I'm tired.' He went to the door, but before leaving he turned and said, 'I'm sorry, sir, for causing you any distress. I hope — very much — that when you've thought about things they won't appear quite so bad. If you meant what you said — about disinheriting me, I shall have to face it. I won't like it, I'm fond of my home, and you and mother. But Jaina comes first now. She has to—'

'And what about her? Does she know? Does she realise the first thing about tradition and background, and what she'd be taking on? Of course she doesn't. How could she — even if we approved. A child — Freddie—'

'Just a few months younger than mother was when you married her I believe—' A sense of physical weakness suddenly overcame the younger man. Sweat streamed from his forehead and the back of his head, drenching his neck and whole of his body in cold chilling waves. He steadied himself by gripping the door knob. Noticing his pallor, Lord de Marchmont stepped forward smartly and took his arm. Freddie winced from a sharp stab of pain cutting through his ribs. The old man grunted.

'Hurts, does it? Calm down, boy. Calm down. Forget all this. We can talk later. As for disinheriting you — balderdash! Couldn't, and well you know it. Wouldn't anyway.'

Freddie managed a smile. 'I'm not sure of anything any more,' he said, 'except Jaina.'

'You may see things differently tomorrow,' the old man said with enforced optimism. 'Anyway you've time for thought.'

'We all have,' Freddie emphasised.

'Hm!'

His Lordship's reflections were at a low ebb indeed as he watched his only son walk slowly upstairs, touching the bannisters every few steps to ease the effort.

At the curve, under the blueish gleam of a high stained glass Gothic window, Freddie's form appeared drooped and saddened; but when he lifted his face towards the landing above, the bone structure was suddenly emphasised. At the top of the stairs light glowed brilliantly from an electric bulb held by the outstretched hand of a marble Aphrodite. Freddie's set stubborn features were clarified briefly, bearing an astonishing likeness to a framed ancient portrait of some bygone de Marchmont hanging on the wall. He had been known as 'Do-or-die Marchmont' during his life and had fought several wars, earning the family title in Tudor times.

For those few moments Freddie's jaw had the same thrust. His profile was almost identical.

Watching him, his father doubted that he would ever give in. The knowledge stunned him at first, then gradually stirred a grudging admiration. He'd always known the boy to be a good sort, keen manager of the estate, with the jovial knack of getting on with the right crowd. He, his father, had never bothered much about what went on in his son's head beneath the general air of sporty bonhomie.

Now, suddenly, he was aware of surprising and rather disturbing potentials.

And Louisa? His wife?

Should he broach the subject or should he keep mum? To stave things off for a bit would be far easier, he told himself glumly. On the other hand Louisa, in spite of her cheerful fussing qualities, had a sixth sense where her only son and child was concerned. She'd be watching and probing if he gave her the slightest cause for disquiet. So in all, he decided, he'd perhaps better prepare her.

The preparation process proved to be more upsetting than he'd anticipated. For once, instead of tears, vapours, and sessions with her smelling salts, Louisa turned into a furious, forthright battling Boadicea.

'I will not have it,' she stated, with indignation ruffling the feathers and beads at her breast to those of some outraged highly coloured mother-bird. 'Neither will you. As you know, I'm not a vindictive woman, I try always to understand and make allowances for the mistakes of others. But Freddie and that girl! Why she's been a − a prostitute or as good as. Imagine it − a life like that, and at her age. It's quite disgusting. I pitied her at first, because everyone knows the Cavannagh man's a savage tyrant, grinding everyone else down when he can for his own ends. I blamed him for his — his bastard's downfall, and although I didn't approve, I admired Freddie for sticking up for her. But to suggest there could be anything between them is — is nothing more than desecration! An insult to our family honour.' She broke off, panting.

Her husband attempted to placate her, but she drew away, shuddering.

'No. I'll never countenance it, never.'

Eventually, after further attempts to soften the situation, his Lordship, realising there was nothing he could do, gave up, and retired to the conservatory. By then Louisa's emotions had got the better of her, and she was crying. Let her sob and storm a bit more, her husband thought philosophically; a little later he'd return and put forward a further suggestion.

The girl! He hadn't really contemplated her views on the matter at all. Did she want to marry Freddie? Of course she'd be a fool if she didn't, but she was obviously the type who wanted colour and excitement in her life, even though she'd appeared a quiet little thing from the few glimpses he'd had of her. And Freddie wasn't one for the bright lights. He was a country lover. Would she ever settle for that? Especially if rumour was true concerning her carryings-on in town.

Maybe she could be induced to see sense, tackled the right way.

Money? But then Cavannagh could so easily put a spoke in there; he could outbid him ten times over. Still, there might be another way.

So the conjecturing continued, while Oliver, preoccupied with further startling ideas for the Torquay project, managed to shut Jaina completely from his mind.

Lisette, at first, went out of her way to brighten Jaina up, trying to stimulate her by talk of new clothes, and suggestions for the future. Knowing that Oliver would disapprove, she nevertheless inferred that if, when a few months had passed Jaina was still anxious to follow the acting profession, she might be able to give her one or two useful introductions.

'Not music hall,' Lisette added quickly,' the *real professional* theatre.'

Jaina merely replied unsmilingly that she wasn't interested in the stage.

Lisette raised her elegant eyebrows disapprovingly.

'But you said you were, my dear.'

'I'm going to be a nun.'

Lisette felt irritation deepening.

'I doubt it. I don't think for a moment they'd accept you. Sins of the flesh are regarded very seriously by those holy women.'

In spite of herself, sarcasm sharpened her voice.

Jaina stiffened, jerking her head defiantly upwards.

'What do you mean? I didn't do anything, not at first anyway. It was that awful man. Besides I could confess and be clean again.' She paused, adding pathetically after a moment, 'Couldn't I?'

Lisette softened.

'Those are mere words, child. Things happen in life that can't be eradicated. We all change from day to day. Anyway it would be very dull if we didn't. I'm not trying to get you to tell me things you don't want to – I was no saint myself when I was young. But you have got to stop moping. When your uncle—'

'My father,' Jaina interrupted bitterly. 'I think I've always known that.'

'Yes – well – when he returns he'll expect you to behave reasonably and fit in with one or other of his suggestions. It's on the cards – providing you don't get into a tantrum and upset him – that he'll suggest a finishing school—'

'You mean the seminary?' Jaina's voice was fierce, her hands clenched.

Lisette waved a glittering ringed hand in negation. How stupid, Jaina thought, for a woman of her age to be so vain. No diamonds or wealth in the world could make her young again. However richly she dressed she was old. Too old to understand about love, because she couldn't possibly feel it any more – not Jaina's kind of love for Freddie, and the terrible longing she still had deep down, behind all her pretences and lies – for him suddenly to appear again. The mere memory of him, of his whimsical smile that brought the tired laughter lines to the corners of his blue eyes was acute pain – such an ache it became the next moment almost hatred.

Oh Freddie, Freddie.

She bit her lip, and turned away as Lisette said rather loudly, 'No. Not the seminary. Finishing school perhaps. What about that? Somewhere right away from here, in France perhaps, or Switzerland. I think I could talk him round.'

'Don't bother,' Jaina said. 'I don't want to be finished — they do that to marry girls off, don't they? And I wouldn't marry anyone — ever, except Freddie.'

Lisette's eyes widened.

'Frederick de Marchmont? Do you mean it was he who—'

Jaina wheeled round, with her tilted eyes blazing in a white face. 'No it wasn't. And don't ever think that — don't ever dare suggest it. Freddie's good, and kind — and — and gentle. But if he'd wanted me enough I'd have let him have every bit of me — every tiny bit. I was longing for him — *longing*, do you understand, Aunt Lisette — Grandmother?' Her voice had become shrill. 'I'm not a child. I know what passion is — a dirty beastly thing unless you're really in love, and I had it first the horrible way. If it had been Freddie—' The shimmer of bright tears blurred her sight. 'It would have been all right. The pain wouldn't have mattered. But it wasn't Freddie. And that's why it never can be now. I suppose I'm what you'd call second-rate — second-hand. A bastard as well. So you see, if it can be arranged I'd be better with the nuns.'

Lisette, shocked at first, was stirred by a strange uncharacteristic compassion, followed by a rising tide of anger against Oliver. This waif, this child of his — to have had to struggle misunderstood through an adolescence bereft of the affection so necessary for normal development. Unwanted. A bastard! How often had the taunt secretly shamed and driven her into her shell?

'Don't be so upset, dear,' she managed to say after a pause. 'We won't talk about it any more. Everything will work out in the end, I'm sure, and when you see Freddie again—' Oh dear! how hopeless words were. And what use was there in offering any false hopes where the de Marchmonts were concerned? However infatuated the young man was with Jaina, they could share no future together. It just wouldn't be allowed. She was wondering how to conclude her unsatisfactory attempt at comfort, when Jaina interrupted. 'I shan't see him again.'

'You don't know that. He's still recovering from shock and injuries. Later he may call.'

'No. If he wanted anything to do with me he'd have written.

And anyhow, it wouldn't have made any difference. Nothing could now. I'm not going to disgrace him, or feel I've always got to feel a sinner, and humble, and in the wrong. I shall lead my own life—'

'You're not twenty-one yet. You'll have to fit in with your father somehow, Jaina—'

Jaina shrugged, sighed, and said in the manner of a completely composed adult, 'We shall see. Thank you, for trying to be kind.'

She moved slowly to the door.

'Where are you going now?'

'For a walk,' Jaina answered.

'Where?'

'Does it matter? I just want some fresh air. Have no fear — I shan't run away again.'

Knowing remonstrance would be of no use Lisette grudgingly watched the girl leave the room, then, resignedly, with a sudden feeling of relief poured herself a madeira, and settled herself on to the chaise-longue for a rest and recuperation from the emotional interlude with her grand-daughter.

20

Sunlight glittered gold from the west when Jaina made her way past the stables up the hill towards the moors. She walked mechanically, as though in a dream — with only one desire — to be alone and at peace for a time with the autumn scents rich and earthy round her, and the brush of air soft on her cheeks. Physically she was stronger, but her brain was tired and bemused. So much had happened; so much to shock and bewilder her. But here, with only the faint brittle crunch of withered bracken and the sleepy chortle of a bird as she passed, she felt able to relax properly for the first time since her flight from Carnack those months — years ago.

How long? She couldn't count, and didn't care. Nothing

mattered any more. Just for the present she was able to forget everything, lost in the dream that was beyond time — beyond even memory of Freddie, except as a haunting image at the far recesses of her mind.

The air freshened as she climbed. The soft stirrings of a gentle rising breeze fanned her forehead, lifting the dark strands of hair like gossamer from her face.

As she approached the copse bordering the pool, a few last leaves drifted from the lean interlaced branches of the trees. Shadows moved delicately and fitfully among the ancient boulders and standing stones. She paused once, turned and glanced back towards the glitter of sea along the far horizon; then she went on again, until the shimmering surface of the pool gleamed bright below the lane above. As she drew nearer, the graceful slender shape of a fox streaked down the hillside, lit briefly to rich gold before its burnished shape was taken into the shadows.

Something melted in Jaina's heart. 'How lovely,' she thought, 'how lovely to be here without anyone at all, just the quietness and the wild things, and the gorse still flowering. And a butterfly too. I thought the butterflies had all gone.' She lifted a hand as a small blue-winged creature fluttered and rested there for a moment. Then it had flown away again, and it was as though, for a second, it took a little of the afternoon's beauty with it.

Jaina pushed a clump of elder aside, and moved slowly, almost tip-toeing to the pool.

She sat down on a bank, watching the transient light dapple its surface. Mostly the pattern was of silver and gold and deepest jade and russet. But when a frog jumped, or a bird rose suddenly from the undergrowth causing a flurry of air, a hundred rainbow droplets seemed to quiver and ripple in a spreading living circle of pale fire.

Jaina was entranced. It was like discovering a whole new world — yet a world of the past; of being born again. Perhaps after all, it was possible to be made new. This might be the truth, and the other dark things she'd pushed away just a silly nightmare that would never return.

She drew her knees up, and sat watching, still as a statue, with her hands clasped together.

And then, with slow lurching sense of fear — a tensing of her muscles and nerves, she saw it.

A shadowed reflection of a form in the water. A quivering dark shape that blotted out the sun and became gradually clearer and larger, looming menacingly, through weed and the quivering shadows of overhanging branches. She dared hardly breathe. She wanted to scream, but no sound came. The shape paused; and she saw its face — a man's face with fiery glowing eyes half hidden by tangled leaves.

The breath seemed to leave her body. She felt the earth shudder beneath her. She opened her mouth uselessly. A hand came upwards from the water — pale, quivering, with immense clawing fingers; a giant's hand.

The world dimmed a little; from somewhere nearby she heard a kind of gurgle — a muffled shout. Jaina's tensed fingers clutched the undergrowth briefly, before everything slipped from light and shade and dancing terror, into blankness and dark. For a moment or two there was a complete silence; then the cool swimming surface of the pool enclosed her, and she knew no more.

Lucas paused only seconds before striding into the water after the tumbled figure of the girl. He managed to grasp her before she went down, and he cursed inwardly as the chill crept upwards, encircling his neck, just under the chin. His first reaction of anger turned to fear and concern when he got her to the bank. She looked so sick, almost dead, with her eyes closed and her skin such a strange colour — greenish white with her hair drenched and streaming like a black shroud over her shoulders.

He shuddered. What would've happened if he hadn't been there? And what had scared her? She must've been scared to go like that? Perhaps she hadn't heard him come along? Maybe she'd seen his reflection and thought he'd come to molest her. As if he'd touch her! He'd liked and respected what he'd seen of her. Anyway he'd never have any truck with a Cavannagh.

Ideas raced through his mind, but only fleetingly.

He got into action quickly, slapping her face and back, sitting her up and shaking her.

'Come on now—' he said, 'you're all right — wake up. What's the matter?'

He paused for a second breathlessly, wondering if she'd had a fit or something. He was about to pick her up in his arms again and carry her to Carnack, when her eyes opened slowly. A little colour returned to her cheeks, but her expression was puzzled and vague. Just as though she was searching for something that wasn't there — something that worried him, because it wasn't real.

Then she spoke, very softly, looking beyond him through the trees.

'Freddie—' Only a whisper, but poignant somehow, scared and lost like a wild thing in search of sanctuary.

His brilliant eyes changed, became velvet-like, gentle with understanding.

'Come along, *dordi*,' he urged, unconsciously using an old Romany word from his youth, 'everything will be all right, Lucas knows, an' I'm telling you. I'll carry you shall I, small one? — Why—' as he lifted her up, 'light as a feather you are — a pretty swan's feather — there's a song I knowed when I was a young 'un — about a milk-white swan carryin' a young queen down the river to a strange land. Like this it went—' and he started singing strange words in a low voice that told of mountains, lakes and far-away magic countries where nights were perfumed with flowers more brilliant than any stars, and streams gushed honey-gold through violet dells.

Jaina did not resist but lay in his strong arms, lulled to dreamlike peace by his voice and body's warmth.

When they reached the house she was asleep.

Lisette was upstairs when Lucas carried Jaina into the hall. There was hurried conversation between servants, the opening and shutting of doors, and then, at last, a figure appeared from the smaller drawing room. She was slim and tall, wearing blue, and holding a flower-crowned blue hat in one hand. Her tawny hair was fashionably piled on the top of her small head, but a few strands had escaped down her cheeks. She looked very beautiful, but pale with shock and distress.

Sabrina.

'She was up there,' Lucas said, before she could speak, 'fallen in the pond she had, but I didn't touch her, so don't you think it, lady. Unless I'd bin there she'd've drowned — sure 'nuff she would.'

'I believe you', Sabrina said. 'Of course I do.' She smiled encouragingly. 'Don't worry, Lucas. I'm grateful — so will her — so will Mr Cavannagh be.'

'Him?' Lucas smiled sardonically. 'It's her I'm worried for. Well? Where shall I put her?'

'Oh!' Confusion sent Sabrina scurrying to a sofa. She placed two cushions at one end, saying, 'Here — just lay her down. And — and I must reward you—'

But when Jaina had been placed very gently on the couch, Lucas contemptuously waved aside the proffered coins.

'I don't want nuthen' for giving a bit of help,' he said scathingly. 'It's no Cavannagh I am.' Sabrina winced. 'So I'll be off back, lady,' he continued, 'or your fine carpet'll be more of a bog than anything else.'

He turned abruptly and left the room, with his boots squelching at every step.

Oh dear, Sabrina thought, staring at the muddied Persian rug, Lisette would be in a tizzy, and Oliver, no doubt, would curse the 'damned tinkers'. But of course, Oliver, as usual, was absent, which she'd known he would be, when she'd made her sudden impulsive visit to Carnack that afternoon.

She sighed, touched a bell, and presently, when Jaina had been carried by servants to her own room, ordered a footman to see the sofa and floors were cleaned, then made her way upstairs.

The ex-governess, Miss Willis, had already taken charge, and was in the process of removing the wet clothes, with a maid standing by holding a nightdress and wrap. Jaina was already reviving, and Lisette appeared seconds after Sabrina. She had one hand to her heart, and immediately took a deep sniff of smelling-salts.

'Whatever's happened now?' she demanded. Her voice was shrill, but quivering from anxiety. For the first time Sabrina saw her as she really was — old and weary and no longer able to keep up the façade of elegant self-control.

'It's going to be all right,' Sabrina said, trying to reassure her. 'Jaina's had a — a fall, that's all. She slipped into the pool. The pool on the moor. Lucas found her and carried her back. It was all just an accident—'

Lisette stood staring down at Jaina, shaking her head slowly.

Then, suddenly, almost fiercely, she drew herself up rigidly and said, 'It was your fault, Sabrina, I hope you realise it. If you'd been here it would never have happened. Your proper place was with your husband and his—'

'Daughter. I know,' Sabrina answered cuttingly. 'I think I know a good deal more about Oliver now than when I married him. But don't accuse me of leaving him. He left me shortly after the honeymoon, if you remember. Anyway I don't think we should argue now. Jaina needs rest.'

'Do you imagine I don't realise it? And do you think I don't need a little quiet? Have you any idea at all what it's been like here since you left? Oliver at odds with everyone and everything — Jaina running away for that long time and worrying us all to death? And the guests! We have quite a number, you know. They deserve a pleasant atmosphere. But how can you prevent gossip spreading?' She broke off, placing a hand against her heart, while her eyes closed briefly.

'Oh, I'm sure the guests are all right,' Sabrina said drily. 'They'll be titillated by any mystery concerning the Cavannaghs. Already news has spread that Freddie and Jaina have eloped.'

'Freddie?' His name echoed softly on Jaina's lips.

Lisette glanced down at her sharply. She was by then lying against the pillows in a quilted bed-jacket over a nightdress, her dark hair smoothed on either side of her face. Miss Willis's lips took a downward disapproving turn as she smoothed the counterpane.

'You can go now, Willis,' Lisette said mustering her old air of remote command. 'If you're wanted again you'll be called.'

Flushing perceptibly, Miss Willis collected the sodden clothes from the wash-basins where they'd been laid, and went to the door. As a parting shot she said, 'I'll see that a hot water bottle's sent up. Pneumonia can be very nasty, you know.'

A little smile twitched Sabrina's lips when she'd gone.

'Poor Miss Willis,' she said.

Lisette gave a gesture of irritation. 'A silly woman. So boring, and such a prude. Still, she has her uses, although I've never been able to call on her when she's most needed — she's either in the linen room, or sewing somewhere, or lying exhausted suffering one of her headaches. She's really too old to assume any proper responsibility—'

'Old?'

'Well — a woman of her type, at the difficult age, as they say, can hardly be relied upon to give practical assistance always in a crisis.' There was a long pause. Jaina's eyes had closed again but her cheeks were now glowing with a delicate rose pink. Lisette's lips softened. 'I wish you would come back, Sabrina,' she said, with a pleading glance at her daughter-in-law. 'We need you. Oliver needs you. Can't you try and forget what was wrong — or at least understand it? Or don't you care at all?'

Did she care? Sabrina's skin pricked. As always, when the mention of Oliver's name took her off-guard, desire flooded her wildly and irrationally. It was as though much of her that had been dead for a long time had suddenly been resurrected to turbulent life. Of course she cared, of course she did. Whatever he was, or had done — however much he'd betrayed her — and she had to accept this — what they'd had together could never entirely be erased. He'd hurt her — not only her flesh, but her spirit. And in her turn she'd hurt him in many small ways. Neither was the hurt yet over. Although since their parting she'd pretended and lied to herself — covered the dark longings under the proud veneer of contempt and wilful nonchalance — of haughty disregard — beneath and beyond the façade, the wounds had still burned and festered. The daylight hours had been bearable; she had attended social affairs, won back a certain esteem from family friends, and busied herself in duties at charitable functions. She had earned her father's full affection, and made uneasy peace with her stepmother. Sabrina Cavannagh had been replaced once more and accepted, however hesitantly, as Sabrina Penderrick.

And so it would go on.

That is — if she could bear it. But could she? Sabrina was brought to herself quickly by hearing Jaina say, 'You do care, don't you?' and then, after an emotional pause through which even the room seemed to wait, and the drift of wind outside the window die into silence, 'Please stay. Don't go, Sabrina.'

'Very well.' Sabrina's voice was a mere whisper. She moved across to the bed, allowing Lisette first to move away. 'I'll stay, for a time anyway.'

Life magically returned to Jaina's eyes, but there was pain there too.

'I thought you would. I knew.'

'How?'

'Because you can't do without him I suppose — without Oliver — my father. And that's what I feel about Freddie. But I don't have the chance you've got, Sabrina.'

'Whatever do you mean?'

'Oh — you know. My age. They think I'm so young. Fancy! after all that's happened. But then there are other things. About being a bastard — and — and—' Her voice shook.

Sabrina placed a hand against the trembling lips. 'Sh — sh — forget, Jaina. It doesn't matter now. And Freddie will come to see you soon. I'm sure of it—' If not, she told herself fiercely, I'll damn well call on him and see that he does.

She didn't have to.

The next day Freddie appeared at Carnack.

The weather had changed unpredictably, becoming colder, and driving a thin rain across the grey sky. Jaina was standing by the bookshelves in the library, wondering whether to take a volume of Keats' poems to the fire, or choose a novel by one of the Brontës. Keats, she thought, would be more to her taste just then, and was about to remove a leather-bound edition when there was the sound of the door opening. She glanced round quickly and saw Sabrina standing there.

'Someone to see you,' she said, and her voice was warm. 'He's come quite a way, Jaina.'

Sabrina's figure receded quietly. Another emerged. The door closed. For several moments nothing happened. Everything was quite still. It was as though time itself had ceased. Jaina could hardly believe what she saw — Freddie standing staring at her with the length of the room between them, his face half shadowed on one side, the other licked to gold from the firelight. His hair was straggling towards one eye, glistening with rain. That wonderful compassionate smile of his touched his lips. She swallowed nervously, as delight, too wonderful almost to comprehend, spread slowly, deliciously through her. Freddie! oh Freddie! She started to tremble, and then, suddenly she was speeding across the floor into his half-raised arms. They enclosed her firmly and drew her close. So close and warm she could feel the damp heather smell of his tweed jacket against her cheeks and forehead. Then he tilted her chin up, and his mouth came down on hers draining all the pain and anguish, the loneliness and shame of the last months away. Everything was hers for that brief interlude — the sweetness of giving and taking, of their two spirits flowering, holding the blossoming of countless spring and summer times ahead.

When at last the long embrace was over, still with an arm round her waist, he led her to an alcove, sat down, and drew her on to his knees. Then he lifted one of her delicate hands to his mouth and looking at her said, 'I couldn't keep away, darling. I should have — I've no right here, an old-stager like me, with a scarred face and swollen jaw, and you so young—' She stared at the bruise which was quite distinct suddenly in the firelight, and the soft palm of her hand was against it. 'Oh Freddie, and it was all for me. I love you so — I love you — *love* you—'

'I know.'

'You love me too, don't you, Freddie?' The question was a whisper, hesitant yet quite certain, because she knew, really. Once again, with infinite tenderness, he kissed her.

'Of course, my darling, my most precious dear.'

'And you don't mind? About me not being a virgin? About—'

She didn't allow him to answer, but got up, and closed her eyes, continuing quickly, 'No, don't answer. I'll count three. If you're smiling when I look up, I'll know it's all right. If you're not, I'll — I'll understand.'

'Very well.' From his tone she could learn nothing. She drew a breath, stood up very straight and started counting aloud, pausing between each word. 'One — two — three—' Then she let out a sigh and very slowly opened her eyes.

Radiance spread in her, quickening her heart again, flooding her with joy.

He was smiling.

Half an hour passed before Sabrina returned. One glimpse of their two figures half silhouetted against the glowing embers of the fire — Jaina crouched on the floor with her head against Freddie's knees, his arm round her, and his lips touching her hair, told her all she wanted to know. Whatever Oliver might say or do, nothing would part them.

This was no passing passion.

It was the real thing at its simplest and best. Something — a quality of life so few found — love.

Shaken, envious in spite of her relief for them, Sabrina left the room, unnoticed, unheard. As she went upstairs to inform Lisette of Freddie's visit a tinge of envy seized her.

She, Sabrina Penderrick, would never know such gentleness or complete mutual peace and understanding — never the awe and compassion of a relationship; only the fire, hot desire, and longing; and perhaps, when she and Oliver were much older, a resignation to their differences.

The truth hit her with a shock. She was wild and untamed, a rebel born; quite incapable of docile submission to any other individual.

That was why, mostly, Oliver had wanted her. To fight and possess her. They were primitives, both of them, needing the challenge and the flame.

The self-admission cheered her a little. The knowledge of Oliver's return any day titillated her senses with even an anticipatory hint of amusement.

When she reached Lisette's room to give her the news, she was already smiling.

Lisette was more resigned to the situation than Sabrina had expected. 'Well,' she said, 'perhaps all that's happened is for the best. Life would be far too hectic here with Oliver and Jaina always quarrelling. These last few months have been too wearying for words. And I'm always the one to blame, in my hardheaded son's opinion.'

She sighed. 'I suppose I shouldn't have allowed her to go out walking alone — especially after that dreadful time when she ran away. But the truth is, Sabrina, I simply refuse to take any further responsibility on that girl's account. If Freddie can be induced to marry her—'

'With Oliver's permission,' Sabrina reminded her quickly. 'And I don't think there'll have to be any inducement where Freddie's concerned. They're quite infatuated.'

'How old is he?' Lisette demanded abruptly.

'Twenty-seven.'

'And Jaina's just sixteen.' A pause, then, 'Of course it's better for the man to be older. But what are the de Marchmonts going to say?'

'I wouldn't worry about that until Oliver's heard.' Sabrina answered firmly.

Lisette's brows puckered anxiously, hopefully.

'You are going to stay, aren't you, Sabrina? Later I mean, when the Jaina business is settled?'

Sabrina flung her mother-in-law a narrowed enigmatic glance. 'We shall have to see, shan't we?' she said brightly, too brightly for Lisette's entire satisfaction. 'So much depends on Oliver.'

Oliver returned to Carnack two days later.

Sabrina was arranging flowers in the hall when he walked in at the front door, appearing very smart in a fur-collared frock coat, followed by a footman carrying his bag. It was late afternoon and, as he removed his silk hat, a dying ray of sunlight turned his luxuriant hair to dark shining copper. He wore drainpipe trousers and spats over highly polished pointed shoes. Sabrina, in a lace-necked tightly waisted blue silk gown under a fitting black velvet coatee, flushed becomingly as he entered, then she drew herself up and lifting her head an inch higher, said primly, 'Good afternoon, Oliver. I didn't know you were arriving today.'

'How convenient,' he said, and suddenly grinned. 'Come here.'

She lifted her long skirts above her slippers with an attempt at dignity, and would have walked defiantly in the opposite direction towards the drawing room if he hadn't unexpectedly taken her hand, pulled her round, and deliberately kissed her hard on the lips. He released her only when a maid came down the hall.

'I hope you have a good fire going in the bedroom,' he said to the girl, 'Mrs Cavannagh and I have things to discuss before dinner.'

'Oh yes, sir – yes—' The maid glanced at Sabrina hesitantly. 'Madam, Mrs Cavannagh's, been sleeping in the spare room, sir, while you were away, and as we didn't know—'

'Then get our usual bedroom ready at once,' Oliver told her unsmilingly. 'In the meantime we'll use the one already warmed.'

As simple as that, thought Sabrina, with a hint of irritation. Oliver all over, do this, do that. But – oh God! how she'd missed him.

The girl, with a dead-pan look on her face, but with a gleam in her eyes that spoke of an inward anticipatory excitement and gossip to come in the servants' hall, hurriedly did as she was bid, leaving Sabrina and Oliver alone together.

'You look well,' he said coolly, straightening his tie. 'A little weary perhaps, under the eyes. But slightly plumper — here and there—' glancing meaningfully at breasts and thighs. 'But I've heard they always keep a good table at Fern Hill, however tight finance may be.'

Sabrina said nothing.

Oliver smiled again, 'Well, my love? I hope things are going to be all right now. Suppose we have a sherry in the library while they get our room habitable. My dear mama's sure to hear I'm back at any moment. The typical greyhound breed with her elegant nose ever on the scent for the first whiff of news.'

Sabrina couldn't help her lips twitching. Greyhound — such an apt description for Lisette.

She followed him to the room, and found her first defences gradually breaking down. Perhaps it was the setting — perhaps that quiet interior still retained a certain spreading glow and aura of the gentle passion left behind by Freddie and Jaina. Who could say? There was simply no way of assessing the unpredictable, wayward, yet all-consuming quality of man's relationship to woman, and her response to its demands.

She moved quietly, automatically to the fire, and stood there with her back to him, hands extended to the flames, the sensuous lines of her body outlined seductively against the glow.

There was the chink of glasses, followed by the firm tread of his feet across the floor. Then another tinkle as he put the drinks down. A touch on her buttocks made her quiver and turn suddenly. Then his tongue was searching hers, and against the wild beating of her heart she could feel the thudding of his own. When, for want of breath, he had to release her, he crossed to the small side-table, poured the sherry, and handed a glass to her.

'To both of us,' he said, with his arm half raised in a toast.

'But—'

'And no buts, Sabrina, no running away, no holding aloof, my darling, or believe me, I'll—'

She waited.

'I'll put you over my knee, and give you the hiding of your life. Then I'll lock you up, and feed you on bread and water until you come to your senses—'

She smiled impishly. 'And what then?'

'Then, you adorable, tantalising witch, I'll show you what it is to have a man like me so damned besottedly in love. Come to that — why the devil should I wait that long?'

Sabrina had no chance to reply. The heady interlude was interrupted by Lisette's entrance, who after an affectionate greeting tinged with subtle reproof launched into a highly-coloured account of Jaina's antics and misdeeds. 'And would you believe it?' she ended breathlessly. 'He wants to marry her — actually. A de Marchmont! Can you understand it at all?'

Oliver shrugged. 'No. But it seems to me quite a good idea.'

'Oliver! that child—'

'She isn't, Mater. Not any more. That's the difference between—'

'Colour, were you going to say?'

'No. East and West,' Oliver replied. 'Three quarters of Jaina may belong to us — the rest was her mother's. And she's no worse for it anyway.' As he spoke he kept his eyes averted from Sabrina's.

Noticing it, and trying hard to stifle the small pang of jealousy that any reminder of Oliver's past always evoked in her, Sabrina said, in level tones, 'I always knew that. The Eastern bit, I mean. And I agree.'

Oliver glanced at his wife in surprise.

'So you guessed?'

'Of course. And I think Jaina's sensed — *known* it — for a very long time.'

'Oh well then—' Oliver's form relaxed. 'There's no more to be said.'

'We shall have to see what the de Marchmonts think about it,' Lisette replied with a certain chilly hauteur. 'Jaina went to meet them yesterday, she's staying at their place for two nights. You can hardly expect them to receive her with open arms. But of course, she's quite an attractive girl in her own way, and from what Freddie said when he left the other day, nothing will make any difference. He'll marry her — even without your permission if you won't give it.'

'She won't have to worry on my account,' Oliver said coolly. 'The sooner she's off my hands, the better.'

'Oh Oliver!' Sabrina's voice held reproof.

'Don't mistake me — I'm fond of the waif. But she's too subtle, too secretive for me to handle. And anyway—' His brows arched whimsically, 'one wayward woman for me to control adequately is more than enough.'

The next day Freddie arrived at Carnack with Jaina, and made a formal request to Cavannagh 'for his daughter's hand'. Beneath the polite exterior Cavannagh sensed a certain stubborn belligerence about de Marchmont that he respected rather than resented.

'I hope you know what you're doing,' he said sceptically. 'Jaina's background is hardly up to your aristocratic standards. She's a mixture in every way, and can be difficult. I'm fond of her though, and I don't want to stand in the way of her happiness — provided she *is* going to be happy. What does your father say? I'm sure—' and his mouth took a fleeting ironic twist '—he can hardly be pleased.'

'No.' Freddie admitted honestly. 'But he'll come round, in time. He'll have to. The snobbery business is bunkum anyway. And he likes her — as a girl.'

'That's something of course.' Oliver's tones were dry. 'He'll have to like her a very great deal to get her accepted by your nobly bred circles.'

'I'm quite aware of it.'

'The hell you are,' Oliver thought with a sudden flash of quick resentment. Nothing showed on his face however. He merely said, 'When do you suppose to get married? How? And where? Do you expect me to give some fashionable flash affair at Carnack? I'm quite prepared to, if you think your parents would appreciate it.'

For a moment Freddie looked mildly embarrassed, which gave Oliver a certain wry pleasure.

'No.' Freddie shook his head slowly. 'Not that. Thank you, sir, all the same. A quiet ceremony at our own small church I think, would be easier — for Jaina and the rest of us, with your permission. You'll give her away, of course? And we shall expect your mother — Mrs Cavannagh — to be there?'

So it was all settled.

Lisette, naturally, was delighted, and proceeded at once to consult her dressmaker concerning a new outfit for the occasion.

That night, following Freddie's visit, Oliver was very quiet at first, as he and his reunited wife prepared themselves for bed.

When he entered the bedroom from his dressing room, she was seated before her mirror brushing the mass of her long tawny-fair hair. The glow from wall-lamps lit its sheen to ripples of dusky gold streaked by intermittent light and shade. The subtle curve of breasts were outlined enticingly through the delicately embroidered muslin wrap.

Oliver felt his senses lurch and a hardening of his whole body.

He came softly behind her, bent down, and pressed his warm hungry lips against her neck, and then her shoulder, while one hand enclosed a nipple, pressing it as though draining honey from an opening flower.

She looked up. Her violet eyes appeared bemused, dreamlike, yet suddenly brilliant with the need and insatiable desire for this demanding arrogant one-man-in-the-world who could move her to submission. He smiled. Her own lips trembled. He lifted her to her feet, then into his arms and carried her to bed.

Outside a soft chill wind moaned insidiously through the trees, whipping a lean branch against the window.

But in the bedroom summer seemed very near, as he took her to him, not only in lust, but with fresh enhanced commitment to their mutual need and overwhelming passion for each other.

In the lazy moments following consummation she recognised that this was for all time. Their future might not be an easy one. There would be misunderstandings and fiery interludes when brief spitting and scratching might bring them to open conflict.

But whatever their differences — and she knew his character could never entirely change — or hers — they would end up together.

'What are you thinking about?' he asked her once.

Through the darkness she smiled.

'I was just recognising what it was really going to be like, as Mrs Oliver Cavannagh,' she answered.

An arm tightened round her.

'You know nothing yet, darling,' he said. 'Every day is different, and every day I'll have something new to teach you, so long as you remember who you are—'

She didn't reply. There was no need.

She knew.